Heaven's Portal: Saving the Presidency

Volume 2

By

Steve A. Day

Illustration by Stuart T. Day

Advok8™

Men are working in scorching fields in the Dominican Republic from sunup to sundown, cutting sugar cane for $3 a day. It has shown me we chose to accept these situations without protest because we get our coffee in the morning and our two lumps of sugar.

Steve A. Day

Heavens Portal: Saving the Presidency

p. cm.

Summary: In the second volume of Heaven's Portal, Masada suffers significantly in its effort to save the US President, who is focused on their destruction. In the meantime, Masada rescues some of the World's most persecuted and impoverished people.

ISBN 978 0 578 76656-0

Labels: Fantasy – Fiction, Fantasy – Portal, Heaven – Fiction, Religion – Fiction, Political – Fiction, Action – Fiction

Printed in the U.S.A.

First American edition, September 2020

Table of Contents

Preface

Shane McNaughton is a Master Judge, appointed by God, of the Order of Masada. Masada's Order is a secretive organization charged with fighting evil and corruption on Earth and all domains. God has empowered Shane to rescue his chosen people from Satan's reach and influence. God has created another universe called Masada, named for a famous Hebrew fortress. The Masada planet is much like Heaven. Masada is abundant with natural resources and incredible, intoxicating beauty. Sadly, this is what Earth once was like before human beings polluted and destroyed much of its natural beauty.

Shane and the other Masadian Judges under his command possess the ability to heal themselves and others. They can reverse the decay of aging. Most importantly, they can travel between all domains in the multiverse. All the Judges have recruited followers from Earth. Thousands of followers, all marked with a small and obscure peacock between their thumb and forefinger, also have incredible powers. Their strength, speed, reflexes, and senses are supernatural. They can see evil and angelic beings, invisible to humans. They can collect energy within their hands and cast the energy as a magical spell; casting fire, water, ice, lighting, and shockwaves. They can also release additional advanced energy through their blessed weapons. They can use this same power to project shields, invisible cloaking, and much more. The Judges include Shane McNaughton, Nancy Stoltz, Mufaro Mavura, Magaskawee (Maggie), Noni Gopal, and Alice MacGiny. They have recently mourned the death of one of their greatest, Joseph Magnum, killed in a great battle with Hell's fallen angels.

They are aided in their quest by their cherubs. They are trained and protected by powerful angelic beings like Michael, Solomon, Thomas, Camuel, Jeremiel, Sri Ma, Barachiel, and Zuriel. They are taught to be warriors but also trained to be righteous men and women before God.

The Order of Masada is fighting evil from all sides. The United States President Jarrod Sands is a driven evil person convinced Shane McNaughton is to be controlled, captured, or worse. Many times, Shane McNaughton has now crossed paths with the President. Each time it has fueled the President's obsession with someone or something he can't control. On the one hand, he wants to recruit Shane and exploit his alleged powers for personal gain. On the other hand, the evil inside him drives him to pursue Shane. To stop Shane McNaughton and those with him.

While many on Earth are possessed by evil spirits that have crossed from the domain of Hell, Beleth is one of the most potent fallen angels in Hell. He has recruited Apollyon (the fallen angel of death), Asmodeus (one of the evilest of fallen angels and viewed as an archdemon), Beelzebub (who was Lucifer's "prince of demons"), Aamon (the demon of wolves), Gusion (a fallen angel who can discern the past, present or future), Mastema (the fallen angel of hostility), Sabnack (the angel soldier with lion's head), and Saleos (the angel soldier who looks like a crocodile) in his quest to attack Shane and the Masadians.

Beleth desires to continue his corruption of Earth and humanity. He is motivated to spite God for banishing him from his home in Heaven. He has discovered Masada, and as it is not Heaven, this paradise could be his to capture. Finally, he has found portals in Masada, leading directly to Heaven. Could he infiltrate these and return to Heaven with his armies?

Chapter 1: Heartbreak and Recovery

Psalm 34: 17 (Old Testament, Hebrew Ketuvim)

"The righteous cry out, and the Lord hears them; he delivers them from all their troubles. 18 The Lord is close to the brokenhearted and saves those who are crushed in spirit. 19 The righteous person may have many troubles, but the Lord delivers him from them all; 20 he protects all his bones, not one of them will be broken. 21 Evil will slay the wicked; the foes of the righteous will be condemned. 22 The Lord will rescue his servants; no one who takes refuge in him will be condemned."

Masada is a domain separate from Heaven, Hell, and Earth. All domains exist at the same time but in different phases or physical states. Masada is a land filled with resources, riches, and beauty. It is a replica of Heaven and Earth. At least it is a replica of the Earth God had created. Today's Earth is polluted, sick, and starving. It is always one heartbeat away from pandemics, starvation, infestation, and destruction. Without a bombardment of artificial chemicals and technologies, Earth could not continue supporting billions of people. Masada has reminded the Judges and their followers of what Earth should be. A place where you can walk outside your house and simply gather the food to make a meal. A place where to simply sit before a stream and watch nature is profound.

In the multiverse, time is irrelevant. A dark expanse of nothingness simply separates the physicality of each domain. Very few can, or have in the past, crossed from one domain to the other. It is possible with multiverse portals to do so. Shane and his Judges have a unique skill in creating portals to travel back and forth and in between.

Many years ago, Shane was in a desperate state. His son was dying from cancer, and he desperately wanted to seek God for help. He dreamt of it. He willed it. God enabled it. Regardless, Shane was able to cross from Earth to Heaven. He saved his son, only to find out this ability was predestined all along. God had selected Shane to be his Master Judge to fight evil. Shane was a descendent of the Nephilim, who once roamed the earth as superhuman.

Shane remains dedicated to protecting God's precious and loved humanity. Unlike popular Western culture where democracies like the United States declare their superiority as God's chosen people. Shane's mission is to save those who are poor, sick, or persecuted. God's chosen people are those who need him the most, not the least.

Shane, his five Judges, and hundreds of followers fight evil. They fight evil crossing the dark expanse from Hell to Earth. They fight evil on Earth. They have more recently even entered into the domain of Hell to carry the fight to Satan.

After a vicious and deadly battle, Beleth and his lieutenants came within one grasp of capturing Masada and kidnapping Shane's infant daughter Christine. Shane and Grace's daughter is the first to be born on Masada. Christine has extraordinary powers and a particular purpose yet undiscovered.

With this said, Shane McNaughton and his five remaining Judges have surveyed Masada. They are troubled by how easy it was for Satan to reach them in a place they previously thought was completely safe.

On Earth, it is the beginning of 2004. The Masada fortress and the villages surrounding it have suffered severe damages. It will take a long time to recover. On this day in Masada, Shane and Grace are on horseback and riding from village to village to check on people. They come across Mufaro, another Judge, helping to repair homes in a war-torn village.

Mufaro greets them, "Hello, we are making good progress on the repairs and should be done in about five workdays. I am changing some things around to ensure we will be ready for any other attacks."

Shane replied, "Good, what changes? Hundreds of powerful evil beings got into Masada through our four physical portals."

Mufaro replied, "When they attacked, we were surprised. We all had to fight past them to get the blessed weaponry in the fortress. This was difficult. Each village should probably have a cache of weapons and a local shelter to keep people safe."

Blessed weapons are the only things capable of killing a demon in any form. All the Judges and their followers are trained to use supernatural speed, strength, and agility with these weapons. Still, even with the swords, shields, spears, and other weapons, it is significant to defeat a powerful evil being.

Mufaro showed Joseph the plans to build stone keeps in the middle of each village. Nothing special, but a keep is a reinforced block building storing what is needed to withstand all sorts of things; enemy attacks, bad weather, or even animal attacks. When not in a battle, the keep can store food, water, and other precious items.

Mufaro is one of the original Judges. He came from Zimbabwe, Africa. He is a large Muslim man and has been one of the most powerful Judge warriors. He has recruited followers from Africa and has often returned to Africa as a healer, protector, and judge.

Returning from the villages, Shane and Grace go up to the sixth-floor apartment to check on Alice. Grace entered after knocking, and Alice is lying on the couch awake. Joseph died roughly two months ago. Alice simply had not been able to engage with her life without her husband. Shane asked if there is anything they can do?

Alice was not unpleasant or withdrawn but simply said, "No, Shane, thanks for asking, but right now, I am just without purpose. Nothing makes sense without Joseph." With that, she teared up and started to cry quietly.

Grace sits helplessly on the couch next to her and leans over to stroke her hair. It is all she can do.

Grace tries to comfort her, "Alice, we are all here for you. This is hard, and Joseph was such a large part of our lives. He would want us to go on with this struggle. You will rejoin us in time."

Alice does not respond.

Grace and Shane try to coax her to engage a bit more, but it does not work. They leave her and continue up to the seventh floor. The good news is Alice and Nancy share the sixth-floor apartment. Nancy will be returning from her duties soon enough. Alice won't be alone.

Alice had such an excellent relationship with Joseph. He was older, a former US Navy Seal, and had lived a tortured life. When Alice was called to be a Judge, she traveled away from her Irish homeland for the first time. Before being called to be a Judge, Alice led an aimless life with her friends. Not a care in the world. She and Joseph were almost opposites but had found each other. Married just a short time. Now Alice is pregnant … and a young widow.

Three weeks ago, Sri Ma, one of Masada's spiritual teachers, had traveled to Ireland to tell Alice she was pregnant with Joseph's baby. Alice is torn into two pieces. The death of her husband and the birth of their child. Devastation and celebration. It was too much. Upon returning from Ireland to the Masada fortress, Alice retreated to her apartment on the mansion's sixth floor. She is guilty of feelings of happiness for her baby. It is tearing her apart.

A few days later, Shane called a meeting in the Masada mansion library with the Judges. Alice managed to drag herself there. Shane had also invited Thomas Black and Jack Dorsey. They are elite soldiers assigned to the Order of Masada by the Catholic Church. Shane also had asked Terry Gault, Joseph's closest follower, to attend. The Judges included Alice, Mufaro, Noni, Nancy, and Maggie.

Shane started, "This is a new day, but the crusade we are on has not changed. We must get back to our duties as we lick our wounds. We have to double our resolve to make sure nothing like the last attack happens again."

There were a lot of comments made to no one in particular. Mostly positive expressing a desire to move on.

Shane has been holding on to a secret. He is hesitant to reveal it, as he is not sure how Alice will react. Shane took a deep breath, and here goes nothing, "The success of the attack on Masada, by Beleth and his evil forces, was precipitated by a spy here in Masada. Jesus revealed this to me, but I have no idea who it is. I am presuming it is no one in this room."

Shane did not need to say anymore. Alice's posture, emotions, and anger shocked her to life. The room was dead quiet.

Alice intensely stated, "Are you telling me one of the people here in Masada was responsible for my Joseph's death! What leads or clues do you have?"

"A set of circumstances led to Beleth and his forces not being detected. It led to the four physical portals, all being opened and unguarded. It led to a moment in time when Masada defenses were almost non-existent. Even without Jesus' revelation, it would be virtually impossible to see all of our vulnerabilities line up into a "perfect storm" moment," replied Shane.

While Alice was exploding back to life, Noni was frantically thinking. He was putting great effort into keeping his emotions in check. Like Alice, Noni was experiencing a wave of memories and emotions all at once. He remembered one of his followers, Sai, had been missing two times after battles in the dark expanse. Sai only returned weeks or days later. He remembered Sai was the one who distracted him. Sai caused him to miss being in the sub-basement, watching the Scrying Mirrors, just as Beleth traveled across the dark expanse to Masada. These few moments prevented him from warning the others of an impending attack. Sai was the spy. Noni was devastated, knowing his first recruited follower may have betrayed him. If he said anything, he was sure Alice would track down Sai and kill him instantly.

Noni was a technologist and a Judge. He was an Indian and Hindu. He was recruited by Shane to this unlikely journey. What would a Christian God want with a Hindu? To his pleasant surprise, when he brought his wife Arunta and his three girls to Masada, they were welcomed without question.

Even more incredibly, Noni found Sri Ma living as a heavenly being assigned to Masada. On Earth, she was formerly an Indian Hindu spiritual leader. God did not look down on any religion which sought out one heavenly God. It seemed God must have whispered each of these religions to life; at the right time and in the right place. While Christianity was arguably his last offer, Noni concluded there was ample evidence God had created other ways to worship and serve him over time.

In the sub-basement of the Masada mansion, Noni is responsible for the operation of the control room. The brain center of Masada. He has the Masada version of a supercomputer with access to infinite data intelligence. Unlike computer terminals, Masada scrying mirrors are controlled by the thoughts of the user. Among other tasks, Noni and his followers typically monitored all movements in the dark expanse to detect evil traveling from one domain to another.

Noni forgot his thoughts and focused back on Shane. Shane was saying, "Before our battle on Masada, we also had a battle with the US government. To date, we have closed the Lakewood Ohio Center. We have all left Earth."

"The only people of significance who are still on Earth are my two sons, Danny and Dalton, and Noni's family, Arunta and the girls. Dalton graduated from college, has a girlfriend, and is working in Washington DC. Danny is in college at my alma mater, Ohio University. Noni's three girls are in school in Lakewood. If possible, I want to leave them alone."

"It is time we turn our attention to the US government and the evil living within. We have all been watching President Sands since he was a New York Senator. We know he is possessed by some sort of evil being, as we can see the invisible red glow around him. He has repeatedly attacked and tried to harm us. It is time to deal with this."

Nancy interrupted, "No way! We can't attack a US President. Isn't this crossing a line? I think we should just avoid him."

Mufaro added, "Remember Russia, China, and North Korea all have the same situation where power, greed, and evil seems to have taken over their government and business leadership."

Nancy continued, "I will admit having the four most powerful militaries controlled by these four evil leaders is scary. Yet, they are the elephant, and we are the mouse."

Noni objected, "I have been watching Jarrod Sands longer than any of you. I have attended his rallies. He is an evil person masquerading as a righteous man. The so-called Christian leaders surrounding him are all false prophets colored by the same evil. We can't ignore it. I agree with Shane."

Shane agreed, "God gave us this ability to see the aura surrounding people. We know blue and green are good and yellow and red are bad. Michael has instructed us in our role to act when we see this. I believe our mission is to cut the head off the snake when faced with the choice. Therefore, we are going to confront and deal with President Jarrod Sands."

"President Jarrod Sands is a conservative US President who has gone out of his way to hurt people. It is not simply a situation of cutting out programs costing too much. It is not simply a belief in trickle-down economic policies that never work. Sands went well beyond this. Inciting hatred, baiting race wars, separating classes, withholding health care, persecuting immigrants, imprisoning children, and on and on. All seemed to stir more and more evil emotions in the United States."

"Even if this is not enough evidence of evil, there is something about him physically and mentally. He always appears hateful, twisted, and angry. He always is pushing blame and attacks towards others to deflect his incompetence. Is President Sands a sick person or an evil possessed person?"

Someone said under their breath, "Or both."

"President Sands is a selfish monster. He single-handily continues to foster white racism, to appoint pro-corporate, Federalist Society judges. To cut taxes to benefit the wealthy while cutting costs to hurt the poor. Most importantly, he is stripping away regulations designed to protect our environment and kill the Earth. He seeks to attack our Democratic-leaning partners in Europe."

"Whether he is sick literally or possessed with evil, no one knows. It is important because every few months, he seems intent on capturing the Order of Masada. Even when he has repeatedly been told we are not for sale, President Sands becomes more aggressive. We have to turn and face this problem head-on." Shane ended his argument.

President Sands' obsession led to the 2003 capture and torture of Shane and his sons. This led to the conservative news channel launching a character assassination of Shane and all the Judges. It led to thousands of hours of surveillance ordered by President Sands. It made it impossible to base the Order of Masada's earthly operations out of the Lakewood, Ohio facility. No longer could Masada work with clinics or hospitals, as they feared being arrested and jailed. This had saddened everyone, as there was no greater joy than to heal someone. A supernatural ability that only the Judges possessed.

Shane changed the subject, "I have asked some of our guests here to meet with the Judges. First, I would like to promote Terry Gault to become a Judge of Masada. I would like Terry to take over leading Joseph's group of followers. Provided the angel council approves this, we will move forward. Secondly, Thomas Black, Jack Dorsey, Grace, Danny, and Dalton will begin as followers within my group. I want anyone engaged with caring for Christine, and Alice's baby, to be fully equipped with our supernatural abilities and training. Is this acceptable to you all?"

Everyone agreed.

"This brings me to my last two pieces of business. First, we have relocated two vast groups of people onto Masada without much indoctrination to our ways, beliefs, or mission. I would like Nancy and Mufaro to work with Sri Ma, Camuel, and Barachiel to now introduce them to the Order of Masada. Discover if they desire to be part of this, or do we return them to Earth equipped to be more successful in their earthly lives?" asked Shane.

Nancy spoke up, "We can't keep calling everything Masada. This is a huge and wonderful planet. I will allow those in the villages to name their cities. I think we should start calling the Masada fortress and mansion by another name. How about calling it Lakewood, as a memory of our now boarded up Earthly headquarters?"

Some laughed, and most remembered their time on Earth.

Shane said, "If we are going to change the name, how about Cuyahoga? That is the county which Lakewood is in, in Ohio. I think it means "crooked river."

Mufaro said to no one in particular, "We have a crooked river behind the fortress; why not?"

No one objected, so the Masada headquarters and fortress were renamed Cuyahoga.

In May of 2003, the Order of Masada had rescued two whole groups of people. The first was a group in Africa who were enslaved harvesting cocoa beans along the Ivory Coast. Tens of thousands of children slaves and their complete families were forced to work in the cocoa fields. The second group was from Central America, where they were forced to harvest sugar cane. Each of these groups of people lived in sub-human conditions. The Judges and their followers created portals and brought these people to Masada. Sri Ma and Nancy had arranged for them to resettle in two remote, isolated village areas on the planet of Masada.

Nancy added, "They have been here almost a year. Every one of them is thankful and completely joyous to be rescued from the existence they had on Earth. We have introduced them to God. We have explained why they are here. We have started to educate them. Just remember, short of their work as slaves, these people were sub-human. No education, no leisure life, and no other purpose. Some of them did not know how to hunt or fish. To garden or to cook. After multiple generations of slavery, these people just had no skills. In this case, they were born again. We are also continuing to introduce them to Christianity, as they had no other religion to speak of."

All agreed it was time to integrate these people into Masada. Nancy, Sri Ma, Camuel, and Barachiel remained responsible for these people's resettlement and indoctrination.

Mufaro had locked all the fixed portals in "Cuyahoga" so no one could get in or out. Everyone helped repair and restore all the damage from a large-scale battle with Beleth and his forces.

Beleth and Beelzebub almost captured Christine, who is the child of Shane and Grace McNaughton. Since Christine's surprising birth in Masada, Sri Ma and Barachiel have reminded Shane that Christine will be unique.

Speaking of Beelzebub, after Shane almost killed him, he dove from the seventh-floor balcony of the Cuyahoga fortress into the river and disappeared. No one had seen him since. Because he was able to shapeshift into any animal or human, this was still particularly troubling. Thus, guards were stationed outside the seventh-floor home of Shane and Grace, and baby Christine always traveled with at least two guards.

A few nights later, Shane is deep in thought in his seventh-floor apartment in Cuyahoga. This is Shane and Grace's home when in Masada. Christine is simply a toddler at this point, living her happy and wonderful life. So many spoil her with attention.

Shane and Grace have not come to terms with Christine's future. Grace is looking at her and says to Shane, "I can't believe this baby girl could generate a massive energy field burning those two monsters. She is just sitting there playing with her toys, happy as a clam."

Shane laughed, "Remind me always to let you discipline her when she comes into her terrible two's."

Grace replied, "Sure, as long as you take on her teenage years. By then, her powers might burn you to a crisp in one teenage freak out."

They laughed, but Shane was also a bit scared.

Across Masada, the Central American refugees decided to call themselves the Creole people. The African refugees chose to call themselves the Baoule' people. Each settlement was equipped to build their own homes and fend for themselves. Mufaro, Nancy, and many others visited them to teach them about the healing and age-reversing properties of the Renovare pools. Each village was built around one of these pools.

In both situations, these people were sickly, tired, aged, and poor. It had taken many months, but they were now emerging as healthy, youthful, and awoke. No longer enslaved to work six days a week for their meager existence, they could now become gardeners, gatherers, hunters, anglers, and craft people. They could make a life in paradise. Nancy knew a governing structure had to be established.

She met with the de facto leaders of each group in a town hall "kind of meeting." The idea was they would self-govern with a structure she developed for them. First, they would have small neighborhoods elect leaders to a governing council. The council would then select a leader for the whole town. The leaders would be called constables. The constables would focus on the operations of society. If they started new towns, the same structure would be in place.

They would also create a similar system for worship. Instead of leaders, they would select pastors to lead them. A lead pastor would manage the localized pastors. The pastors would rely on Camuel and Sri Ma for spiritual growth and religious instruction. Each society was free to select the religion that most suited their worship of God.

Finally, Nancy taught them about the Judges and the followers. She asked the constables and the pastors to nurture and submit any person suited as a follower of the Order of Masada. Of course, with the general thankfulness towards Masada, Nancy knew she could ask and receive everyone as a volunteer to be a follower. She wanted them to find those who were viewed as physically, mentally, and spiritually gifted. They seemed to understand. Nancy knew if they did not evolve, the angels and Sri Ma would help them.

Nancy wondered how many more villages would be started. She knew the planet of Masada was as large or larger than Earth. Of course, natural resources were unlimited. Could they rescue millions of people or billions of people?

Masada now had a formula for this type of rescue. With the Creole and the Baoule' groups; the Order of Masada had placed followers inside the villages months ahead of Earth's journey to Masada. The followers came alongside Christian and Catholic missionaries to identify those who were spiritual and godly. The Catholic Church Missions had been of help by placing a formal presence in or near these groups on Earth. There were still many more opportunities to rescue groups of sick, poor, and persecuted people.

On Earth, as 2004 came around, President Jarrod Sands was pre-occupied with Masada. He watched the video of Shane McNaughton's capture repeatedly. He was fixated on two particular points in the video. The first was when the US forces kidnapped Shane, brought Shane's younger son Danny into the room, and sliced his arm open. Sands loved to watch the part where Danny was suddenly healed. He also liked to watch the part where Shane, who was placed in chain and iron shackles, effortlessly removed them when he decided to get up. What powers.

Like the evil demon who possessed him, Jarrod Sands feared this power. If he could not control this power, he at least wanted to find a way to destroy Shane. President Sands was like a petulant kid who wanted his toys, and if he could not have them, no one could.

It was time for his "meditation." In his bedroom, President Sands had a wardrobe closet. When closed, it merely looked like a piece of furniture. It was behind and off to the side of a two-chair sitting area. Yet, Scott Stanfield had it built to specifications. When opened, the doors each had a flat-screen television. He turned the television audio off in his private quarters. The middle section had a large mirror. One of the chairs swiveled around. When opened, President Sands could sit immediately in front of the mirror. His meditation involved him having his favorite conservative television news channels on each of the side screens. However, in the mirror, he could look squarely at himself.

President Sands had not fully understood, but it began a few years before being elected to the United States Senate from New York. Back then, he had been a typical real estate billionaire. The family business. Regardless, he would stare in this mirror until he was in a trance. He would see himself first as he was. Gradually, he would feel euphoric and see a younger version of himself staring back at him. It seemed to be him, but it had glowing eyes. It had more sinister mannerisms than he remembered as a young man. The way it suggested things, in his mind, did not remind him of his voice. When it first started, he thought it was some split personality. As time went on, he came to realize it as a secret weapon. The vision in the mirror, the conversations in his mind, and these meditations all gave him strength. The visions were his guiding voice, which hatched some of his greatest successes.

President Sands began meditation the same corny way he had for some time. He spoke to the mirror, "You look like a winner, and you feel like a winner. Mirror, Mirror on the wall who is the fairest of them all. Jarrod Sands! Jarrod Sands!" He would repeat this mantra as he stared into the mirror. At some point, he was entranced. Today, meditation led to one of the frequent topics.

The younger version of himself replied, not out loud, but somewhere within his mind. "You must capture Shane McNaughton. He has the power to kill us. You must destroy him. Your conservative backers will all abandon you if they see weakness. You must destroy any who challenges us. No retreat, no empathy!"

14

As President Sands heard this message, a private intercom announced Mick Gallow was on his way up to the private residence. No one knew about President Sands' "meditation" sessions, and only Scott Stanfield knew the contents of the wardrobe. President Sands was irritated by the interruption. He often spent from 6:00 AM until Noon in his private residence. Watching the news on two television screens and meditating within his mirror. Yet, the next meeting was very much related to the meditation message he had just received. He got up, closed the wardrobe. He locked it and made sure the chair was turned around. He double-checked, as he always did. There were no telltale signs of his sitting in front of the wardrobe. Perfect. He headed out to his sitting room to greet his guests.

Mick Gallow was escorted into his private quarters. Mick Gallow was the President's personal attorney from his days before he was a politician. Soon after Mick arrived, Scott Stanfield also had walked upstairs from his office. Scott was the executive assistant to the President. Both men were the most trusted confidants to President Sands. As such, he felt comfortable with any conversation.

Pleasantries were exchanged. President Sands began, "Before I leave office, I want to accomplish one specific thing. I want to have Shane McNaughton and his team of rejects dead. No excuses, they either work for me or they are dead. This has to be the agreed-upon outcome. I have some of the most powerful, intelligent people in the world looking for them. When they are found, I would like you two to have a clandestine security force ready to capture them. Take whatever we learned and work up a plan. I don't trust the people working for me in the government to get this done. Also, use our back channels to Russia, China, and North Korea to ensure we have visibility throughout the world. Only two years left."

Mick Gallow added, "We can get this done, but we need all the classified and current intel on Shane McNaughton. Scott, can you get this for me?"

Scott Stanfield thought about this as he was answering. He was once again violating his oath of office by releasing classified information to Mick. President Sands had peddled some of the United States secrets to his buddies around the world. To him, it was merely more bargaining chips. To the recipients, they were learning precious lessons about the United States intelligence community. It was borderline treason.

Scott said, "Yes, I will get the information forwarded to me and then will provide you periodic updates. If there are sightings of these people, I will get the information via a private burner phone.

Scott paused for effect and then asked the million-dollar question, "Why all the cloak and dagger? Dalton McNaughton is working here in Washington, DC. He is Shane McNaughton's son."

President Sands jumped in, "Are you nuts! Did you see what happened when we went after his family? He did not take it very well. This cannot be tracked back to us anymore."

Scott protested, "That was different, twice we have paraded his family in front of him as a threat. Both times he reacted badly. Dalton is working as a political lobbyist for clean energy. He is in our world. There are ten ways to play this. We could buy him off. We could grease his career. We could kill his career. Well, you get it. My suggestion is just to wait for his dad to show up. No threats. No drama."

Both other men were quiet. President Sands finally spoke up, "I think we need to be careful here. Let's spend a few months with Mick working in the background, pulling strings to help Dalton's career along. Get Dalton to a point where he has a lot to lose if things go South. Then let's spring the trap. Mick, can you do this?"

Mick agreed, and the meeting was over.

Most of the White House staff did not like to see Mick Gallow in the offices. It typically meant President Sands was doing some harm or damage somewhere in the world. Later they would have to clean it up. The efforts they had been through to cover up President Sands' illegal, unethical and immoral activities had been continual since he took office. Most of them were career government workers, albeit conservative. During President Sands' tenure, most of them swallowed their ethics and principles to pander to him. All of them had broken their public service oaths. Most of them had now broken the law many times over. Republicans were supposed to be the good guys, the guys riding the white horse in their minds. These days, it was precisely the opposite. They still talked about their great values, but it was now a complete con job. To the most optimistic Republicans, they were now much more defective than any of their liberal counterparts.

The White House staff had a saying for the continual screw-ups they had to cover up for the President. "They were as numb as President Sands was dumb." At least it was the saying used outside of the White House.

As for Dalton, he had graduated from college with a degree in political science. He had planned to get a law degree, but he just was not ready. Having a father and mother off fighting real evil had soured him to pursue a law degree. He saw how trivial this might be as compared to his parent's struggle. After college, he looked for a nonprofit doing good in the world. He had come across the Alliance for Free Energy, which was promoting fossil fuel energy alternatives. He had been an intern and was now working in donor relations. It was a sales job.

As a struggling college graduate, he could only afford a shared apartment with three other guys. Dalton's life's sweetener occurred a short time after coming to Washington, DC when he met Sarah Carbetto. Sarah was a dark-haired, olive-skinned Italian girl who was also on a very similar career path. Things were going well with her, and it made everything else feel great. Dalton was in love for the first time in his life.

A few weeks later, Dalton and Sarah wrapped up a workout in the gym after work. They decided to go to dinner. They chose to eat at Sarah's favorite place, Etrusco, on Dupont Circle. It was not expensive but was rated as one of the better Italian restaurants around Dupont. They were eating and laughing.

As a side point, at the insistence of his father, Dalton had gone through the transformation of Masada. He had been bestowed with strength, speed, agility, energy casting, and all of the other skills. Unlike other followers, Dalton could create portals and could heal. Going to work out at the gym was somewhat a fool's errand since he could pretty much-set world's records in almost any aspect of physical competition. He faked it. It was worth it because it was an hour he shared with Sarah most nights. Both his brother Danny and he had these powers.

Etrusco entrance on 20th Street NW was a walk down. While Dalton and Sarah dined, they did not notice Bob Jones watching them from the median strip in the road where a small park existed. Beyond being a somewhat athletic type of build, the man was non-descript. He simply looked like a man smoking a cigarette in the park. Only if you saw him periodically putting a small monocular to his eye would you have wondered what he was doing there? Mick Gallow had started to put people in Dalton's life and work.

Sarah asked Dalton, "You had a good day, and you are probably going to get a promotion in a year. Can we go to visit my parents and your parents this summer?" She paused and saw a blank look on Dalton's face. She asked, "Too soon?"

Dalton laughed and said, "You think I would take a strange girl home to meet my parents?"

He got kicked under the table.

18

Dalton suggested they take a mini-vacation to Lakewood, Ohio. Sarah had never been to the Great Lakes region, and as the weather warmed up, he would plan a trip. Sarah asked Dalton if he had to make arrangements with his parents? He told her his parents were not in Lakewood very much, and he owned the house.

Sarah asked, "Can't you just phone your parents and arrange a date when we all can get together? Why do you own their house? Are they older?"

Dalton laughed; at least he laughed inside. "No, my parents travel, and it is hard to get ahold of them. We will just have to risk it. Maybe we will have the house to ourselves." He smiled slyly.

Dalton had already asked his Cherubs to determine if his parents could make a trip to Lakewood for a week to meet Sarah this spring. Grace, his mom, was now chatting in his head … a hundred questions about the new girl.

As they left the restaurant, they had decided it was too late for both to go their separate ways. At least it is what they told each other. Instead, they decided to go to Sarah's place for the night, and Dalton would leave early in the morning.

They decided the cold night air was perfect for a walk home. The man observing them got into his car and drove to Sarah's house. He knew by their direction where they were going. He might as well get a good parking spot until his relief showed up. They had twenty-four-hour surveillance on both Dalton and Danny. Each of Shane's sons had a four-person team rotating through six-hour shifts. It kept them fresh and gave them time to go back to their hotel room/office to relax and file reports.

Bob Jones had only been on this gig for about two weeks. He knew the routine by heart. Dalton and Sarah would go back to her place. They would watch television and work on their laptops for about an hour. They would most likely have a bottle of wine. At around 10:30 PM, they would go to bed. They would make love. Sarah would come to the kitchen for a glass of water. Dalton would turn the sports news on the television. By 11:30 PM, the lights were out, and they would be off to sleep. Dalton would get up at 6:30 AM and head back to his apartment to get ready for the next day.

Bob sighed. Young love. He hoped this job would not turn into something where he had to harm these two. He thought of them as good people.

One last occurrence was happening on Masada. Since the meeting, Alice had slowly raged at the thought of a spy responsible for her husband's death. It shook her to the point of insanity. She returned to work with a vengeance. She trained harder than anyone. She pushed her followers harder than anyone. She engaged evil beings found crossing in the dark expanse. Killing them was not enough. She started to enjoy torturing them before death.

Alice continued to travel to Ireland to visit hospitals and clinics she routinely helped. If she found a possessed human in the course of this, she did not hesitate to chase the fleeing evil being down into the dark expanse and kill it mercilessly. Alice was on a mission to the point of scaring a lot of those around her. They reminded her she was pregnant, and it did not seem to register with her. She did not sleep, and she did not slow down. Her mission was to find the spy and kill him. She dreamt of a day she finally met up with Beleth and could have the satisfaction of a battle to the death.

She only kept up healing people and caring for her contacts in Ireland as a slim lifeline to the goodness she used to feel. Goodness, that was her's, not theirs.

Alice told herself she would stop all this and focus on her child in a month or so. After the child was delivered, her plan was to return to her private war. Sri Ma, Grace, Nancy, and the staff could care for the baby. Once she saw and held her baby, Alice wondered if she would feel differently. She did not know. She was too filled with hate and rage to slow down. She did not connect with the baby like a normal mother. Perhaps it was the warrior in her, or maybe it was the absence of Joseph.

Noni had also been keeping a secret. He already knew who the spy was. It was his follower Sai. All the necessary boxes were checked. Three times before the attacks, Sai had been missing. Immediately before the final attack, Sai had distracted Noni from seeing Beleth's evil forces on the scrying mirrors as they left Hell and headed for Masada. Sai was the spy. Noni did not know why, but he had to tell Shane.

Shane was out in front of the Cuyahoga mansion on a Spring morning when Noni asked to talk to him. Noni began, "I owe you an apology, and I hope you can someday forgive me. I have wrestled with this for weeks and see no other way but to confess."

Shane was shocked as Noni was so serious, "What are you talking about? Things have been returning to normal."

Noni went on, "I know who the spy is. I know who betrayed us to Beleth before we were attacked last year. I have been wrestling with this for some time."

Shane's mind was racing as he had no clue who the spy was, "Who and why?"

Noni quietly motioned to move to a side of the main pathway, "It is Sai. It was Sai Chanda, my follower."

Shane asked, "How do you know, and what evidence do you have?"

As Shane said this, he heard Alice approach from the rear. She said, "Evidence of what?"

Neither Shane nor Noni wanted to speak. Their minds had raced from the explosive information about the spy to the second explosion, which would occur once Alice knew who the spy was.

Shane looked at Alice and calmly said, "Alice, you have to stay calm if you are going to join this conversation. Do you agree?" She said she would. Shane continued, "Noni has discovered the identity of the spy who betrayed us."

Alice's subtle physical changes gave her away. Her breathing was more deliberate. Her eyes and pupils had gotten twice as large. Her body had tensed up. She was gathering energy, like a human spring, ready to explode.

Shane asked Alice again, "Alice, are you sure you want to be part of this conversation?"

Alice almost shouted, "Hell, yes! Noni, if you know, I want you to tell me right damn now!"

Noni looked at Shane and then back at Alice, "I believe, with 95% certainty, the spy was Sai Chanda. He was one of my followers, and I am so sorry. I feel responsible and want to do whatever I can to make this right."

Shane took hold of Alice's shoulder and turned her squarely towards him. "Alice, there will be a time to deal with revenge, but for right now, I would like you and Noni to track him down. Capture him without indicating what you know. Put him in the jail down in the sub-basement. Before anything dramatic happens, I want to question him. I want to understand everything about this. Can we agree on that?"

Alice had a tear running down her cheek, but she shook her head yes.

Noni and Alice walked off to track down Sai. He was not in the sub-basement, on duty. He was either at his house or out in one of the wilderness areas.

Noni used his telepathy to ask one of his followers in the sub-basement of Cuyahoga to locate Sai. They used the scrying mirrors in the control room to find him. It took only a few seconds.

Noni had a strange look on his face. He told Alice, "It is strange because the fixed portals in the Cuyahoga guard towers are locked, but Sai is in the West tower. I think he is trying to escape."

Noni did not even get it out of his mouth. Alice disappeared instantly. She raced to the tower and found Sai at the bottom.

Alice asked, "What are you doing, spy? Are you trying to sneak off? Do you know the damage you have done?"

Sai was startled but replied with hate, "My master will come for me. We know you are preventing a reunion with our God. You are all doomed to ..."

That was the last thing Sai got out of his mouth before Alice drove her sword into his chest. He was not dead but was close to it.

Noni carried him to the healing pools and saved his life. He then was thrown into the sub-basement jail cells until they figured out what to do with him. Shane wanted to see if there was intelligence to gather.

As the dust settled on his capture, Shane looked at Alice and asked, "Do you feel better?"

Alice smiled and said, "No, I don't, but driving a sword through him did not make me feel any worse."

Chapter 2: Family is Precious

(Psalm 128: 1-6, Jewish Ketuvim, Old Testament)

"Blessed are all who fear the Lord, who walk in obedience to him. 2 You will eat the fruit of your labor; blessings and prosperity will be yours. 3 Your wife will be like a fruitful vine within your house; your children will be like olive shoots around your table. 4 Yes, this will be the blessing for the man who fears the Lord.

5 May the Lord bless you from Zion; may you see the prosperity of Jerusalem all the days of your life. 6 May you live to see your children's children—peace be on Israel."

It was May 2004 when Dalton and Sarah Carbetto had traveled to Lakewood, Ohio. Dalton's father, mother, brother, and baby sister had abandoned Lakewood. This happened because the United States government slandered his family on television. Armed forces attacked and kidnapped his father, his brother, and himself. Despite being US citizens, they even tortured them. He was also present when the Masadians showed up in force and neutralized the military forces which had illegally taken Shane.

Dalton expected the US armed forces had been waiting for the family's return to Lakewood. While it was not perfect, the way he felt about Sarah was worth the risk. He loved her beyond the risks associated with his family.

Dalton drove up to the Lakewood house. His parents had put the house in his, and his brother's, names to keep it in the family. If the US government seized all assets from Shane and Grace McNaughton, the thinking was at least Dalton, and Danny could preserve their childhood home.

As he got out of the car, he saw the lawn mowed, and the house looked alive. It looked like people lived there. Sam Van Dorn always kept crews working at maintaining various Masadians' residences, and maintaining the Lakewood Center, while all were away. Many of these were followers who had chosen to live on Earth and go about their daily lives.

Dalton and Sarah got their bags and went into the house. It was pleasant, and Sarah was nervous. She was let down when no one was there. Dalton told her his parents had let him know they would meet at the Lakewood Center for dinner. They had a few hours to freshen up. He gave her a tour of the house.

Sarah again asked, "I don't understand. Your parents do not live here? They live across town?"

Dalton just shook his head.

Outside, a sedan had predictably pulled up to the curb. Inside were two military types monitoring the trip taken by Dalton and Sarah. A report would be sent to Mick Gallow and Scott Stanfield. There was an anticipation Shane and Grace might show up to greet Dalton. Mick Gallow instructed additional men to move towards the Lakewood house and the Lakewood Center.

A few hours later, Dalton and Sarah got into the car and headed to the Lakewood Center. When they arrived at the compound's gate, Dalton had a garage door opener he pressed to open the gate.

As the gate opened, Sarah's mind was spinning, "Who the Hell are you? What is going on?"

Dalton did not feel like explaining anything right now and just laughed. "Relax, no big deal."

The Lakewood Center was designed to replicate the Masada fortress and mansion, which was now called Cuyahoga. Instead of the Masadian facility's beauty, Shane and Sam Van Dorn had designed the facility as a replica inside but completely stark and austere outside. As Dalton drove up the driveway, just a simple light at the front entrance glowed.

Dalton and Sarah got out and walked to the front door. There was a keypad, and Dalton put in his code. The front door unlocked. Dalton opened the door to allow Sarah to enter. Upon entry, and like in Masada, the first thing you see is the great hall. The front part of the hall is like a ballroom, open and ornate. The back part of the hall is a dining area. At the very back is a small elongated stage and places to sit.

To the left is an opening to a large study and library. To the right, the doors were closed. Dalton watched Sarah take it all in. As she did, she eventually got around to looking at the winding staircase, seeming to go up forever. It only went up for seven floors. Unlike Masada, the Lakewood Center facility at least had an elevator.

Dalton asked Sarah, "Shall we?" He motioned to the elevator.

They arrived on the seventh floor and looked down a hallway to eight doors. The four middle doors were wide open. As they entered, it was a replica of the apartment the McNaughton's had in Masada. The only difference was the Cuyahoga mansion did have a fantastic view out the rear of the balcony to Masada. Lakewood, Ohio did not.

Dalton was pleasantly surprised as the whole family was there. Shane and Grace were now up and moving to the door to greet them. Danny was on the balcony playing with baby Christine. Thomas Black and Jack Dorsey were standing towards the sides of the room. Dalton understood they were there as bodyguards.

After Sarah was introduced to everyone, they sat down at the dining room table in the main salon for dinner. Sarah sat with Dalton on one side and Grace on the other. Christine was in a booster seat sitting between Grace and Danny. Sam Van Dorn had arranged for a chef and wait staff to be here. The conversation was pretty good, and most of the secrets remained buried and far from daylight.

Yet Sarah had an instinctual way to ask just the right question, "So Grace, why do you live in this large apartment on top of an ugly building, when you could live in your home across Lakewood?"

Grace said, "We are either busy traveling or are busy with our holistic health business. It keeps us on the road. This apartment allows us to be here, when and if, the Lakewood Center opens back up."

Sarah asked, "Why is the Lakewood Center closed?"

Shane injected, "We have been so busy in other very needy places of the world. We have not been able to return and operate this facility for the last half-year or so. And since you can find this information in any library, you might as well know Dalton's family is running from the law."

There were nervous laughs around the table. Sarah was not sure if this was a joke or not.

Shane continued, "Last year, President Sands called us an "enemy of the state" on television. This has been a running feud for many years. We refuse to work for him because we view him as a … jerk. It has caused a bit of a problem with the US government."

Sarah continued, "What does he want you to do for him, and why is it so special?"

Grace took over, "Sarah, we are simply healers, with blessings from God. Think of us like Mother Theresa. The President desires us to be part of his team of people. On the other hand, we believe our value is to focus on places in the world where people are incredibly sick, poor and persecuted. He can't understand this and is not accustomed to being turned down. Nothing more than a tantrum. Better you heard our version."

Sarah concluded out loud, "Well, I don't like President Sands, anyway."

Everyone laughed, and that was the end of it. They enjoyed dinner.

That night, the US government agents assigned to watch over Lakewood were all outside the Lakewood Center. They knew Dalton had gone into the compound through the gates. They were expecting other family or Masadians to do the same. However, no one showed up. This left them sitting in their cars outside the compound. Frustrated.

After dinner, the McNaughton family enjoyed a night of being together in peace. In the mansion apartment, baby Christine was the center of attention. They laughed and played and joked. These types of nights did not come along very often for the Judges of the Order of Masada.

Sarah was sitting on the couch with Grace. Dalton was on the floor, in front of her, playing with Christine. Sarah looked at Grace for a long moment and then blurted out, "I guess you to be around fifty years of age, how do you look like you are as young as me?"

The room got a little quiet, as if other activity did not stop, but everyone had an ear tilted to hear the conversation. Grace had a rehearsed reply, "I guess it is good genes, and if not, Christine does keep me young. She was a surprising addition to our family."

That was true. Shane and Grace had no idea the healing of their own bodies would include repairing Grace's reproductive organs. She had a hysterectomy in her forties and had not even considered the healing properties of Masada would make her fertile again. It was a surprise.

When the night was over, Dalton and Sarah said goodbye headed back to the Lakewood house. Danny chose to go with them to the house for the night. Dalton could tell Sarah had been overwhelmed with questions and worries. He let her sit silently in the passenger side of the car as they drove home. Dalton did notice a car was following them from a distance. He telepathically told his father of his suspicion.

Back at the Lakewood home, the three of them got into the house without any worries. One of the things Sam Van Dorn had done before their arrival was sweep the place for listening devices. He had hired a reputable firm out of Cleveland to come in and accomplish this. He wanted the house to be safe for them. Danny went off to his room, and then eventually got in his car to go see friends. Dalton and Sarah sat on the back porch and enjoyed the night air.

Sarah finally was ready to speak, "I guess I will just say it, your parents don't look like your parents. The massive compound and building were very strange. Outside, it was like a fort. Inside, it was like a palace. There is something you are not telling me."

Dalton had been rehearsing the response since before dinner. He knew Sarah well enough to know she would not simply enjoy the night without question. "Sarah, my family has some very unique skills. When I was in high school, I had terminal cancer. My father came to the hospital and laid his hands on me. He took the cancer away. There are other examples of him doing this. He is what the Bible would call a healer. No tricks, no jokes, and no catches. My parents are part of a small group of people in the world having this skill. A group of them travel the world, work with the religious organizations, and heal people."

Sarah was now a bit scared. "There is no such thing as healers. Come on? Your parents seem like very nice and down to earth people."

Dalton continued, "You are right to doubt. My father was simply a retail store manager before all of this. He was not a holy man, a pastor, a prophet, or any other unique thing. This was a surprise to him as much as anyone else."

Sarah asked, "What about their age? They look almost younger than us."

Dalton replied, "Part of the healing process allows them to continually heal themselves. If you think of aging as a disease, then it is easier to understand. They are at their optimal age and optimal physical selves. Let just enjoy the night for what it was. You met my parents and my brother and my baby sister. We had a good time."

Sarah dropped it and headed to the bathroom. When she came back out, she was ready for bed. She was in a black negligée and went into the kitchen to get a bottle of wine. Dalton did not need to be asked as he headed for his bedroom to freshen up as well.

That night, they made love with an intensity that was simply Lakewood magic. Sarah was tall and lean but was also naturally proportioned. She had long but naturally curly black hair. Her eyes were grey, and in the moonlit room, they seemed to glow. For Dalton, this night was worth the trip by itself.

Somewhere in the middle of things, Sarah whispered for the first time, "Dalton, I love you." She had said it before, but it was always like a friend saying, I love you. This was different. Her soul was speaking to Dalton. Dalton knew their relationship was now bonded. He could envision being husband and wife.

For the next few days, Dalton took Sarah around Cleveland. They visited the typical attractions. First, they visited the Rock and Roll Hall of Fame, and one of Dalton's favorites, Mabel's BBQ.

Mabel's BBQ was famous for their BBQ meats. However, Dalton loved their poppyseed coleslaw and their fried potatoes. Their key lime pudding was heaven. Mabel's menu was wall to wall goodness.

The next day was warm. Dalton had arranged to go sailing. They had a 1995 Hunter 36 Legend sailboat moored at the Rocky River Marina. Dalton, Danny, and Sarah were going to go to Put in Bay Island for a day cruise. If it got late, they could sleep on the boat. The boat had been a graduation gift from Shane and Grace to both boys. They always made sure it was cared for it and took at least a few summer trips together.

As it turned out, they spent way too much time on the Put in Bay Catawba Avenue winery and found themselves late at night at the Boathouse. Dalton and Danny could have predicted this, as they found themselves in this same situation many times before. They were too intoxicated to boat home. They would spend the night on the boat. Get up the next morning and have breakfast before heading out.

The next morning, they headed into Delaware Avenue to find breakfast. Sarah was holding a table while Danny and Dalton were waiting in line to get food. The man sitting next to her caught her eye.

He said, "Nice morning. Are you from around here?"

Sarah replied, "No, we came here to visit my boyfriend's family. We are from Washington, DC. How about you?"

He replied, "What a coincidence, I am from Alexandria, Virginia. Just came over on the Put in Bay Ferry to see the sights."

At that point, Danny and Dalton arrived at the table with their hands full of breakfast sandwiches and coffee. They sat down as best they could. The place was crowded. People desperate to get breakfast after a night on the town.

Danny notice the man chatting with Sarah and said, "Hello, how are you?"

The man replied, "I am fine, thank you. Just getting my morning started. My name is Bob Jones, by the way."

Dalton said, "Danny, Sarah, and Dalton." As he casually pointed to each person.

31

For Bob Jones, this was indeed a coincidence. He had followed Dalton from Washington DC to Lakewood. The last time he saw them was when they left the marina on the sailboat.

He had followed them by driving along the coast and spying on them through binoculars every so often. He finally guessed by their destination as Put in Bay.

After sitting in the DeRivera Park watching their boat most of the night, he had come into the restaurant. He just wanted coffee. For the first time, he was within touching distance of Dalton and Sarah. While it was not his team's responsibility, he also got to meet Danny. Another team in Ohio was watching Danny.

Sarah added, "Dalton and I are a couple. We came here to meet Dalton's parents for the first time."

A perfectly harmless statement made by a happy girlfriend. Yet, it put Dalton and Danny on guard.

Bob Jones had just made his trip worthwhile. He got a piece of intelligence no one else knew. When they all went their ways, Bob Jones forwarded this piece of intelligence to his boss. Mick Gallow would know via text message Shane and Grace McNaughton were in Ohio.

As for Shane and Grace, they were still at the Lakewood Center. They had planned to remain available as long as Dalton and Sarah were in town. This would allow them to present some resemblance of a typical Lakewood Ohio family. While Dalton and Danny were on Lake Erie, Shane and Grace decided to go over to the house. It had been a while, and Shane wanted just to make sure the home was in good shape. He would enjoy any yard work or chores around the house, even if it were only for a day.

In a car down the block, the US government agents had also forwarded a message to their bosses of a Shane and Grace McNaughton sighting. They observed them driving into their Lakewood home neighborhood.

At this point, Mick Gallow, Scott Stanfield, and Rick Jones, Us Marshall's (Director of the Special Operations Group (SOG)) all were informed of the sightings. For months, everything was quiet. Now within hours, there had been a sudden return of all the McNaughton's to Ohio. Should they just observe? Should they engage? Should they simply ask for another conversation? The clock was ticking, and the three senior DC leaders knew they would have to inform President Sands of this development.

Upon requesting an appointment, all three men arrived at the White House around 12:30 PM. It had been two hours since field reports had been forwarded up the chain. They were to meet President Sands in his private residence.

President Sands was sitting at a table doing some sort of paperwork. As the three men came in, they each found comfortable chairs around the room. President Sands came out from around the table and sat in the fourth chair.

President Sands started, "So we have our prey in our sights. What has happened?"

Rick Jones replied, "It seems this started when Shane and Grace's older son took his girlfriend home to meet the parents. At first, this was simply the two of them staying at the Lakewood residence. However, it appears they went to the Lakewood Center compound for the evening. From there, we monitored their return to their home. Danny, the younger brother, was with them."

Mick Gallow interrupted, "It seems the trigger was Sarah Carbetto. It was Dalton's need to bring her home."

Rick Jones continued, "Dalton, Danny, and Sarah went to Put in Bay for an overnight stay. This morning we observed Shane, Grace, two bodyguards, and their baby girl arriving at the Lakewood residence. It seems they are just doing chores and home repairs. Much like any American on this summer Saturday." Rick Jones added the last sentence because it was his plan before this meeting ruined his day.

President Sands turned red as he heard something entirely different, "You mean to say that Shane met them, but your teams did not even know he was in Lakewood. How did he get there without being detected? I am paying a lot of money and getting no damn results!"

Mick Gallow interrupted again, "We also had an unusual encounter with the boys on Put in Bay. One of our men was eating breakfast, and the McNaughton's sat down next to him in a crowded restaurant. They had a conversation."

President Sands listened for about two minutes. This was his tolerance for not being the center of attention in any room he occupied.

President Sands said, "Here is what I want you to do. Let's order a drone strike on the Lakewood home when they are all confirmed at this location. Take them all out at once."

Mick Gallow was an old Jarrod Sands crony but was new to the government. He laughed, "Are you crazy? I don't think you can do that on American soil."

Ultimately, Rick Jones interjected the minimum measure he thought would satisfy President Sands, "Without drama, we will send someone Shane knows to have a conversation with him. Simply a reconnection after our last encounter. Will Shane kill the guy or be civil? It would be nice to know."

President Sands was not satisfied and added, "Second, Mick Gallow, you now have a man in the life of Dalton and his girlfriend. See if you can penetrate further with this person. Could we put him in their work-life or their social circle? Get in a position to be able to take advantage of them somehow? Thank you for coming. You all are excused."

With that, everyone left. Later Saturday, Cleveland Office US Marshal Arlen Wright pulled up to Shane and Grace McNaughton's old Lakewood Ohio home. Shane was in the side yard working on a garden bed, and Grace was inside. Arlen slowly walked up to Shane in the yard. Thomas Black was with Shane as they worked in the yard. Jack Dorsey was in the house primarily assigned to Christine.

When the US government first got interested in Shane McNaughton, Arlen was the first marshal who had questioned Shane many years ago. Shane looked up at Arlen and then back to his garden.

Arlen started, "Hello Shane, it is a nice Saturday to do the yard work. We had thought you moved on."

Shane did not look up but replied, "No, this is always the home where we raised our children. We always will try to keep it in the family. Why are you here?"

Arlen replied, "Last year, my boss tried to kidnap you, and it did not end well. One thing you can count on is the incompetence of the US government."

Shane laughed and got up to greet his old adversary.

Shane asked if Arlen wanted a beer. He accepted. He was on duty, but it was his Saturday too. They went into the house and to the kitchen island. Grace did not come over. When she saw Arlen, she said a curt Hello and continued with her chores.

After a long swig on the beer, Arlen said, "So what are we going to do with you? I am here because they have us watch for you constantly. President Sands seems to be obsessed with you. Why is that?"

Shane thought about it for a minute and said, "I have no idea, as I have never met the man. He does look like a horse's ass every time I see him on television. So, no great loss on my part. I cannot answer your question."

Arlen did not say anything.

After some time, Arlen finally spoke, "You know he is going to order us to come and get you again soon."

Shane said, "I won't be here. After fiddling around the house today, Grace and I will head back home. Is that OK with you?"

Arlen asked, "Back to somewhere tropical, I hope. Just where is home these days? Give me some bit of intelligence to take back to the bosses."

Shane smiled, "There is nothing to say. We operate all over the world to save people who are sick, poor, or persecuted. Here is a riddle for you. What do sugar, alcohol, chocolate and soda pop all have in common?"

Arlen shook his head.

Shane said, "Slavery is the key ingredient."

Arlen shook his head, put down the beer bottle, and headed out the door without saying another word. As Arlen left, he was upset. How could they continue to harass this man? In all the years, he had never seen Shane McNaughton preemptively do anything illegal or threatening. What was the comment about slavery?

Arlen looked down the street to see another car parked. He was not the only person dispatched. He wondered who it was?

After Arlen left, Grace came back into the kitchen area. She bluntly asked, "How much time do we have?"

Shane knew what she meant. How much time until some US government types come banging on the door. Since Arlen left, Thomas and Jack had been standing guard at both the front and rear of the house. Periodically, they would do sweeps both inside and outside. Both Thomas and Jack had noticed another sedan parked down the street.

It was decided Jack Dorsey would investigate the sedan. Jack slipped out the back door and walked through the neighbors' back yards until he was slightly behind the sedan. He then approached from between two houses at lightning speed, crossed the street, and slowed to a walk by the car's passenger side. Jack had a small camera with him and set it to take a picture every two seconds. As he walked by the side door, he started taking pictures.

As he got to the front of the vehicle, he casually crossed over to the other side of the street. It was unusual, but not beyond belief, Jack was simply out on a walk. Regardless, he got pictures of the two men sitting in the car. He then walked down the street and again cut between two homes, and through the backyards to the McNaughton's home.

At least now, they would have pictures of whoever was sitting in the car. One of the men was none other than Bob Jones. The images would be taken back to Masada and turned over to Noni. Noni would do the necessary detective work to find out the who's and why's of these people.

Soon after this, Grace left a note for Dalton and Sarah on the kitchen table. It said how much they enjoyed meeting Sarah and were happy to see the boys again. To stay safe and call if they needed anything. With that, Shane created a portal to Masada. Grace and he would travel back to their home. Grace always felt like she was abandoning her family when leaving Lakewood, Ohio. She hoped for a day when the US government was not pursuing Masada.

A portal is like a wall of water. If you look through gently rippling water in a clear lake and see the bottom of the lake, it is what a portal looks like. In the case of moving into the dark expanse, it is entirely black. It was like walking into a dark closet and then closing the door.

Grace, Christine, Jack, Thomas, and Shane stepped through the portal. They were now in a vast dark expanse. Tiny lights were seen, all representing portals to other universes. The universes were all part of a common construct—each with its own physical, time, and spatial nature. When crossing from one to another, you left through a portal, floated in the dark expanse, and were attracted to a destination portal. It was as if a strong magnet were pulling you. You could maneuver in the dark expanse, to some degree. Not like flying, but instead using this magnetism to pull or push from or to other portals. Shane often wondered why they did not notice cold or heat or even oxygen. He believed it was because as long as they were in the dark expanse, time was suspended.

There are three types of portals; fixed portals, locked/hidden portals, and temporary portals. All spiritual beings travel between fixed portals. The locked, hidden, or guarded portals all had restricted access. For instance, Heavenly portals were always protected by a guard angel. The guard angel was responsible for keeping everyone out who is not in God's Book of Life. Locked portals are portals with a physical, locked door preventing access to the domain's entrance. There are temporary portals. Shane and his Judges could create these. None of Masada's other followers could do so. None of the evil beings in Hell could create temporary portals, either.

Since Beleth's attack on Shane's group in Cuyahoga, the Masadians had put up doors with locks on the four fixed portals.

In Hell, Beleth was angry and anxious. As one of the greatest fallen angels to have been cast out with Satan, Beleth had become a feared and indulgent being. He commanded all of Satan's armies. With the existence of Masada, Beleth had a war to fight. While precluded from entering Heaven, Satan and his followers had no such rules regarding Masada. Masada was a paradise unto itself, and Beleth viewed it as a grand consolation prize.

In the last battle, Beleth had just missed accomplishing two of his three goals. The first goal was to discover a portal from Masada to Heaven. He had accomplished this, even though he found it was guarded by several guard angels. The second goal was to find and kidnap baby Christine. He had Christine in his arms when she suddenly was surrounded by a force field, burning him badly. He had the scars on his arms to prove it. The third goal was to conquer Shane McNaughton and the Order of Masada. To take their paradise for his own. He had failed at this completely. Beleth underestimated these humans. They were vastly outnumbered by Beleth's forces, but the Masadian warrior's skills were incredible. They managed to win when he had five of his warriors to every one of the Masada warriors. This was amazing.

Beleth would begin immediately to assemble and train an even bigger and better army. His generals would come up with an even better strategy. He would not be discouraged by this setback. In fact, if he were defeated twenty times, he would try again. Being imprisoned in Hell for thousands of years teaches you this patience.

Meanwhile, on Earth in Brussels, Belgium, a group of men and women met secretly at the Steigenberger Wiltcher's Hotel in the royal suite. They were representatives of the seven most powerful sugar crystal and cocoa agricultural families. They had more power than governments, more power than world trade organizations, and more power than any other of the world's corporate associations. The world needed its sugar, its Coca Cola, and its chocolate.

They were also joined by two additional guests. One was Tucker Drake from British MI-6. The other was Colton Lake from the US CIA. Drake and Lake. These two gentlemen provided an update on last year's exodus of the African and Central American workers. In this case, workers were a bullshit term used to describe the hundreds of thousands of people enslaved to work in the sugar cane fields of Central America, the Dominican Republic, and the cocoa fields of Africa's Ivory Coast.

In these places, Masada had migrated over seventy percent of the workers and their families to Masada. To have most workers disappear was catastrophic to the people in this room.

Generations of slave families had been trapped in these fields. Harvesting the basic raw materials for candy, sodas, syrups, sugar, and much more. These "laborers" worked six or seven days a week. They started as mere boys and worked until they died. Their payment was for pennies a day. If they desired a better life, they could not achieve it. Many were now multi-generational, undocumented laborers. They could not escape anywhere.

Today's mystery was how did these uneducated, unorganized people simply disappear from the face of the Earth?

Tucker was speaking, "Our operatives have talked to the people left behind in the villages. They reported the presence of outsiders before the disappearances, working within the Catholic and evangelical missionaries. They seemed to target the workers who were actively worshiping with the churches. Two words came up in our interviews. Loosely translated, the word Masada and the word peacock came up."

"It seems these people all were in large lines heading into the churches. Once inside, they did not come back out. We discovered no direct witness to anything. The entry into the church was the last time many of these people were seen."

One of the men, Stanton Rockefeller, asked, "So how did so many of them disappear so quickly. These churches must have been huge."

Tucker and Colton both laughed, and Tucker said, "Sorry for the laugh. We did not mean any offense."

Tucker paused and then stated, "This is a small conference room in the hotel. Most of these churches were no bigger than this room. One of the things we did learn was none of the people who disappeared took anything with them—no pots, pans, bedding, and clothing."

Colton continued, "While this is confidential and classified, the US Government has been investigating a group called the Order of Masada for almost eight years. This investigation comes from the top. It seems President Sands has been personally involved. There have been other cases of people disappearing associated with this group."

Another woman, Margarete Stallings, stammered, "We pay President Sands millions upon millions of dollars to ensure our interests are protected. How the Hell did this happen, and what is he doing about it? We need to get in to see him immediately and understand what he is going to do to compensate us?"

Stanton added, "I think the damage is done. We cannot simply go into the impoverished, backwoods areas of Haiti, El Salvador, Zimbabwe, and Congo to get more slaves for our farms. Despite the billions we have paid politicians to look the other way, I am not sure we could block these actions from public exposure. We have to face a harsh reality. We will have to pay for the harvesting of our crops. This will eat into our profits, and it will dramatically increase the price of our products. This will be devastating to world economies."

Margarete disagreed, "I am not going to let it impact my family or me. Not one red cent of the money is going to be diverted. We spent five generations building this business into one of the largest in the world. We have fought off governments, Wall Street, and all bleeding-heart liberals constantly wanting to paint us as slave owners. We have spent hundreds of millions of dollars to whitewash it all. I am not going to be the generation destroying this monopoly for my family."

"Stanton, you need to talk to our Washington attorneys. I want the United Nations and the US Department of Agriculture to grant us additional funding to offset this tragedy. I don't care if we have to say these Masada people kidnapped and killed our workers. Just get this done."

During the whole meeting, Masada was talked about over and over again. Colton Lake had several private thoughts during the meeting. The first was simply how lucky he was to even be in the room with twelve of the wealthiest people in the world. Second, he was bound to be promoted as a result of this interaction. Somewhere down the road, he had to engineer his role in all of this.

Tucker Drake was thinking about something different. He was thinking about how these twelve influential people worth billions upon billions did not address the neglect or poverty of these enslaved worker families. Not once did they talk about those people who did remain in the sugar cane and cocoa fields. People were still forced into this slavery, and still, these twelve simply did not care.

Tucker looked down at his hand, between his thumb and forefinger. Barely noticeable was a tattoo, which was a combination of black ink and gold ink. If put to the sunlight, it would subtly reflect. He had gotten this tattoo three years ago. It was a peacock.

With this said, Tucker was a follower of Masada. Based upon the tattoo, he was more specifically a follower of the now-deceased Joseph Magnum. As such, as Margarete was talking, he could certainly see the reddish aura around her. She was not merely angry. She was evil. She was very powerful and wealthy.

A few days later, Rick Jones and Sterling Lindquist, a Deputy Direction in the Central Intelligence Agency, were among a group sitting in the White House Oval Office. It was a briefing for President Sands on the Shane McNaughton issue.

The first briefing from Rick Jones simply outlined a sighting of Shane and Grace McNaughton in Lakewood, Ohio. They had come into town to visit their son Dalton. They stayed within the Lakewood Center residence, although no one saw them enter. They then drove to their old Lakewood, Ohio home. They did some regular chores around the house. Arlen Wright, the US Marshall in Cleveland, made contact with Shane. There was little to report.

Sterling Lindquist provided a second report of a Meeting in Brussels, Belgium, with the sugar and cocoa industries' controlling families. This was an understatement to those in the room. It would be like a meeting between the Saudi Family to discuss oil production if oil production was ten times as important as it currently is. Regardless, Sterling did not divulge the CIA was actually in attendance and had an agent provide information. It was not relevant at this point.

Instead, Sterling focused on the message. The disappearance of thousands of workers is somehow linked to Masada. Somehow linked to Shane McNaughton. We have known that Shane McNaughton and his people suddenly disappear from the face of the Earth. It seems that on a much larger scale, this is what has happened here. Tens of thousands of these people walked into tiny churches and were never seen again."

President Sands laughed, "Do you think we could pay Shane McNaughton to vanquish all the liberals and their fake press. That would be worth millions to me."

No one laughed, particularly Sterling. He knew the rest of the story, "The wealthy families are saying any hardship or financial burden caused is something the US government must compensate them for. They know you have been aware of Masada for some time. They are holding you responsible for not dealing with it."

President Sands was not laughing anymore, "You get word back to them to go screw themselves. This is the United States of America, and we are not beholding to them."

Scott Stanfield interjected, "Well, we kind of are. Not only are they one of the leading donors to most of the conservative politicians in Washington, but the two industries also represent trillions of dollars in economic value. Clear back to the 1981 Farm Bill, the US government provided over four billion dollars of subsidies to the sugar farmers alone, and there is the catch. We have very few independent sugar farms in the United States. Also, even though we have a tariff program dating back to 1789, these billionaires' sugar imports have been exempted. Whether you like it or not, these people own you, Mr. President."

Jarrod Sands did not like to hear this. Later, he would find a way to punish Scott Stanfield for this disrespect.

A few days later, Tucker Drake was meeting with Terry Gault. He had asked Terry to meet with him in London. With a few of his followers, Terry had taken a portal to London to meet with Tucker. Tucker's briefing was very different than President Sands' briefing. The outcome was the same. The wealthy sugar and cocoa billionaires wanted the US government to compensate them for the lost laborers. Masada was viewed as a US problem. The workers were gone from the fields, and now their businesses were disrupted. Someone had to pay.

Terry Gault asked, "Did they trace this back to Masada?"

Tucker replied, "Yes, they did. And my CIA counterpart told them the US government had knowledge and interest in Masada. The common interest has been established, which does not bode well for us."

They discussed this a bit further. Tucker did mention the red glow on some of the people in the room. But for the most part, it was just another adversary to put on a list of evil influencing the world in ways society generally ignored.

Chapter 3: The Dragon Rises Again

Revelations 12 7 – 9 (New Testament)

7 Then war broke out in Heaven. Michael and his angels fought against the dragon, and the dragon and his angels fought back. 8 But he was not strong enough, and they lost their place in Heaven. 9 The great dragon was hurled down—that ancient serpent called the devil, or Satan, who leads the whole world astray. He was hurled to the Earth and his angels with him.

When Terry returned to Masada, he briefed the other Judges. Shane was tired of this. He was tired of the constant persecution. Deep down, he had been as troubled as Grace when they could not visit with their sons. They could not return to their earthly home. They had done nothing wrong.

As the Judges met, Shane posed a question, "What stops us from attacking President Sands and trying to exorcise the demon living within him. We did this with others, with a very positive outcome. Remember the Tolberts? They were just greedy millionaires who thought only of their glory. We killed the demons within, and they went on to live productive lives. Why can't we do this with President Sands? Just look at him every time on television. He seems to be continuously tortured and filled with venom. He seems to want to pick fights with everyone. Don't we think a powerful demon is driving this? Isn't our responsibility to attack this?

Alice replied, "Yes, let's go get it done. My suggestion is we attack him where he least expects it. If he dies, it is the will of God."

Terry cautioned, "I agree with you both, but I think we need to remember this is the most guarded man in the world. How are we going to manage this?

Noni answered, "The news reports President Sands spends hours locked up in his residence. What is he doing in there? They seem to think he watches television nonstop. He is obsessed with his image and fragile ego. He only comes out of his rooms when there is a specific need. After all, his wife lives apart from him. I think the only time they are together is during specific public appearances. After that, I think she lives her own life. She even has a boyfriend she spends more time with. I think back in New York, where they are from.

I agree with Alice. Let's just get the pattern of his hours in the private residence, and we can attack him there.

Maggie commented to no one in particular, "I hate the guy. But I also don't want to portal into his room and see him doing weird sex shit in there. He is rumored to be quite a sexual predator. What is he watching on television all day, porn? Or is he watching reruns of himself on television? I am not sure which is sicker?

Everyone laughed, just a bit.

Shane told Noni, "You plan this over the next few days, and let's figure out how to accomplish this."

It took Noni a great deal of research. He looked at the White House night routines. Support staff like cleaners, cooks, waiters, butlers are all gone. Just a skeleton crew is left overnight. Once the President is in the private quarters, the secret service will guard entry points but not enter. Also, in President Sands' case, his family is removed from him. They do not visit him, and often the First Lady will travel back to New York on the weekends. Noni created portals to peer inside the White House to confirm every detail. The ideal for Masada would be a weekend night attack. It was settled.

Noni worked with villagers to construct a mock-up of the President's suite. The sitting room, the bathroom, the closets, the entrances, and the bedroom. The ideal would be to get the President isolated to the bedroom. The seven Judges would all have to be involved, as well as a few followers. They rehearsed all the situations they thought could happen. They rehearsed finding him in one of the other rooms. They rehearsed him being in the bathroom on the toilet. They rehearsed the surprise of a secret service agent being in the room. They went through every situation.

Noni and Shane discussed it. The worst thing which could happen is their failure. The second worst thing which could happen is for them to be seen by a second human being. It was important they were quick, thorough, and back out the portals in less than a minute. This was the goal.

Once they had rehearsed, and all had their roles perfected, Noni scheduled a weekend. Noni verified the President would not be traveling. It was time, and it had taken them less than two Earth weeks to get ready.

At 10:00 PM, Noni was the first to open a portal and enter the White House. His mission was to open an obscure portal, for a few seconds, in the President's bedroom. Just enough to get a peek to see if he was there and alone. Noni did this and found him strangely sitting in a chair and facing a mirror in his wardrobe. He confirmed to the others.

Thirty seconds later, Shane and Terry did the same thing in the other rooms. They found no one there. At the same time, Mufaro and Alice did the same in the master bathroom and closet area. They found no one there.

Maggie remained within a dark expanse guarding the pathway from Earth to Hell. If the demon possessing President Sands escaped, it would be headed back to Hell. Maggie would intercept and kill it.

Everything was good. Shane and Terry stepped through the portal. Terry would guard the doors, and Shane would move into the President's bedroom. As he approached the door, he found it locked. He created a portal to silently get to the other side. Mufaro would guard the doors to the hall, and Alice would move through the bathroom. Noni and Nancy would come directly through Noni's portal to the bedroom. All happened as planned.

President Sands was in a trance, and it took him a long time to sense movement at his doors. He was both startled and angry. He had always gone to great lengths to protect his secret. Now some secret service agent was about to get fired. He turned with a growl and was shocked.

He did not know three of the people in his bedroom. He scanned them, and then his eyes fell on Shane McNaughton. It was a face he recognized instantly.

President Sands shouted, "What the Hell are you doing in my bedroom? Get out before I call my agents!"

Shane did not say a thing but instead walked quickly towards President Sands with a dagger extended. Quickly to a Judge of Masada was moving so fast as to be almost invisible to the human eye. Shane drove a blessed dagger into President Sands' abdomen right below the rib cage and up into the lung. At least this would silence him.

Everyone stepped back with the expectation of an evil being emerging from Sands, as only they could see it. It would take on its physical form for a few seconds before its travel back into the dark expanse. They would try to kill it, and if not, Maggie was waiting.

What happened next was not anticipated. A full-sized dragon emerged from Jarrod Sands. It threw his limp body aside as if it was merely dirty clothing to discard. This dragon had no intention of escaping.

The dragon hissed, "I am Typhon, and why have you come. You surely will die here and now."

The dragon had a cobra snake-like head. It had two wings and two arms. The wings were large, but there were claws at the top and bottom edges. The muscular arms were inside the wings, and each hand looked like an eagle's claw. The talons were sharp and long. The legs were short, and the feet of the dragon were strange. They seemed to shapeshift so the dragon could stand upright on any surface or structure. The dragon was green on the bottom with leathery skin, but on top was covered in bright red scales.

This dragon immediately grabbed Noni and moved towards Alice as it seemed to glide over the bed. Nancy used an energy burst to block its path to Alice. Noni was in anguish as he tried to free himself from the dragon's grip.

Shane stepped forward and drove a spear into the dragon. The dragon whirled around, shattering the President's poster bed. Shane held the spear in place with one hand. As the dragon moved towards Shane, he reached out with his other clawed arm. The dragon also swung a wing with outstretched talons wrapping up Shane's arm and aiming the claws at his back.

Just before he was in the dragon's grasp, Shane grabbed the dragon's arm and held it midair. It took all of Shane's strength to hold this arm in place. Shane fully expected to be seriously injured by the wing tip talons coming towards his left side. At the last minute and out of nowhere, Terry had come through the door. He blocked the death blow from landing on Shane.

The dragon's attacks were all countered except for Noni, who was still in the grip of the dragon's left arm. Shane felt they were regaining control of this fight. He tried to leverage the hold he had on the dragon's right arm. If Shane could twist, he might get the arm to buckle. He would have to let go of the spear to use both hands.

As Shane was thinking this, he did not see the dragon's head tilt backward. The dragon dropped Noni as he did this. His back arched, and he took a breath in. His head immediately came down, and three searing beams of energy were cast from his eyes and mouth. He swung his head to scorch each of the Judges. The game was over unless any of the Judges wanted to be burnt in half.

At this point, Shane signaled a retreat. Their time was up, and the noise they made was not going to go unnoticed. The room had been scorched by the fire. Alice, Mufaro, Noni, Nancy, and Terry all escaped through portals. Shane was about to turn when the dragon grabbed him again.

The dragon said, "McNaughton, do not attack me again. I am not like the other evil beings you so easily defeated. I am Typhon and have survived for thousands of years. This man's skin is mine. I will do with him as I choose. Do not return. In time, I will come for you, and it will be your end."

Typhon picked Shane up and tossed him towards the door. Shane took a portal and disappeared.

Each of the Judges exited their portal, as arranged, where Maggie was waiting. They were defeated and devastated. Noni was crushed from the grip of Typhon. Alice, Nancy and Terry had searing burns across their bodies and faces. Shane had all of those wounds. Instead of chasing down an evil being, Maggie was now the primary healer getting the Judges back to Masada.

Mufaro shouted at no one in particular, "What was that? It seemed like a dragon."

Nancy gasped from pain as she added, "This was not demonic possession. The dragon and President Sands seemed to be the same being."

Shane replied, "Let's just get back to Masada and figure out what to do about it. If this dragon is running the US government, this could be trouble for the entire world."

For the next few weeks, Masada held its breath. Did the President have a memory of the attack? Did the dragon kill the President? About two weeks later, President Sands was at a public press conference. Noni attended and captured the President with a video recorder. He showed the Judges. First, President Sands showed no ill effects from their encounter. Second, Noni witnessed Sands still had a bright red aura around him. Third, he was even more aggravated than usual.

Shane watched President Sands' speech as he angrily spewed, "The United States of America must support our sugar and cocoa corporations. I am announcing a multi-billion emergency fund to help the corporations hurt by the unexplained exodus of their labor pools in Central American and Africa. As to my liberal and conservative colleagues pointing out this is none of our concern, they are simply all too ignorant and too anti-business to recognize these international corporations are vital to our economy."

"In fact, Senator "Do no good" Gudnou is an example of the lazy, socialist, and liberal malcontent. He is not a true patriot, and I encourage him to leave. His stupid comments about the US paying for continued slave labor are untrue. These comments will cause his voters to throw him out in the next election."

Shane thought, "Well, the President has not changed much. He is still a horse's ass. I am not sure he even remembers our attack."

The President droned on. Congratulating himself and spewing venom at all those he viewed as opposing him. Over the next few weeks, the President did find a way to break with protocols and pay the sugar and cocoa companies their bailout money. In return, these companies announced automation plans for their agricultural "partners." They would use the bailout money to develop and purchase automated ways for harvesting their crops. Simultaneously, the agrarian partners spent their time quietly chasing off the remaining workers in their fields. This created large pools of refugees, now the problem of other countries such as the Dominican Republic, Haiti, Columbia, and Ghana.

President Sands was asked about the international crisis he had created when giving billions to these large and powerful corporations. He replied, "This is not a United States problem. This is the problem of third-rate countries with third rate citizens." He completely ignored the starvation, persecution, and social problems he would cause in the years to come.

Back on Masada, Shane, Noni, and Maggie had healed up. They decided to take a trip across Masada, as they needed to clear their heads. It was a vast land with riches beyond belief. They decided to go to an area not previously explored by anyone. They headed for the opposite side of the planet. When they arrived through a portal, they did so within a mountain meadow surrounded by mountain ranges. There were a large number of both prey and predator animals within this meadow. A lion pride occupied a small hilltop on the far side of the meadow. Deer, goats and buffalo were grazing in the meadow. As the three Masadians exited the portal, they scared off some of those grazing. There were birds overhead, and there were large animals along the borders of the meadow. Giraffe could be seen far off grazing on trees at the edges of the forest. There was a stream in the middle of the field, and a few bears were fishing.

The three simply remained quiet, looking at all of the wondrous things occurring in nature just within this one simple mountain scene. Maggie whispered, "This is what my ancestors experienced every day of their lives. The cycle of life. Why go back after this possessed President, when we have all of this to enjoy? He will be out of office in a few months, and we will have to see who replaces him. It might solve itself."

Shane asked, "How will we defeat the dragon? Do you think the dragon will remain with the President once he leaves office? My belief is this President will exit and live only a short life afterward. I think Typhon will depart to go find another host powerful enough to corrupt the earth. What if Typhon possesses a Saudi king? A South American dictator? How long will it take us to find him again? How much more damage will be done?"

Noni thoughtfully added, "Shane is right. We have the dragon right in front of us now. We are going to have to take another and a more successful approach to killing it. I just hope when this is accomplished, Jarrod Sands is still alive and well. Perhaps without the dragon, he would find some peace and way to repent for his life."

As Noni was saying this, the lions took off after a small deer which had wandered too close. It was nature's theater being played out. They watched in silence.

Maggie broke this silence. "I want to use this same meadow as a relocation for my followers. We will call it Dakota. I will bring those most broken here to heal. When I have time, I will find a Renovare Pool somewhere near here to be the center of my new city. It will be glorious."

"Imagine my people being able to live as their ancestors did in a paradise providing for everything. Native American Indians are one of the most persecuted and sickly societies on Earth. They are a supreme example of how modern civilization uses people and then destroys them. If this valley contains only a fraction of those suffering on Earth, it is a victory. It is allowing a small fraction of people to live out their lives with dignity."

Shane said, "I would like to get up on that Mountain to see more of this area. Let's portal up to the ridgeline over there." He pointed generally. Shane created a portal.

Now their view had changed. The Masadians could see perhaps twenty miles of the valleys as they looked out over the base of this mountain range. As the elevation changed, there was a vast body of water. Perhaps a large lake or even an ocean in the distance. There were numerous changes in nature's carpet; clumps of trees, forests, meadows, streams, and eroded crevasses in the land. This is what Earth used to look like.

Shane wondered out loud, "If people on Earth could see what I see, I wonder how many of them would continue to pollute, corrupt, and overbuild the Earth. If people on Earth were to realize their Heaven was already given to them by God thousands of years before, would they still neglect it? If people on Earth were to realize their Earth will rapidly become what Hell looks like today, would they continue to deny Global Warming? If they really understood this, would they continue down the path of rampant consumption they are on?"

Noni replied, "Those with religion always believe Heaven will be created for them. They will get a bright and shiny new place to live in. I don't think they understand how precious Earth is to them. While I don't presume to know God's plan, I do know what I have seen. Earth is now closer to Hell than it is to Masada. Shane, you have seen Heaven. What is it like?

Shane thought, "Heaven is very similar to Masada. It is most likely very similar to Earth thousands of years ago. The main difference is Heaven, like Masada, is a gathering place. You simply gather what you need. You leave no footprint destroying nature. There was one difference. Heaven seems to have an unseen network connecting all living things to God. The network brings family and friends together. That network seems to even arrange the villages and cities in their proper places. My belief is God designs everything within Heaven using a network of intelligence and purpose."

"Honestly, I made it to God's Temple. It was beyond words to describe. My belief is that God is not simply a person or being. God is not some raw power. He is interconnected with everything. The alpha and the omega. He is the source of power, but also seemed to promote the networking of it."

"I think he gave humans Earth, and they have chosen to do what they do. I think humans are designing the Earth without purpose or vision. In the end, they are choosing to be farther away from God's design. They are doing this without understanding the glorious future he might hold for them. Lastly, there Heaven is Earth. Perhaps God will restore it. It is not some magical, distant place."

They sat in silence with their own thoughts for quite a while.

Finally, Maggie spoke, "It is time to go. I have demons to kill."

Chapter 4 – Sioux Rescue

(Islam Quran 2:177)

"Righteousness is not that you turn your faces toward the east or the west, but [true] righteousness is [in] one who believes in God, the Last Day, the angels, the Book, and the prophets and gives wealth, in spite of love for it, to relatives, orphans, the needy, the traveler, those who ask [for help], and for freeing slaves; [and who] establishes prayer and gives zakah (obligatory charity); [those who] fulfill their promise when they promise; and [those who] are patient in poverty and ailment and during battle. Those are the ones who have been true, and it is those who are the righteous."

Back at Masada, everyone was healing up. No one really understood what had happened with the President Sands mission. Michael, the archangel, and Shane were discussing it.

Shane asked, "We were destroyed by this dragon. Our weapons had no effect. It was able to defeat all of us. It just cast-off President Sands like he was simply a shirt. It was not like anything we have ever seen before."

Shane continued, "When we exorcise a demon from a human, it has a physicality we can attack. Yet this lasts for only a minute or so before the demon becomes a spirit. This dragon was very physical. There was no sign it was trying to escape or that it would morph to a spirit form."

Michael listened, "Shane, what you are describing is impossible. The twelve dragons were vanquished into the bowels of Hell. God locked them in Satan's jail with him. If they did escape, they would be more powerful than any of us. They would not possess a human. They would devour the human from the inside out. If they do exist, their power and their intent would be total destruction."

"Typhon was one of the most powerful dragons. They were on Earth before humanity when the Earth was simply a floating rock. As God created Earth as the paradise for men, God made an agreement with the dragons. They agreed to remain hidden and consume only what they needed. Their nature was to turn all to ash. At some point, humans grew to cover the Earth and inevitably ran into the dragons. A great war ensued. The humans were no match for the dragons."

"God returned and imprisoned them in Hell. As an additional way to keep Satan's jail secure, they were put in chains around his jail. Each powerful enough that if Satan ever did escape, they would destroy him. Both evil, but not necessarily allies."

Shane warned, "If these are on Earth and hiding as humans, then how do we detect and kill them."

Michael said, "I am not sure."

For the first time since Shane began this journey with the Order of Masada, the teacher did not have an answer. He would be on his own. But he worried. Did President Sands know who attacked him? Was their attack observed by the Secret Service? Would the conflict with the US government escalate? They were soon to find out.

Across Masada, life was getting back to normal in Summer 2004, Earth time. Masada has seasons, but time moved at the will of the Judges. Two years ago, Frannie had been merely riding on a Cleveland city bus one day, and Shane McNaughton had given her a business card. She was an old lady who worked hard most of her life. Shane brought her to Masada. After many months, Frannie was a healthy and beautiful young lady, literally wise beyond her years. Her Masadian village had made her an informal leader.

On Earth, she was an honest, God-fearing, little old lady. No one would notice. As a black woman, she had always excelled at blending into the background. Yet on Masada, she was a fierce and bold leader. She had found her voice, as it should be. She even had a romantic crush on Judge Mufaro. They both had grown close. Would it go to the next level? Anything is possible on Masada.

On Masada, the abundance of riches allowed them to quickly make clothing or shelters for themselves. If a house was needed, the village people simply got together for a few days and constructed it. If they needed a grain mill, they did the same. No one exchanged money. If a person was good at making clothing, the villagers would ask for them to make clothing. If a person was good at baking, the same was true. It was not even a barter system. It was a society where each person looked out for all the others. Occasionally, technology was needed. In these instances, Judges were enlisted to bring the technology through a portal to satisfy the need.

This had become a really popular thing. Judges would occasionally honor a request to bring back Twinkies, potato chips, a toy, or a board game. Sometimes, a village would request some horse tack, tools, electronics, or engine parts. It was problematic as Masada did not have processed fuel. Electricity was always an issue, Judges would bring back solar panels and wind turbines to compensate. A little bit of Earth could go a long way on Masada.

Relationships were the same. As Masada matured, two things evolved. The first was changing relationships. Marriages, children, and families were forming. Also, religion played an essential part in Masadian life. On Earth, belief in God, Jesus, and religion were predicated on faith. On Masada, the presence of heavenly (and evil) beings eliminated the unseen need for great faith. A different and more profound love for God emerged.

On Masada, all religions worshiping one God were deemed acceptable. Native Americans, Indians, Asians, Middle Eastern, and European people brought all sorts of beliefs with them. Creole and Baoule's people brought even more. It was as if many roads diverged to one point.

Shane had taught Heaven was an original version of Earth and of Masada. It was mankind that corrupted Earth, polluted Earth, and destroyed this basic tenant of society. It was essential to preserve the human relationship with nature in Masada. It was as important as the love of God.

For the most part, even if the concept of a gatherer society was strange, followers would be thrilled with the advantages. An abundance of everything. Want for nothing. Health was perfect. Relationships were pure. While the domains of Hell and Earth burned with discord, Masada's domain was tranquil and alive.

Sri Ma had enlisted Frannie to teach these principles to the Creole and the Baoule' peoples. In their existence on Earth, these people had such a rudimentary understanding of the Earth's natural role in their life. Here they needed to adopt conservation of nature. They needed to resist polluting the environment they lived in. They could not live a primitive life. Unlimited time and no disease demanded a strategy of living for the long term. Frannie and the other teachers from Masada began teaching these societies the basic lessons of life.

Interestingly, introducing them to Christianity in the context of Masada was also very different. Creole voodoo and Baoule' idol worship were still fresh in the minds of many people. The idea of a single God and a savior was essential to them. As they were saved by this God, their love and gratitude were eternal. Most thought they had already found paradise, and in fact, that was partly right.

The Order of Masada did not discourage false religion but instead nurtured people to love the one living God. The one God making all possible. After all, Shane McNaughton had been to the Temple of New Jerusalem. Angels and heavenly beings were always around. Faith was not an essential ingredient in religion. Righteousness and love were the measures of a person.

In the Creole villages, one man stood above all the rest. His name was Jonas. He was a big man by Haitian standards and well-liked. He was always part prankster and part wise man. He seemed to have experience and intelligence, which was significantly greater than those around him. As such, he was emerging as the leader of Creole. Sri Ma was excited by this and had hoped Jonas would be one of the first rescued Masadian's to join the Order. She was continually looking for those special people who would take the next important step.

It was also getting closer to the time when Alice would deliver her baby. Since their attack on President Sands in Washington DC, Shane grounded Alice. No traveling, no patrols in the dark expanse, and simply rest. Alice was instructed to rest in her apartment on the sixth floor. Others would take care of her for now.

In July 2004, Alice gave birth to a baby boy. His name was Joseph Junior, named after one of the greatest Judges of the Order of Masada. Joseph Junior's deceased father. Alice actually let her wounds heal, and her anger diminish as she enjoyed caring for her baby. At the same time, there were plenty of surrogate mothers. Grace, Nancy, Maggie, Arunta, old Christine, and many others cared for Joseph Junior. Shane vowed to raise him as his own son, in honor of his dead friend Joseph Senior.

While Alice was recovering, Maggie took Mufaro and Nancy on a trip to the Dakotas. The goal was to work on all nine of the Indian reservations. To do what they could for some of the most neglected citizens of the World. Over half of the people live well below the United States poverty line. Nine in ten people did not have a job. Eight of ten people suffered from debilitating alcoholism and addiction.   Life expectancy was just about half the life of a typical adult in the United States and was the second lowest in the Western hemisphere. Tuberculosis, diabetes, and cancer were as common as a cold.

Maggie said, "The news in the United States can dramatize the plight of one lost soul. Everyone cares. People rush to help. Yet, Native Americans living on reservations are the most tragic story of a society in the World. The average US citizen doesn't even think about it. Why is that?"

Maggie had an impossible goal. She wanted to heal everyone. Upon arriving in Pine Ridge, South Dakota, Nancy was shocked. Both Maggie and Mufaro had life experiences living in this type of poverty. Nancy did not. She certainly did not believe it existed in North America. The best of the homes here were still well below the worst of the homes in Nancy's hometown of Buffalo, New York.

Nancy whispered, "Oh my God. I can't believe this."

While it was summer, there were merely many children, women, and men just propped up against buildings. They were breathing, but most suffered from prolonged or permanent physical disabilities. Children without the ability to move around had limbs curled up under them. They just laid in the dirt.

Maggie had already arranged to meet with the eighteen-member Oglala Sioux Tribal Council. This was the governing body on the reservation. Maggie had made a deal. If the tribal council arranged a pow wow for the entire community, Maggie would work miracles for those in attendance. She would heal them all. They agreed to do this at the Oglala Lakota Nation Wacipi Rodeo Fair. This was the most extensive collection of people from the reservation.

Privately, Maggie had no idea how this would work. She had been praying to God silently to show her a way to do what she promised.

It was arranged at 6:00 PM, the pow wow would begin. Maggie was Sioux, which gave her the advantage to get up in front of the group at the Rodeo Fair. They were hopeful at least some of the townsfolks would show up. Maggie had explained to Mufaro and Nancy most of the native American people had given up on government. When your starving, hungover, and dying, government meetings do not mean much.

At 5:45 PM, Maggie and her group walked to the campfire. The Masadians were shocked. At least one thousand people had made the trip. It would take them a week to heal all of these people. Maggie did not know what to do. Nancy smiled and told her it was not a problem.

Maggie got in front of the people and tried to talk so they could hear her. It was just too large of a crowd. A minute later, the sheriff drove his Ford Escape through a hastily made opening in the crowd and parked it in the middle next to the large campfire. He jumped out and handed Maggie the microphone for his public address system.

Maggie began, "My brothers and sisters, I come to you today with an offer from the Great Spirit. I would like to heal you from your sickness and sadness. I would like to soothe your wounded spirit. My only hope is to return, to you, your dignity and pride. I want to allow you to relive life with love for the earth, the sun, and the sky. I want to give you the healing of your children. Your poor children are suffering and sick with the white man's diseases. It is time the Sioux people are reborn to discover both old traditions and new truths. If you are wanting my help, remain, and move closer. If you do not, you can be on your way with no hard feelings. I love all of you."

Surprisingly, there were at least two hundred or so people who got up and left. Many just wanted to continue to enjoy the Rodeo Fair. Many were men still having an ability to walk away, to return to a bar, or to their bottle. This was simply the most significant offer of their lives, yet they did not understand. Maggie did not fault or blame them. Perhaps she would return to help them another time.

After about fifteen minutes, the crowd had gathered closer. Those who could stand did so. They propped others up, or they carried them in their arms. Some remained on the ground. Nancy climbed on top of the Ford. She meditated and then launched healing energy as if she was the transmitter of a radiating and robust signal. Nancy's power to cast energy was greater than all the other judges. She was casting healing energy and saturating everyone within the Pow Wow. Nancy maintained the energy for roughly twenty minutes. After that, she gave up in exhaustion.

Maggie addressed the crowd with the microphone, "Go now, enjoy yourselves and be at peace. Gradually, you will be restored. Tomorrow, we will be here again at this same time. We will heal those who need more help."

Some shouted thank you but most just left. Since the healing was not instantaneous, they were disappointed. The Native Americans did not realize God's power was already working within their cellular structure. They were being healed from the inside out.

The next morning, Maggie, Mufaro, and Nancy returned to the Pine Ridge administration building. John Standing Bear, the current President, was there to greet them. He said, "I have heard already this morning many people are feeling the effects of the service you performed last night. It is too early to tell, but I do think you have healed many. I have never seen anything like this."

Nancy spoke, "We can heal them, but what will they do with themselves. There are still no jobs, no wealth, and no means to live off the land. What can we do to fix this?"

John thought and said, "Well, I am not sure. Other tribes have built casinos or dug for oil. No United States corporations are going to build any factories or warehouses on a Native American reservation. Native Americans all over the United States know two things. Reservations are prisons for the Native Americans. No reservation will ever allow them to achieve wealth. We can't even buy or sell the land we work and die on. It has been this way for hundreds of years."

Mufaro got up to excuse himself. He walked to the restroom. No one thought anything of it.

A few minutes later, Mufaro came back. He looked at John, "Are you an honest man, John? Do you have the best interests of your people at heart? We can help you solve problems, but it has to be a relationship of trust and confidentiality. Do you need some time to think about this?"

Actually, everyone in the room was surprised by this direct conversation. John did not know how to answer.

Eventually, John said in a measured tone, "I did not take on this job or work this hard without wanting the best for my people. I am an honest man, and you can trust me."

Mufaro said, "Good! I want to give you something to help you. It will provide you the money you can use to improve the life situation here. I have a business card for you. On this business card is a name and phone number. You are to call it. Whenever you need money, take some stones from the bag and call this number. They will sell the stones you give them and provide for you."

Mufaro handed John Standing Bear roughly $10,000,000 of rare gemstones. John Standing Bear did not fully comprehend what he was looking at. The bag was filled with precious stones. His mind was processing the idea this would become funding for his people. Funding for health care, retail services, jobs, and education. It would allow him to address parts of the problem.

Mufaro had more to say, "After we have healed your people, there are going to be some of them simply destined to come with us. Maggie will evaluate each person we see today. If they are chosen, then we will take them with us. We will take their families too. We will give them a new life, at least for some time. Beyond this, there are two additional things we must agree to. You will be contacted by the Commission of Catholic Missions to place mission churches on each of the nine reservations in the Dakotas. We will use these churches as future bases of operation. We will heal the people, heal the land, and create a new life story for your people. Is this acceptable to you?"

John Standing Beer was not accustomed to being given so much. Was this a trick or a false promise? He did not know. He did know, without a doubt, some people had been healed the night before. Yet, somewhere deep in his heart, he believed this large, powerful man sitting in front of him. John said, "Thank you, and I believe you will do all you say."

At 6:00 PM, Maggie again gathered for the pow wow. This time, there were five thousand people who were circled around. When Maggie gave the option for those to leave, this time, no one left. The circle of people grew closer to Maggie. Nancy once again used a massive energy burst to heal as many as possible. By 6:45 PM, Nancy had exhausted her ability to cast energy.

The Sioux people who had gathered were healthier, younger, and stronger. Addictions and crippling physical deformities had disappeared from some of them. Less obvious, diseases such as tuberculosis, diabetes, and cancer had disappeared from the bodies of these people.

When Nancy had concluded, the people did not disperse. Instead, the pow wow turned glorious. The circle once again expanded. The hole in the middle was filled with Native Americans in their ceremonial costumes. They began dancing in celebration and thanks. The people on the inside of the circle sat, and all began singing or chanting. The healing might have come from Nancy, but the thankfulness came from the people.

Maggie was thankful beyond measure. She prayed to God for thanks. She prayed for her people. She was somewhat guilty as her own beliefs had merged with Christianity since becoming a Judge. It had allowed her to move on from a vague image of God to her own personal image of God. A God who created her and loved her. Nonetheless, in her prayers, God provided a message to her.

Maggie again took the microphone from the Sheriff's truck. She asked all to be quiet for a moment of thankful prayer, and she said,

(Great Spirit Prayer)

"Oh, Great Spirit, whose voice I hear in the wind, Whose breath gives life to all the world. Hear me; I need your strength and wisdom. Let me walk in beauty and make my eyes ever behold the red and purple sunset. Make my hands respect the things you have made and my ears sharp to hear your voice. Make me wise so that I may understand the things you have taught my people.

Help me to remain calm and strong in the face of all that comes towards me. Let me learn the lessons you have hidden in every leaf and rock.

Help me seek pure thoughts and act with the intention of helping others. Help me find compassion without empathy overwhelming me.

I seek strength, not to be greater than my brother, but to fight my greatest enemy Myself. Make me always ready to come to you with clean hands and straight eyes. So when life fades, as the fading sunset, my spirit may come to you without shame."

With this said, Maggie had accomplished her mission. She had given the people of Pine Ridge Sioux Reservation the first gift to help them heal their spirits, minds, and bodies. If that had been all, Maggie would have been satisfied. This barren reservation was now filled with life and hope.

(Old Testament 2 Chronicles 7: 12-14, Jewish Ketuvim)

12 the Lord appeared to him at night and said: "I have heard your prayer and have chosen this place for myself as a temple for sacrifices."

13 "When I shut up the Heavens so that there is no rain, or command locusts to devour the land or send a plague among my people, 14 if my people, who are called by my name, will humble themselves and pray and seek my face and turn from their wicked ways, then I will hear from Heaven, and I will forgive their sin and will heal their land."

Suddenly, Maggie was surprised as she was forcefully lifted into the air. She was floating at about a hundred feet high. Her mind was filled with a vision of the New Jerusalem mountain top in Heaven. Much like the mountaintop palace of God, Maggie suddenly shot a massively bright light that seemed to come from her head. It was too bright to look at directly. If Shane had been there, it would have reminded him of his first trip to the palace of God.

This light basked over the land within the reservation. Trees, bushes, and grasses magically grew. Water flowed from creeks long dried up. Birds and animals were seen habituating this new lush virgin landscape. Buffalo were seen grazing in the grasses. The barren landscape was being transformed into grasslands, forests, and wetlands. This was impossible to comprehend, even for Mufaro and Nancy. They had not seen this, but Maggie had exploded with an ability to heal barren land. The Native Americans were scared and fearful. Like Nancy's healing energy, Maggie projected this energy for roughly thirty minutes. During this time, plant life grew at accelerated rates. Animals came from nowhere. As the people had been healed, so had the land. A bird's eye view of South Dakota would have shown this as an oasis of natural beauty against otherwise barren geography.

Maggie returned to the ground. The Sioux were very excited and fearful. What had they witnessed? Was this good or evil? Nancy and Mufaro rushed to Maggie, who had collapsed on the ground.

Nancy shook and woke her. Nancy asked, "Are you all right? What did you do?"

Maggie weakly said, "It was not me. I have no idea what caused this energy."

Mufaro exclaimed, "Amazing!"

Maggie, Nancy, and Mufaro left the Pine Ridge Reservation the next morning. It was very different from when they came. Almost everyone came out to wish them well. Most had been restored to a healthy version of themselves. Others had been cured of disease. Finally, the lush and rich landscape seemed to grow instantly throughout the reservation. Where a barren hill existed, there was now the saplings of a young forest. Where a barren dust bowl had existed, there was now a rich meadow. All had been restored as far as the eye could see.

John Standing Bear escorted them inside the Pine Ridge administration building. They asked him to give them a room they could use. They hinted they would use this room as a departure point on their journey. He was well beyond questioning anything they asked for or did. Maggie had six hand-picked followers with her.

Maggie took the team to the other eight Dakota reservations. They accomplished the same at each of these. Mufaro also made sure to arrange for the follow-up with the Catholic Church mission group, building a mission center on each of the reservations. These mission centers would allow Maggie to return and have a base of operations. Jack Dorsey had personally traveled back to the Vatican to ensure this was handled promptly.

For the Order of Masada, they had now begun a project to focus on the Native Americans' stranded on dying reservation land. They would do what they could to heal the people and the land. Maggie was dedicated to starting progress to a better and independent future.

Upon return to Masada, Maggie was content. She felt she had now achieved one of her most important personal accomplishments. Beyond this, Maggie had brought back from the Dakotas six followers. These were all expert trackers and skilled hunters. Half men and Half women. She had known four of them from her former life and determined they were all sufficiently righteous and good. She also allowed the reservation leaders to provide her roughly five hundred people with no family in the reservations. These people were to be her first settlers in the Dakota of Masada. They would be given a new start.

As September 2004 came around, Dalton and Sarah were getting ready for the Fall in Washington DC. Dalton had returned from Ohio to find he was being promoted to a Director of the company. How could an entry-level college graduate be promoted to Director? As it was explained, their new demographic was young adults, and they wanted a fresh face to spearhead this donor initiative. It came with a huge raise, and company car and several perks Dalton was excited by. His new boss was a gentleman named Robert Jones, a brand-new officer of the company. The morning after Dalton accepted the position, he was heading to work. He was groggy from Sarah's promotion celebration arranged the night before. Today, he was worried about meeting his new boss.

Dalton got to work, grabbed a strong cup of coffee, and settled into his new office. It was pretty barren as his personal things were still downstairs in his cubicle. He would get them later. He heard a knock on the door and signaled for the person to enter.

Robert Jones came in and said, "Hello, I am Robert, and I wanted to meet you. I suppose we are both new to our jobs. I am just getting acclimated to the organization. I will give you some space."

Dalton's mind was racing. Where did he know this man from? He could not place it.

Robert was walking out the door when he stopped and said, "Wait! This is too good. I know you. We met in Put in Bay. We were both getting breakfast, and I was talking to your girlfriend. What a coincidence!" Robert laughed and left.

Dalton had been trained by his father, and their shared experience, to not believe in coincidence. He was laughing on the outside but was suspicious on the inside. Rightfully so, as Robert was a Mick Gallow plant, who had previously been stalking Dalton and Sarah.

For Robert's part, his running into a McNaughton in Put in Bay was fortunate for his career. It allowed him to parlay his basic investigation role into a corporate espionage role—better pay, hours, prestige, and career outcome. Robert was thrilled and just kept telling himself not to screw this up. Play it cool. His company, hired by Mick Gallow, had done an intensive job of training him to be a "pretend executive" of a green energy nonprofit organization. He knew he could fake it for a while.

Robert and Dalton met up for lunch. Dalton asked Robert, "What were your experiences before coming here? Are you new to the DC area?"

Robert replied, "Checking out the boss already, good for you. I traveled a lot and have only been involved in nonprofits for a short amount of my overall career. Mostly in sales. I found this job interesting because it was about building communities of interest. I suppose you are excited to be focusing on the young adult?"

Dalton said, "Yes, I am excited to be focused on my age group. In donor relations, the young adult is only just waking up to a topic such as ours." Dalton noticed Robert spoke but did not answer the question Dalton asked him.

Robert got up to leave as he was late for a meeting. Dalton thought a nice guy, but the coincidence was bothering him. Soon he would forget this, as his first day in the new job was filled with all sorts of new challenges.

Later that night, Dalton met with Sarah, as was their routine. Workout, dinner, home. At dinner, Dalton asked Sarah an overly casual question. "What are you doing this weekend?" He knew the answer, as they always hung out together. Yet Sarah said she was open.

Dalton said, "With this new job and new money, I think it is time we move in together. I think we should spend the weekend looking for a place of our own. What do you think about that?"

Sarah could not contain her smile, but wanted to be cool at the same time, "Are you sure? You just got the job. Don't you want to settle in before taking any big steps?"

Dalton replied with a laugh, "Sarah, I am asking you to start a life with me. I love you. The job is a coincidence, and truth be told, my parents are sort of wealthy."

Sarah agreed. That weekend they searched for a new place to live. They found a beautiful row home near Lincoln Park between North and South Carolina Avenue. It was on 10th Street SE and was one of the more unique homes in that area. As each building shared a common wall with the next, this house had a small walkway on each side of it. It was not connected to the adjacent houses. A bit more money, but it gave Dalton and Sarah a good vibe.

As the realtor asked them if they wanted to put an offer on the home, Dalton told the realtor they would buy it now. She was baffled. Dalton gave the realtor a business card for Van Dorn Holdings, Ltd in Cleveland, Ohio.

She asked, "What is this for?"

Dalton replied, "Contact this office. They will purchase the home for us and arrange for payment."

Sarah was again surprised and had a million questions. She had envisioned Dalton, and she would be looking at homes for a few weeks, then stressing over how they could afford it, and then cosigning a home loan together. This was unexpected.

As they left, Sarah asked, "What just happened? I thought we would discuss how to buy it and be going to the bank for a loan."

Dalton laughed and said, "Sam Van Dorn is a man in Cleveland working with my Dad for years. He takes care of all of our business affairs. Things like large purchases, insurances, and taxes are handled by Van Dorn Holdings, Ltd. It makes life simple."

"If you don't like the home or want to look some more, I will cancel the process. I don't want to force you into a purchase you do not like. I just thought we both liked this home. That is what you said, or did I misunderstand?"

Sarah just shook her head, "No, I love the home. It is the one I told you I wanted. I will stand by that. I will go with the flow, even if I don't know where it leads to."

The realtor called that night and said everything had been taken care of. They could move in two weeks if they wanted. Dalton was pleased and knew he would have another thing to explain in a moment. Movers would show up at Dalton and Sarah's apartments in two weeks to move both of them. He had planned to take Sarah out of town while this happened. He knew Sam Van Dorn would move them with the utmost care and security. It would be swept for any unwanted electronics or listening devices. Masada would put in their own electronic security package in the home. Furniture would be in place, and all would be good. Typically, it was a team of Masadian followers doing the work.

Dalton got a phone call and re-entered the living room. Sarah was packing clothes in boxes.

Dalton said, "By the way, everything is set for a move in two weeks. Promise you will not freak out?"

Sarah did not say anything but looked at him, waiting for what was next. She was not upset. It was more like waiting to open the next Christmas present on Christmas morning.

Dalton was a bit cautious, "We don't need to be here for the move. There will be a group of my Father's associates coming to pack and move us. We simply need to be out of their way. What about a weekend vacation while this is happening?"

She smiled and just said, "I will go with the flow."

Dalton was now hearing Sarah's question almost every day. He did his best to always deflect, but soon he would have to reveal more. He would have to figure a way to tell her about Masada without losing the love of his life.

Shane had planned a rare day of relaxation in Cuyahoga. He planned a Daddy day with Christine. He just wanted some alone time with her, as his current "job" often did not allow for this. He and Christine hiked to a nearby pond. He had brought a few balls and a couple fishing poles. He was not sure what they would want to do.

Christine was most happy to be out in a field running. Daddy chasing her was the best, as she giggled and giggled. Occasionally, Christine would lose interest and stop to examine some meadow flowers. Then she would want to play chase again until she saw some bugs.

Finally, Shane got the fishing rods out, baited the hooks, and cast them into the pond. It did not take long to snag a fish. Shane called for Christine, "Christine, come here. Quick, I have a fish on the hook. You can pull it in."

Christine came running over and took the rod. She did not know how to use it, but he loved the idea of playing tug of war with whatever was pulling it underwater. She giggled. Finally, to end the poor fish's suffering, Shane reeled the fish in to show Christine.

For some reason, Christine was not happy. Shane did not know if she was mad at him or the fish or that tug of war was over. She growled. She raised her hand and pointed at the lake. Within ten seconds, about fifty fish were floating in the air. Shane was shocked and a little scared.

Shane slowly approached Christine, put his arm around her, and lowered her outstretched arm. The fish slowly floated back down to the water. Shane gave her a hug and a kiss. She changed her demeanor immediately into Daddy's little girl. They had lunch … not the fish … and then hurried back home to show Mommy the fish in the bucket.

Chapter 5 – Alice the Warrior land

(Hindu Writings, Mahabharatta, Section CXI)

"The man who becomes guilty of ingratitude O King, has to go to the regions of Yama and there to undergo very painful and severe treatment at the hands of the messengers, provoked to fury, of the grim king of the dead. Clubs with heavy hammers and mallets, sharp-pointed lances, heated jars, all fraught with severe pain, frightful forests of sword-blades, heated sands, thorny Salamis--these and many other instruments of the most painful torture such a man has to endure in the regions of Yama, O Bharata!"

(Hindu Vedic Hymns in the Rig-Veda, describing the Hindu Hell)

"Burn him not, scorch him not, O Agni, consume him not entirely; afflict him not

May your eye go to the Sun, to the wind your soul

Or go to the waters if it suits thee there or abide with thy members in the plants."

Alice had enjoyed motherhood. Joseph Junior was a reminder of her husband. It brought her back to Joseph and their time in Masada. Times when they simply hiked to a beautiful stream or overlook. Where they laid on the ground and just remained silent. Alice tightly held on to the joy of holding each other and moments of deep love. These feelings were slowly transferring to her son.

She also took comfort because, even without Joseph, she was part of a strong community. Grace, Nancy, Maggie, Noni's wife Arunta, and many others served as surrogate mothers to Joseph. They served as sisters to her. Even more important, Shane, Mufaro, Terry, and Noni were her fellow Judges reflecting parts of Joseph's masculine character. While motherhood was her joy, the Order of Masada was her soul.

Junior was a redhead. A good Irish boy. He was also pudgy and seemed to have an unlimited appetite. As he moved to solid food, he gave his mother a break. She was certainly grateful for that. The other thing noticed by everyone was the bond developing between baby Christine and Junior. Christine never wanted to go out without Joseph, somehow tagging along. Even if she was simply a toddler, Joseph was her best friend. Conversely, beyond his love for food, Joseph's only other real interest was watching and reaching for Christine. They were almost always joined at the hip.

At the same time, Alice started to find more and more time to regain her training. She and her followers restarted the most grueling training regimen in all of Masada. While they kept it a secret, they knew Alice's mission was to go into Hell, find Beleth, and kill him. To exact the revenge she had sworn at Joseph's gravesite. This vow would be fulfilled, even above her duties as a mother.

Alice began her mission with a team of forty of her followers. All were trained and excellent warriors. The initial goal was simple. Alice was going to enter Hell through the fixed portals and start reconnaissance on evil beings. By watching their movements, her theory was she would soon find Beleth.

Alice arrived at a fixed portal for Hell. While there was a break in the evil flowing out, Alice moved her group in. As they got into Hell, they broke off into six teams of six. Alice and three of her more senior people were in reserve. This first mission was to be easy. Simply head out in six directions from the portal to discover anything they could.

Hell was not what people talked about in storybooks. It was not lakes of fire or masses of people being tortured. It was more like Afghanistan's Sistan Basin, which is dry and arid. The heat was uncomfortable but not overwhelming. In the distance were mountains. These were not majestic snow-covered mountains but simply barren rocks. There were footpaths or animal paths still within view of the portal. Each of the six groups followed these. If there was a split, they would divide and continue.

In each group, one follower could cast the invisibility energy. If they detected even a hint of movement in front of them, the group would move off the path. They would huddle under a blanket of invisibility. They would not reappear until it was safe. Sometimes, they could find a grouping of rocks or higher ground to disguise their movements.

Alice had no goals except discovering the pathway to Beleth. Every thirty minutes or so, a group would telepathically report into Alice. If a scout team found something interesting, Alice and her three followers could head to this group for further exploration.

In this first mission, they discovered a town. It was a grouping of old, run-down wooden frame buildings. Human beings were living there. The humans were starving, wounded, and barely alive ... yet they could not die. They were immortal skeletons of their earthly selves. They huddled in these buildings.

The team watching the village was hidden off to the right on a hill's rocky outcrop. Alice got to them in a few minutes. As they watched, a wolf pack came down from the mountains to the village. The wolves looked for anything to eat. There was a man out in the open and not fully protected. They got to him and tore into his flesh. They ripped a large chunk of his abdomen right off of him. Another ripped a chunk of his thigh from him. At that point, other people emerged from their houses with sticks or clubs. They chased off the wolves and carried the man to a broken-down table. They had a bit of water and some dirty cloth they used to wash his wounds. One of Alice's followers had been a nurse. Her name was Trudy.

Trudy whispered to Alice, "Look at those people and their wounds. I bet most of those wounds are chronic wounds that never truly heal. Each one just continues to cause inflammation and pain. The person loses motion and eventually is debilitated. All those people show evidence of continual rot. This is pure torture."

Another follower close by added, "I bet those wolves feed on the humans which continue to heal enough to provide meals over and over again. The wolves just keep taking chunks out of the humans. It is a terrible form of torture. Can we help them?"

Alice replied, "No, we can't get involved. I don't want anyone in Hell to be aware we are here. More importantly, I don't want those wolves coming after us. Let's retrace to widely circumvent the wolves and this village. Keep going deeper into Hell."

Alice's' teams remained in Hell for roughly an earth week. They had done some amazing scouting. They discovered four specific things. First, the portal came out on a small landmass, perhaps a large island or peninsula. When they moved to about a hundred miles away, they found a body of water. The water was acidic, and parts of it were on fire. The aquatic life all seemed to be dangerous. There were small wooden boats simply left onshore.

Secondly, the teams found several more of the villages. All the villages were in terrible shape. The wildlife they observed was very similar to a desert on Earth. Wolves, snakes, predatory birds, scorpions and spiders, beetles, and an occasional sizeable feral cat were all discovered.

The first week was done, and the groups had created maps of all they saw. The knowledge they now had would allow them to create portals deeper into Hell. Each visit should enable them to penetrate deeper and deeper. Upon return to Masada, Shane and the others had been worrying and waiting for Alice. As the group of forty emerged from their mission, the Judges rushed to greet them.

Shane greeted them, "Welcome back. You all look like you have been out too long in the hot sun. Get refreshed, and let's have dinner to celebrate your safe return. You can tell us what you found."

Alice and some of her followers briefed the Order of Masada in the Cuyahoga dining hall later that night. Alice explained, "Our notion of Hell is flawed. It seems to be the worst or harshest version of Earth. It is hot, barren, and hostile. It is not the proverbial Hell's fire pit. I guess it reminded me of what an overheated, empty Earth would look like. Global warming and pollution at their greatest extreme.

Someone in the crowd joked, "You mean the Earth in about fifty more years."

Many sadly laughed.

Alice explained her next mission would be to create portals to the edges of their initial search. At those points, the hope was to move even deeper into Hell. Alice expected once they got on the other side of the body of water, the population density and activity might pick up.

On Earth, President Sands, Mick Gallow, and Scott Stanfield were huddled in a meeting in the White House oval office. Mick was providing an update on all activity regarding Masada. They briefed the President on their observation of Shane McNaughton and his family. Shane and Grace had disappeared. Danny was in college. The team following Danny said he was living an "everyday collegiate" life.

Dalton was much more interesting. Mick Gallow reported, "We have been able to reach out to one of the officers in his nonprofit. We arranged for Dalton to be promoted from the mailroom to the boardroom. We also were able to plant one of our team into the nonprofit as Dalton's boss. We have been quite successful in getting next to him."

"Also, with his promotion, he is demonstrating a real desire to move up in the world. This is something we can work with. He just bought an $800,000 townhome. Of course, we connected this to Van Dorn Holdings Ltd. As you may recall, Sam Van Dorn is the money guy behind Shane McNaughton. We have dots we are connecting through our efforts with Dalton."

"There is something else working for us we did not anticipate. Dalton's girlfriend is noticing the strangeness of his family. She seems to be asking the same questions we are asking. He has not answered her directly, but it is getting close. If we keep our surveillance in place, we might get the answers we need. Because Masada protects Dalton by sweeping his locations for listening devices, we can't get really close. But we have placed surveillance and listening devices outside of his office and residence. This is, of course, five times as expensive as normal surveillance would cost. Sarah has been the key to finding things out."

Scott Stanfield interjected, "That is not good enough. Let's see if we can give her a new friend to push her to ask more questions. Is this possible?"

Mick Gallow replied, "No problem, it is your money?"

President Sands laughed, "Not exactly. We are using the slush fund built in our re-election campaign to pay for this. So, it is someone else's money."

Scott Stanfield just shook his head. President Sands just announced his participation in another unethical and illegal activity. Scott just wished he would shut up.

On Masada, Alice had waited a few weeks to recharge the team. They had mapped their progress and believed Hell was a world, much like Masada. The goal now was to create portals at the furthest spots they had explored and continue from those points. Alice now needed some help. She enlisted Maggie and Terry Gault to help her. If the three of them worked together, they could get everyone into the right locations quickly.

The team of eighty was again split into groups. It was double the size of the first expedition force. Alice, Maggie, and Terry each controlled their own groups. The goal of the Judges was to quickly set up portals and get the teams safely through. Based upon discoveries as they moved, the three Judges would take turns investigating with any given scouting group.

The teams were following six paths, then twelve paths, and it continued to expand. Two groups decided to use the small wooden boats they found and push to cross the large body of water. It was slow going, and they were very fearful of being discovered. Yet, within a few hours, they had rowed across the body of water. The other teams continued tracing the pathways to more and more villages. They were moving closer and closer to larger cities of people. Again, these cities resembled battle-ravaged ghettos or slum areas. They were infested with rodents, bugs, and other animals. They even witnessed cannibalism amongst the people. They saw a lady laying out on a board, and some people were simply carving portions of meat from her body. It looked like they were in a line, waiting. People were fighting and stealing from one another.

Troy, one of Alice's leaders, cautioned his team. "Be very careful. If they see us, we would most likely look like a very attractive meal. Let's stay hidden as we travel."

Another group came to a valley area. What they saw was completely different. In this area, there were thousands of warriors training. There were blacksmiths, mess halls, livery stables, and all sorts of support activity. This Masadian team was led by Jason, one of Maggie's trackers. This team was the first to be faced with grave danger. This training location sent out patrols and had guards posted. The patrols were not looking for them, and it appeared they were most interested in hunting and gathering food. Whether animal, vegetable, or person, it did not seem to matter to them. Jason was particularly bothered because they appeared to be using some breed of a large wolf as their guard dog. He was worried the wolf might pick up the Masada team's scent.

In the meantime, Alice's group and a group led by Peggy had disembarked after crossing the body of water. Peggy was going to go left. Her goal was to see if the water ended at some point. Alice's group was going to push straight forward along the footpath from the boat moorings. Alice had a target of mountains in front of her.

Alice's group traveled straight towards a mountain range. When they got there, Alice noticed a canyon opening to the right. Alice decided to break the group up. One group would move down the canyon. The other two would climb high up to provide overwatch as they progressed. They would stay abreast of each other as they went.

As they moved, they were going deeper and deeper down while moving into a canyon with steeper walls. This was not ideal. Alice also started to notice there were additional ledges and entrances to caves as they moved. The groups traveling at the top of the mountain ledges could see down, but it was getting more difficult. The face of the cliffs often hid a ledge below. The groups at the top had to move slower and more out in front of Alice's group on the canyon floor. This left Alice vulnerable to someone traveling from the rear and bumping into them.

At one point, a group of roughly fifty evil beings came down the footpath from the rear. They were traveling at a fast pace and almost ran right into Alice. Alice moved back against the canyon wall and cast invisibility to cloak the group at the last minute. Alice was anticipating; they were getting closer and closer to Beleth. Follow the traffic, and it would lead to him.

Peggy's group had found the edge of the water. It revealed the remaining groups to the left could circumvent the water and still get to this canyon. Peggy turned around. One of the other groups joined up. They were headed towards the canyon to join Alice.

Troy was one of the scouts on top of the canyon. He had scouted ahead, found a ledge, and entered an uninhabited, large cavern. They had been moving for at least two days. It was time for a break. At this point, Troy signaled Alice. Alice created portals to the cave entrance, avoiding the inconvenience of climbing the canyon wall. Three teams were in this cave. Maggie created portals to retrieve her group. Thirty of the Masada warriors had gathered in this cave and exchanged what information they had discovered. The two remaining sets of groups were scouting cities and were observing the army training grounds. Maggie and Terry took two followers and joined these groups, still doing reconnaissance.

It was agreed when Maggie and Terry felt they had nothing more to learn, they would portal back to Masada. Alice would remain with the larger group in the canyon and continue the search forward. After four hours, Alice was ready to move forward again. They decided the two teams scouting above the canyon would leave first. Alice created portals to get each team in position. Alice returned and took the last team towards the canyon floor.

It was a big surprise when they had traveled no more than five miles to find a large clearing in the canyon. It was several miles wide and long. In the center of this valley was an army fortress. There had to be five thousand evil beings roaming this canyon. Alice and her team stayed close to the right wall and carefully moved to circumvent the inhabitants.

About midway up the canyon wall on the right side were three large cavern openings with an adjoining ledge. It was easy to see this was important, as it was illuminated with torches. Also, a significant number of guards were standing in front of these cavern openings. Alice needed to see more. She could not move fast, and she could not create portals large enough to bring her whole team.

Jason had been leading the groups at the top of the canyon. Alice set a portal to his position.

Alice instructed him, "Jason, we have gotten as far as we can go with the number of people we have. I want to take two followers and move into the caverns. What I would like you to do is get everyone else back to the cave we found. When I am done, I will return to you. Then we will set a portal and head to Masada. If I am not back in the next two hours, march your way to the fixed portal we first entered. Take it and go back to Masada. Is this clear?

Jason acknowledged, and their plan was in place.

Alice picked two followers, and the remaining people headed back to the cave.

Alice observed the far-right side of the ledge. The guards did not protect it. Who breaks into Hell, anyway? Most of the guards were either asleep or in small huddles talking. So, Alice set a portal for the far right. When Alice got to the ledge, it was relatively easy to sneak into the right cavern opening.

Once in the cavern, Alice discovered it was like a huge great hall. All three cavern openings led to this hall. Beyond was simply one non-descript tunnel. Alice headed for this tunnel. It was difficult because the tunnel narrowed. Many evil beings were traveling in the tunnel. Alice and her team moved from one small hiding space to another along the walls. It took Alice about an hour of travel downwards until she reached a second hallway. They found new tunnel openings to the left and the right. By observing the foot traffic imprints on the cavern's floor, Alice could tell one of the two tunnels got the most traffic. Alice's instinct told her to keep moving forward and downward.

At the two-hour point, Alice arrived at a large interior cavern. Looking across this canyon from Alice's ledge, there was a massive fortress with a mansion. Before the mansion was a village, and across the canyon floor were other towns. This was not a cavern but a massive underground world. Alice felt she might have found Beleth.

Off in the distance, there was an enormous procession, with a large, golden litter in the middle. It seemed whoever was inside the litter was important. Alice wondered if this was Beleth? She could end him right now.

Ron, one of the followers, guessed what Alice was thinking, "Alice, we have to go. Teams are waiting for us. This is not the time. We can't be discovered right now."

Alice begrudgingly created portals to the cave and then subsequently got everyone through portals to Masada without being discovered. There was only one problem. Maggie had not returned.

At that moment, Maggie and her group of the original eight ran for their lives across rocky terrain. At some point, a wolf had picked up their scent. Now they had many wolves tracking them. Because of their abilities as Masadians, they could easily outrun the wolves. Yet, the objective was to not be discovered.

Maggie had spread everyone out in a fan. They would run when they had a clear path and shelter when they did not. The wolves continued to come without stopping. Maggie had hoped they would lose interest. They did not. All Maggie needed was a fifteen-minute gap, where she could create a portal and get everyone home.

Maggie could not know one of Hell's demons, Aamon, had discovered their presence. By his wolves, he was informed of the discovery of a fresh, living, human scent. Hell typically smelled like dead, rotting flesh, mixed with burning Sulphur. This new scent was a unique and wonderful smell to the wolves. Aamon himself looked like a large man-wolf and had joined the pursuit. These wolves would not give up until they found their prize, or the scent disappeared.

Maggie and the team were in shelter when the wolves appeared coming over a hill about five hundred yards away. They were too close. Yet, Maggie could not move. In front of her was an army on patrol or training. From their protected position between a group of rocks, Maggie calculated the army would pass in two minutes. The wolves would be on them before they were clear to move.

Maggie had eight with her. She devised a plan. As the wolves approached, she would attack them. It was attack or be discovered by the army in front of her. She had no choice.

Maggie searched the horizon and saw a small indent with a rock formation hiding them from the army's view. The distance and the rock formation would create a perfect place to draw the wolves into their trap. Maggie signaled everyone to backtrack to this location quickly.

Two of Maggie's followers, Hansko and Mato, were to move ahead of the others. They were to make sure to give the wolves a target to chase. The wolves finally came close enough to see the two native American followers. They howled, and the chase was on. The other six followers were now hidden in ambush. Seven wolves were now running full speed. Hansko and Mato ran right through the group of hidden Masadians.

Maggie now stood up, and the invisibility faded away. She gathered energy, pushed it forward, and focused on a large water pulse to wash the wolves away. She screamed, "Buwa!" The water crashed down in a massive wave, seeming to come from the sky. Two leaping wolves were slammed into the ground and motionless. The next three lost their footing and were being carried away in the surf. The last two halted upon seeing this and scurried away.

Now! Maggie signaled her group to attack. The wolves were not used to this. Most human beings would retreat and hide. It caught them off guard. Aamon was not with this group of wolves but was on a hilltop and could see what was happening. His seven wolves were all wounded and now running away with fear. He could not see who did this, but there were brief glimpses in the rocks of humans. Strong and healthy humans. Interesting.

Maggie quickly headed to the defensive position. Hansko and Mato were right behind her. She opened a portal to Masada. Everyone got through. It was closed. Back on Masada, Maggie was the last to come home. For those observing her and her team, it was clear they had been attacked. Maggie sought out Alice and told her what had happened. It was quite possible Hell now knew humans were there.

Later that night in Hell, Aamon traveled to the mansion Alice had seen in the underground world. He had decided it was a night to eat and drink with Beleth and his group. Aamon did not want to immediately reveal what he witnessed through the eyes of his wolves. Instead, he tried to pick a time and moment to inform Beleth of this great discovery. He wanted to find favor with Beleth.

Aamon had always been a fallen angel that was not well respected. A dog. A wolf. Not a grand angel. Not a lion or a bear or some other magnificent creature. Discovering the humans was his one special thing. A piece of information which he alone had. He would not give it away so easily.

The moment came after they dined. They were in the large living room of Beleth's apartment. Some of Beleth's personal guards were playing a card game around a table. Some had taken slaves into the lounge area and were having fun playing with them. There were still a few sitting with Beleth, making polite conversation. Aamon cautiously approached Beleth and sat near him.

Aamon leaned into Beleth, "Lord, I have some news for you."

Beleth nodded to indicate he was listening.

Aamon said, "My wolves picked up a fresh human scent in the plains today. It was just beyond a city they were hunting. I instructed them to give pursuit. They chased them for quite a long time. These humans were very fast to outrun my wolves."

Beleth simply said, "Interesting."

Aamon went on, "You know, Lord, I can have visions of what my wolves see. At some point, a woman stood up and turned to fight them. Whoever was with her ambushed my wolves, and they got away."

Beleth was now interested, "In the plains? That is a desolate ground. I wonder what they were doing out there. Tomorrow Aamon, take your wolves and try to discover where they traveled. Find out what they might have been doing."

Aamon had been given a mission. He nodded and was thrilled Beleth had entrusted him with this small task. He would be thorough.

Chapter 6 – Engaged and Threatened

Sarah and Dalton were settling into their newfound life together. Dalton has asked Sarah to go on a weekend getaway. Dalton had planned a getaway to The Homestead, a luxury resort located in Virginia's Allegheny Mountains, in Hot Springs, Virginia. The Homestead had been around since 1766 and was on roughly 2,000 acres of land. The resort was in the middle of nowhere but offered many activities including; swimming, a spa, an equestrian center, canoeing, hiking, and golf.

On a Friday in September 2004, they drove up. As night approached, driving was difficult on two-lane roads in the hills. They got to The Homestead, and Sarah was impressed. When they drove up, they went into a large circular driveway in front of the massive resort's main building. It was lit up like a Christmas tree. They got their hotel rooms and then took a walk around the hotel. They saw the pool areas. The indoor pool was large and uncrowded. They saw where the spa was, and Dalton had booked them a couple's massage on Sunday.

The next day they went hiking on one of the moderate trails. The Homestead provided them a trail map, and they were having a great time. They were a bit early for the fall foliage. Yet, it still was beautiful and healthy to be outdoors and away from Washington.

They got to a rest point on a bluff overlooking a beautiful valley. Sarah had been carrying the sack lunches provided by the resort. They sat and were going to enjoy lunch.

Sarah reflected, "This is great. I am so glad we decided to take the weekend off. With the new house and the moves, we needed to get away."

Dalton replied, "Yep. This is just what the doctor ordered."

They sat in silence, enjoying the rest and the view. They were about done with lunch when a little dark flash caught Dalton's eye. He turned around to see two young bears. They must have smelled Sarah and Dalton's food. It did not take long for a mother bear to emerge from the trail. Dalton knew there was nowhere to go. They could jump down the bluff. Best case, they would break some bones. They could stay where they were and hope the bears would go away.

Dalton got up and yelled while waving his arms. It scared the younger bears, and they hurried on. Dalton had inadvertently separated the mother and her cubs. The mother bear would have to cross Dalton's path to catch up with her young children. The mother bear got up on her hind legs, growled, and came towards Dalton. Sarah was behind him. Sarah was terrified and screamed.

Before the bear could close the distance, Dalton shocked Sarah by rushing to the bear. Dalton grabbed each of the bear's front arms and held her in place. The bear reached out, bit him in the shoulder, and shook him to tear the flesh. Dalton responded by pushing the bear back about ten feet. Dalton then pushed the bear's arms quickly down and towards the path where her bear cubs had gone. He moved with lightning speed to her hindquarters. Dalton now hugged her along her rear. He picked her up and pushed her. She could not twist around to attack. Soon she was ten yards closer to her cubs. The mother bear ran off. Dalton had executed this move in a matter of seconds. As if he was moving a small dog along its path.

Dalton returned to Sarah and sat down. He was not winded, but he did have a lot of blood on his shirt where the bear had bitten him. He asked Sarah, "Are you all right? I thought if I did not act, the bear might charge over here. Sorry to scare you."

Sarah was shocked, "How did you do that? You moved so fast. How?

As Sarah's composure returned, she asked more probing questions. "Let me see the wound. Should we call 911 to get you help? What if that bear returns? How did you lift a grown bear? You smell like crap. How did you move like that?"

Dalton was stuck. He felt he did the right thing. The bear was not hurt. Sarah was protected. Yet, Dalton exposed his true speed and strength. Now he had a gaping wound he had to heal before he passed out.

He might as well start with the obvious. He took off his shirt to expose two four-inch deep wounds below his shoulder blade, and he was sure there was another grouping in his back. Sarah saw them. Dalton took his opposite hand and put it over the wound. He focused, and his hand produced a barely discernable glow. In roughly thirty seconds, he took his hand away. He was healed, and there was no sign of the wound. Just blood to clean up.

Sarah sat silently and just stared.

Dalton said, "Let's start back, and I can explain this to you later."

Sarah growled, "Hell no. Explain this to me right now. I asked you these questions for months, and you were perfectly fine, letting me think I was crazy. When we were in Ohio, you answered me like I was in grade school. I am an adult. I want honest answers to all of this now."

"There are things you are not telling me. Secrets existed way before the damn bears—the secrecy surrounding your family. I looked on the Internet and saw the press reports on your family from a few months before. They actually called your dad an enemy of the state. I have not judged or allowed any of this to impact the way I feel about you. You are going to have to tell me the truth. If you don't, then we are finished."

Dalton was now forced to try and explain, "Sarah, as we go through this life, we do so and are privileged. We both have good jobs. We go out to eat great dinners when we want. We have our laundry sent out and delivered. We have all sorts of amenities in our life. Do you not agree?"

Sarah was puzzled, but she agreed.

Dalton continued, "Yet, there are millions of people caught in terrible poverty. Half the things we ate today were sourced from these places, all exploiting poverty to serve us our food. Less than 5% of the world's wealthiest people own most of the riches. Even with us both having good jobs, we are a few paychecks from homelessness."

Sarah interrupted, "What the Hell are you talking about? Is this your way of changing the subject?"

Dalton replied, "Give me a minute, and I will answer your question. What if this human tragedy was all part of a design. What if it were this way because of a struggle between good and evil? What if we were all pawns in a fight between God and Satan? Do you think this is possible?"

Sarah thought about it and said, "No, I don't think people are poor or sick on purpose. I don't think a puppet master is playing out some sick game. In fact, I am not sure I even believe there is a God."

Dalton continued, "What if one day God says, "I am tired of the rot, the corruption and the exploitation of my people. I love the people, and I designed the Earth to be their paradise. Why are they being mistreated on Earth? I am going to enlist some exceptional warriors to fight against this corruption. People to fight for the poor and the sick."

Sarah listened but was growing impatient.

Dalton finished up, "Sarah, my father, mother, and family are part of a group of people who are fighting against evil every day. Superhero's. They have rescued hundreds of thousands from the slave fields in Central America and Africa. They are right now rescuing the Sioux Native Americans from South and North Dakota."

"Take a guess who is persecuting my family as we are accomplishing this? The United States Government. They have been to our home and took our dad for questioning. They have kidnapped our family and tortured us in prisons. Guess who else is persecuting my family. Those huge corporations providing you with sugar and coffee, and chocolate. This is what is going on."

"Sarah, I have received the powers and the training to simply be my father's son. I am not involved in anything he does but have had to accept the risks and the threats. I have had to prepare. You are seeing just a glimpse of this."

Sarah responded, "Thanks, but this is full of bull. Prove it.

Dalton simply said, "OK. Let's go."

Sarah and Dalton picked up their stuff and started to leave. Dalton blocked Sarah and grabbed her around the waist. He opened a portal, and they suddenly were on the front lawn of The Homestead Inn.

Sarah was shocked, "How did we get here? What did you do?"

Dalton said, "I can transport myself instantly to any place I have ever been. I don't need a car or an airplane. All my family can do this."

Sarah slowly backed away. It was too much. She looked at Dalton and said, "I want to be alone right now."

Dalton let her go.

The weekend had not gone as planned. Dalton had an engagement ring. Before the bear incident, the plan was to ask Sarah to marry him, after lunch, on the bluff. Now he was unsettled.

That night, they went to dinner in the main dining room. They dressed for dinner and even got someone to take their picture in the lobby of the resort. Sarah had calmed down, and Dalton was glad he gave her some space and quiet time.

At dinner, Sarah finally said, "Dalton, I love you. Is there more to this story?"

Dalton thought for a moment and slowly talked, "I love you, too. I have all of these superpowers, but I have not acted on any of my family's things. I just wanted a normal life and have been crazy about you since I met you."

They enjoyed the end of their dinner and then went to their room for the night. Dalton's weekend was ruined. Sarah was withdrawn. When they fell asleep, each was facing the opposite direction in bed. Dalton had no idea about the future. The next morning, they packed up and headed back to Washington, DC. The trip back was quiet and subdued. They did not avoid each other, but they simply listened to music to pass the time on the drive back.

When they got home, it was to their new townhome. The move had been completed. The place looked as if someone actually had lived there for some time. Even their clothes, trinkets, and dishes were washed and put away. The refrigerator was stocked, as was the pantry.

Sarah got a couple of beers and asked Dalton to join her in the living room.

Sarah sat and began her well-rehearsed response, "OK, superman, this is how it is going to go. First, I want there to be no more secrets. If there is more to tell, then I want to hear it. Second, I will choose the when and where of how we are involved with your parents or your family business. Third, you are going to man up and give me the engagement ring you have been carrying around all weekend."

Dalton was bright red in the face. He was utterly unprepared for anything she said. He stammered and stuttered, "I, I, um, OK."

Sarah was going to obviously enjoy this, "OK, what?"

Dalton replied, "What you said." He dug into his pocket for the ring box.

Sarah took the box and got down on her knee in front of him as he sat on the couch, "Dalton, will you please marry me?"

Dalton laughed and said, "Yes!"

Sarah continued, "OK, now it is your turn. What else are you not telling me?"

Dalton thought for a minute, "OK, let's start with me. I will not age. I can heal myself from most wounds, as well as others. I have superhuman senses; smell, taste, hearing, touch, and sight. I am strong and very, very fast. I can teleport from any point to any other point, as long as I have a vision of it. I can take things and people with me. Finally, I can harness energy to create magic."

Sarah was genuinely excited, "Whoa, magic? Like a wizard?"

Dalton, "Yes, watch this." He held out his forefinger and put a candle in the other hand. He sent a gentle but small stream of flames to the candle. It lit the wick. Once done, he pushed a small stream of water droplets to the wick and flame. He then held up one hand and again created a stream of fire. He directed this to the other hand. However, before it reached the other hand, it seemed to reflect off an invisible wall about halfway between his hands.

Dalton explained the last trick, "I used one hand to push the flame and the other hand to put up a shield. Now I will show you a neat one. Dalton put up both hands and simply disappeared right in front of her. Sarah waited there for him to reappear. Instead, he reappeared across the room.

Sarah was impressed, "You really have some skills, superman. That is so cool."

95

Dalton felt relieved, and Sarah was in the moment. They hugged each other as they returned to the couch. Sarah got on the phone with her parents. At the same time, outside the apartment, a van was parked along the sidewalk. A telephone listening device at Sarah's parent's location picked up the news. A new report would be filed with Bob Jones.

It did not take long for Bob Jones to report the engagement to his superiors. In the following weeks, he also noticed Sarah had quit her persistent questioning of Dalton about his family. Bob suspected something had changed on the trip. Sarah must know who and what the McNaughton's are. Sarah now had a target on her back.

Maggie continued to work across the country, helping to set up Catholic Missions on Native American reservations. As with other distressed groups, Masada sent followers down to the reservations to work in the missions. It allowed them to assess the good, the evil, and the needy within the populations. Regardless, each of the first nine Dakota reservations were experiencing incredibly good health and good fortune. Their land was healed. Their people were healed. They had hope for the first time in hundreds of years. Maggie recruited at least fifty Native American followers who she took to Masada for training and service. The Dakota village on Masada was up and running.

It did not go unnoticed. The Bureau of Indian Affairs and its sister agencies noticed all nine of the Dakotas' reservations being completely transformed. Natural resources, agriculture, and the people had all changed in a matter of weeks. The health care services on the reservations were no longer seeing any patients. Addiction and crippling diseases seemed to disappear. The wealth and fortunes of the Native Americans had somehow multiplied. They no longer settled for living on a reservation. They no longer agreed on "tiptoeing" into the white man's world. Twenty or thirty families would leave the reservation and purchase all the homes and building lots in a nearby city. They had the strength and power to now overtake those who had ignored them for years.

In fact, local farmers had started to complain about their barren land. The reservations had somehow transformed into a fertile and unusual paradise. Local farmers began to shout at their politicians, demanding grazing rights on the reservations. Reservation land produced tenfold the agricultural output of the local farmer.

Maggie noticed something interesting. As the reservations evolved to a natural resource paradise, it seemed to have bled the life out of the areas surrounding it. Farms twenty miles away had reported that grazing and planted fields had turned to dust. Maggie suspected the healing of the land drew its energy from the surrounding areas.

Local farmers screamed when Dakota Native Americans would purchase their bankrupt farms and their farm equipment for pennies on the dollar. Every farm a Native American owned seemed to instantly transform itself into a fertile paradise. They started to buy up land, equipment, and commercial centers in North or South Dakota.

Where was this wealth coming from? No longer was the Native American simply housed on dead reservations … on land the government-owned and would not sell to them. These Native American's could now afford to use this land or not. They could now afford to live in the cities, enjoy the white man's schools, and do whatever they wanted. Who allowed this to happen? Conservative politicians were screaming. Their way of life in North and South Dakota was being destroyed. Native Americans laughed on the inside as they remembered how this way of life had put them on death's doorstep. At least before Masada rescued them.

The Assistant Secretary – Indian Affairs for the U.S. Department of the Interior in Washington, DC was reading regional reports on the issues. One word popped up that she had never heard before. It seemed a group called Masada was somehow helping these people. She did not know whether to feel good or threatened by this. After all, she had once lived on these reservations. From her perspective, she secretly wanted to meet these people from Masada and ask for their help in other places. Unknown to her, Maggie was already moving across the United States to other Native American ghettos ... or, as the white man says, reservations.

Mufaro continued to work in Africa. He had extended his reach from Zimbabwe to Cote' de Ivoire. Again, Masada used the Catholic Mission system for help. It allowed for bases of operations where Mufaro could recruit and place his followers. Mufaro had incredible freedom to interact and heal people. There was no government pursuit in these areas. There was little press or media which noticed him or his actions. What Mufaro did not know was he was in a significantly more dangerous position than he thought. The cocoa field billionaires were progressing in their investigation as to who took their slave labor. In a few more months, they would have enough information to understand exactly what Mufaro was doing.

A few weeks later, President Sands met with Mick Gallow and Scott Stanfield. Mick explained they had continued their surveillance. Dalton had progressed in his career. Their undercover agent had got hired as Dalton's boss. They confirmed Sarah Carbetto was engaged to Dalton. They suspected she had become aware of the family secrets. On the other hand, Danny McNaughton was still a normal college kid focused on friends, alcohol, and fun. Beyond this, there had been no sightings of the primary targets at the Lakewood Center or Masada.

President Sands was disappointed. He did not have a clear memory of the initial Masada attack upon him, but his hatred burned even brighter for Shane McNaughton and the Lakewood Center. When Sam Van Dorn closed up the Lakewood Center, it created a continued reminder to Jarrod Sands. These people could disappear and escape his power. It also was a raw and festering itch he could not scratch.

Jarrod Sands concluded. He wanted action. Sarah Carbetto was the only vulnerable and innocent link to Shane McNaughton. Perfect. As a wealthy man, and except his mother, all women were simply ornaments to President Sands. They were things to play with. Money had taught him for every dollar he had, there was a woman to be bought. The First Lady, his wife, was a perfect example. He did not so much as marry her but signed a contract with her.

He told Mick Gallow to get to Sarah Carbetto anyway he could.

Scott Stanfield objected, "Wait a minute. What are we talking about? As a US President, you would be breaking a dozen laws doing anything to hurt an innocent US citizen? Let's be clear what you are saying."

Jarrod Sands was not used to being challenged, "This family is an enemy of the US, and they are not true patriots. I think bringing her into custody and extracting information is acceptable. If she is somehow injured in the process, it was her choice to associate knowingly with these enemies of the state."

Mick Gallow knew better than to question the President. Besides, he was secretly taping all of the conversations, should he ever need the recordings. Sarah Carbetto was a means of staying relevant and getting paid. Mick Gallow would do what he had to do.

In the Fall of 2004, Masada, Shane, and the Judges had discussions on what to do next. Sri Ma and Nancy were working with the Masada settlements from Africa and Central America. It was significantly more challenging than they had thought. These people needed slow and careful nurturing to become a functional society. Mufaro and Maggie were continuing to work with groups in Africa and the US Dakota reservations. At this point, the mission was to heal, extract people from terrible conditions, restore their lands, and protect them from criminal threats.

Shane recognized a need to find more Judges. After Joseph had died, he had continued to put off the need to recruit more leaders for the Order of Masada. Now, things were getting complicated. Judges had picked up missions taking most of their time.

This brought the discussion to Alice, Terry Gault, and Nancy. Alice wanted to continue to conduct patrols in Hell. She argued they had just gotten close enough to be in the underbelly of Hell, and she needed to return before things shifted or changed. Terry commanded Joseph's followers. He was going with Alice on missions no matter what. Shane agreed to this with the stipulation Alice would be cautious and keep risks to a minimum. As this conversation ended, Shane pulled Terry aside, "Keep an eye on Alice and make sure she doesn't do anything crazy."

Terry simply nodded.

Meantime back on Earth, Sarah and Dalton were settling into a great life. Good job. Good friends. They used their house to entertain and to promote their standing in the nonprofit world. Despite Dalton's career being something orchestrated by Mick Gallow, Dalton was very good at it. He had outperformed all of his peers and was recognized in the Washington DC circles as one of the most promising liberal, nonprofit marketers. Bob Jones had been a great boss in allowing Dalton to simply do his thing. Sometimes Dalton was not sure Bob had any technical knowledge for marketing nonprofits to donors. When they did interact, it was mostly conversations leading to Dalton's personal and family life.

Sarah did not have a high-profile job. She was a grant administrator at a local college. She had a few friends, mostly from her own college days. College friends who had all moved to or found each other in Washington, DC.

On this night, Dalton had to work late. Bob Jones had asked Dalton and his team to stay late for a meeting. It was an opportunity for Sarah to invite her circle of friends over to their new house for a girl's night. There would be about ten women, and Sarah was excited to host her first party. It made the place feel like Sarah's home, not Dillon and Sarah's house.

The ladies arrived. The entry fee for the party was a bottle of wine or an appetizer. Everyone stood or sat around the kitchen island while stories and gossip flowed like wine. Sarah was having a good time. The women all expressed their envy of Sarah's sudden good fortune. Several commented about the move up in the world reflected in Sarah and Dalton's pricey new residence. Of course, there was a great deal of conversation around Dalton and Sarah's engagement. The typical questions.

"How can you and Dalton afford this place?"

"How did Dalton propose to you?" One of the questions Sarah did not exactly answer truthfully.

"When are you getting married, and where?"

Jackie Snowdown was the life of any party she went to, "So Sarah, how are you and your new boy toy getting along in this place? When is the wedding? We need to set a hard date for the bridal shower. I have seen Dalton, and you damn sure need to close the deal with him."

Everyone laughed.

Nancy Tolton, who was the newest member of this group, asked, "How have Dalton's parents accepted you? What do you think of the McNaughton family? Does Dalton have brothers and sisters? I know that there is always the "meeting the parents" drama."

Sarah did not know Nancy well but deflected the questions for the most part. She was not yet ready to put her relationships with Dalton's family into words.

The party moved from the kitchen to the living room. Everyone relaxed and enjoyed the night. Sarah played some good music. The women talked about a range of things. Politics, fashion, gossip, and their old college days were all subjects of the night.

Even President Sands came into the conversation. Most were disappointed, as they thought he would do something good for their lives. In the end, the group seemed to conclude he only helped his rich buddies.

At roughly 10:30 PM, the party started to wind down. Sarah had planned this. Dalton would be coming home soon. At some point, only Sarah, Nancy, and Jackie were left. Jackie got a call, and she had a babysitter problem. She had to go. Nancy took the opportunity to say she would be leaving too. Things were wrapping up. Sarah was walking Jackie to the door and was a bit worried. Jackie had too much to drink.

Sarah turned around, expecting Nancy to be right behind her. Instead, Nancy had gone back into the kitchen. Nancy emerged with two cocktails.

Nancy said, "I brought this dessert wine with me, and we never got to it. I hope you don't mind. I opened it. I wanted to toast your engagement and how much I have enjoyed getting to know you."

Sarah was turning her thoughts to clean up, as Dalton was surely on his way. She wanted to get this over quickly. She took the drink, they bumped glasses, and she chugged it. Sarah enjoyed the wine and said as much. Nancy said she would help her clean up a bit, and before Sarah could comment, Nancy headed to the living room to gather glasses and plates. Sarah was okay with it and started to get to work in the kitchen.

Within about ninety seconds, Sarah felt dizzy. She feared she was going to pass out.

Nancy said something to her, what was it? "The house is clear. Come in through the front door."

It was the last thing Sarah remembered.

About twenty minutes later, Dalton came home. He was surprised the house was relatively cleaned up. He was thankful. Yet it was quiet. Dalton called for Sarah but did not hear her respond. He walked the house and could not find her. This was strange. Maybe she had to take someone home. Dalton got undressed and in comfortable clothing. He turned on the television, expecting her to be home soon. He tried her cell phone, but no answer. He was worried, but he resisted jumping to conclusions. At an hour, he was now more than anxious.

Dalton knew some of the women at the party, so he started to call. He had reached four of them he knew, and all said the party was great. They said they all left between ten and ten-thirty. Sarah was fine when they left. He did finally discover the last two people at his house seemed to be Jackie and Nancy. Dalton knew Jackie but would have to go upstairs to get her number. He did not know Nancy.

Dalton called Jackie, "Hello, this is Dalton McNaughton. Is Jackie there?"

"This is her husband. I think she is on the bed in a drunken stupor. I guess the girls had a nice party," said Jackie's husband.

Dalton should have laughed at this point, but he didn't, "Jackie was one of the last people to leave the party. Is it possible to could talk to her? I can't find Sarah, and she should be here."

"Sure, let me wake her up."

Jackie got on the phone, but was a bit groggy, "Hey Dalton, what is up?"

Dalton repeated, "I came home and can't find Sarah anywhere. She is not answering her phone. You were one of the last to leave, was there anything unusual. Did she have to drive someone home?"

Jackie thought for a minute, "Nancy and I were the last ones at the party. We left together. Sarah walked us out, and everything was fine."

Dalton said, "Well, thanks. She is not here, but I am sure she will show up."

Dalton was about to hang up the phone when Jackie said, "Wait a minute. Nancy did not actually leave with me. I thought she was right with us, but when I turned around, she must have doubled back into the house."

Dalton said thank you and hung up. He picked up Sarah's iPad and looked for Nancy's phone number. He found it and called it.

Dalton said, "Hello, is this Nancy Tolton? I am Dalton McNaughton. I returned home and have not seen Sarah. Can you tell me if she is with you?"

Nancy said, "Sure, she is with me. For now, she is fine, but if you want to see her again, you will open the door."

At that point, Dalton heard a knock. He opened the door, and Bob Jones was there with three other men. They greeted him and asked if they could come in. Dalton let them in, with the phone still to his ear.

Nancy said, "Don't worry Dalton, after we question Sarah for a bit, you can have her back. But for now, if you want to keep her safe, please do what Bob asks you to do."

Bob Jones said, "Sorry Dalton, but we are going to find out what Sarah knows about you and your family. Once it is done, you and I will have a few things to talk about. Until then, she will remain with us, and she will be safe. So please behave. Now the first thing we should do is get all your communications devices. Then why don't you and I get comfortable in the living room."

Chapter 7 – Beleth is captured – Dragon weapons

In November 2004, Alice assembled a team of eighty followers. Terry Gault and she were going to lead them on another patrol into Hell and target the underground valley they found deep in the caverns. The meeting's objective was to ascertain who was living in the large mansion, what other fallen angels were in this cavern, and if this cavern led down to other parts of Hell. Alice and Terry laid out a plan.

Alice and Terry split the teams into two, forty follower units. Alice would travel directly down the canyon and into the caverns. Terry would provide overwatch and backup. They would get into Hell by using a portal to the cave where Alice had gathered the followers on the last trip.

Once everyone was through to the cave, they sorted themselves out. Everyone had blessed weaponry, and all were some of the most trained warriors in Masada.

Silently, everyone moved cautiously to their designated starting points. Alice took her forty followers down towards the canyon floor, down the right-side walls, and stopped when they were at the foothill leading to the cavern above. They created a portal to get up to the cavern entrance by watching for a gap in the guards. Like before, the three openings to the cavern all led to the same great room. As the followers exited the portal, they paused and then quietly moved into the cavern through the right opening. No one noticed, and there were very few evil beings in sight.

It was time to move down the tunnel. Moving forty followers down the tunnel system was going to be risky. The tunnel was very narrow. Even with invisibility, there was a lot of evil beings to slip by. They decided to use small indentations in the tunnel system as collection points. The forty were organized into teams of four to create a relay of sorts. They would move through the tunnel in these small groups, stop at the indents. When it was safe to go forward, they would do so. They would signal the group behind them to move forward as well. If faced with evil beings, the groups of four would attack. Upon neutralizing them, they would carry them along to dispose of them when they could.

The forty advanced to through the tunnel system quickly and without being discovered. They were now on the ledge overlooking the great underground valley. Light seemed to come from rocks or molten streams periodically visible in the valley. Yet, it was still dark, humid, and dreary.

They quickly descended the valley wall to the base. Eight evil beings were dead and discarded. It was easy to move through the right side of the valley to the fortress wall outside the mansion. They climbed the wall and found no guards or people inside the compound. Terry's group was now entering the caverns, as well. His group would secure the exit route while surveying the world in front of him. He actually could just make out the Masadians as they scaled the fortress wall and entered the mansion. He guessed they were at least a half of a mile away.

When Alice got inside, she was surprised. Unlike the squalid exterior, the inside was richly decorated and actually clean. Emaciated human beings were cleaning everywhere. There was no way to move without them seeing Alice and her team. One of the humans moved towards Alice and her team. The human looked up and looked back down. No expression. No reaction. Alice now believed this slave labor would be no threat. In a variety of locations in this great hall, there were small seating areas. In these areas, evil beings were resting and socializing. They seemed to be enjoying and indulging themselves in the meager luxuries which the mansion did provide them.

Alice found a pathway to the stairs. Her strategy was to move up and search floor by floor. She moved her group to the stairs and started upwards. About halfway to the second floor, as Alice turned to climb the winding stairway, she came face to face with a demon. The demon was about to raise an alarm, when an arrow whizzed by her head. One of her team had shot and killed the demon. The team used its relay system to dispose of the body.

The second floor had doors to various rooms. Some of the rooms were sitting rooms. Some of the rooms were apartments. At each room entrance, Alice stopped. If the door was open, they cautiously peered inside. If the door was closed, they cautiously listened for activity. There was little to discover here.

They were now on the third floor. At this point, they had confronted and dispatched five demons. Yet, the third floor was almost identical to the second floor. There was nothing noteworthy.

Up to the last and final floor. The fourth floor had one large room on the right and one large room on the left. On the right, one of four doors was open. Looking inside, roughly fifty evil demons were entertaining themselves. They were playing games. A few of them were wrestling. A few of them were throwing knives at a human target on the wall. The noise was loud.

On the left side, the doors opened to a large salon. At the far end of the salon, Beleth was sitting in a large chair with a group of females tending to him. Alice decided she was going to attack. She got her team arranged in the dark corners of the hallway. They got ready for battle.

Terry Gault heard Alice call him to the fourth floor of the mansion. She also telepathically gave him a vision of the layout. She created a portal from her to his location. He was on the way. Alice then telepathically informed all of the other judges. As she expected, Shane immediately asked her to stand down.

She was excited but took a few deep breaths before replying to Shane, "Shane, I am within a few feet of him, and we can easily penetrate the room. I can kill him and be out before anyone knows."

Shane asked, "If it is easy, then do not kill him. Bring him out of Hell so we can gather information. I know every bone in your body wants to kill him but let's be smart."

Alice almost expected this from Shane. It was the smart play. It was not their mission to kill beings. It was their mission to advance God's battle. Killing was only reserved for life and death situations. Deep down, Alice agreed with Shane. It is why she was a Judge.

Terry had arrived on the fourth floor. Alice and Terry looked into the room. There was a group of twelve evil beings sitting right in front of the middle doors. There were eight guards armed and stationed along the sides of the room. There was a game table at the far left. At this table were some rather large evil beings eating and talking. Then at the far right was Beleth and his women. Terry and Alice agree to create one team of twenty that would move straight to Beleth.

The other sixty followers were broke into groups. Two groups would move down the walls and engage the guards. Another two groups would engage the large evil beings at the far-left game table. One group would engage the huddle of twelve sitting closer to the doors.

If they moved fast enough, no alarm would be raised. If an alarm was activated, the Masadians could expect a swarm of combatants. Those from across the hall would be the first to respond. Any follower completing their primary assignment was to return to guard the doors. The risk was the doors would remain unguarded for too long and leave them exposed to a rear attack. It was a risk worth taking.

Alice and Terry lined the teams up in the right order, first to last to move into the room. Alice looked at everyone and saw all were ready. Alice was about to issue a command when Terry signaled to wait. He whispered to four of his followers closest to him. They peeled off and left the formation. Terry held up a hand. Alice watched the four. They quietly approached the doors on the other side of the hall. Gently closing them, and then securing the doors with rope. Terry smiled at Alice.

Alice directed the groups to start the attack on Beleth. The teams to attack the guards along the wall were first in. They silently moved in a crouched position. Their dark-colored clothing blended with the darkness along the walls. Everyone waited until they hit the first set of guards. These guards did not see them coming and were silently killed or taken down. Next in was the team attacking those closest and sitting together in front of the doors. When they attacked, it was unavoidably noisy. Within five seconds, the lightning fast Masadians were in the room and engaged with all targets. The evil beings in this room had very little time to react.

As Alice moved past the first group, her peripheral vision saw the first six perimeter guards go down. She saw those sitting evil beings sitting closest to the door were neutralized, as well. Alice was quickly beyond this group and halfway to Beleth.

Beleth and the evil beings at the table had a few seconds to process the sudden activity. They recognized the Masadians moving forward. The evil beings around the table moved as quickly as the Masadians to get in front and surround Beleth. The Masadians were now fighting one large group.

The Masadians were trained, and this reaction did not slow them down. The Masadian group heading for the far-left table did not collapse their path but instead moved as far down the left side as they could. They then turned into evil beings in a flanking move. It was like a dogleg right in golf.

Alice's force of twenty moved straight in. They crashed into the large guards with speed and power. It was an intense and very quick moving skirmish. Half of those between Beleth and Alice were now dead or down.

Before they could get to Beleth, he had raised a trumpet and blew it loudly. It was an ear-piercing sound. The good news is the blast only lasted a few seconds. In another few seconds, Beleth's guards were overpowered, and Beleth was captured. All the other evil beings in the room were caught or killed. Alice had accomplished her goal. Beleth was tied up, and two Masadians held him in place. Alice was proud as she believed they executed this mission in less than twenty-five seconds.

One of the followers ran from the doors to Terry. He shouted, "There are hundreds of evil beings coming up those stairs. That trumpet must have been an alarm heard all across this valley. What should we do?"

Alice signaled thirty of her team to attack the advancing evil beings moving up the stairs. The battle's first attack could be heard like an explosion of contact, motion, and weapons all colliding at once. They would make a stand there. If they piled up enough dead evil beings on those stairs, it would slow the pursuit.

Alice looked at the windows, moved to a few of the chairs, and started to break out the six windows in the back of the room. It was four stories down, but they could easily repel to the ground level. The followers moved quickly down the back wall, as Alice got Beleth ready to be sent to the ground. Half of the team was now at the bottom of the building.

In the room, Alice gave her team the signal to retreat and move out the windows. In one effort, the remaining followers raced across the room, littered with dead or wounded. They picked up the few wounded Masadians and got out the window as quickly as possible. Alice sent Beleth with them. The doors were breaking from the evil forces, on the other side, desperate to get in.

Alice remained behind. She gathered energy and cast a massive fireball at the doors across the room. Alice channeled the energy from the death of Joseph. The thought of Joseph Junior never meeting his father. The hurt caused by many battles with these evil beings, and any other idea to build upon her energy. The fire cast was devastating. Alice's rage turned the fourth floor into a fireball. Afterward, for a few minutes, there was simply silence. This would give them the time they needed.

Alice jumped out of the windows. The groups were well ahead of her heading towards the cliff leading to this valley's exit.

Beleth seeing Alice's approach, shouted, "You will not escape here. Thousands are standing in your way. I look forward to slowly killing you, myself."

Alice saw Terry ahead of her, and he was stalled. He was in an outcrop of rocks on a small hill, and he was surrounded by evil beings. She looked up to the ledge above the valley and the tunnel openings. Hundreds of evil beings were waiting on the ledge. In a few seconds, Alice caught up to Terry. The entire group of Masada was now surrounded at the base of the valley wall. They would have to make a stand and open a portal to Masada from there. Hold off the hordes until as many as possible got through. The ones who did not have enough time to get to the portals would be slaughtered.

The Masadians were now in a desperately formed semi-circle. Surrounded by hundreds of evil beings. Alice guessed they had about two minutes until the enemy gained enough courage to charge them. Just as Alice was thinking about the options, bodies from the ledge above start falling all around them. Dropping to the valley floor. Thud, thud, thud. It was like an unexpected hailstorm.

Alice got a message from Shane. "We are on the ledge and have control. Get up here, and we will cover your retreat."

Alice had never been so glad to hear Shane's voice in her head. Archers from above sent volleys of arrows into their enemy. Evil beings were dropping over dead or wounded. The confusion gave Alice and Terry the time to get everyone up to the ledge.

On the ledge, the followers had barricaded the tunnel and secured the ledge. They now had a reasonable time to portal directly to Masada from this location. Mufaro and Shane were both there. Shane was leading the attack to gain time for the retreat. Mufaro, Alice, and Terry created portals for the escape.

Portals throughout Cuyahoga were opened as the followers streamed through. A successful mission was cause for celebration, but at this moment, the adrenaline from the battles was running high.

Just before one of the portals closed, a wolf ran through and off to the hills in confusion. Aamon had disguised himself and had boldly seized the initiative. He had followed Shane and Mufaro to the ledge. None of the Masadians had taken notice of him, as a scared wolf cowering off to the side. He had dove headfirst into one of the portals just before it closed.

Now in Masada, Aamon used a moment of distraction to escape to the outside of the fortress. From here, he watched Beleth being led away in chains.

Back in Masada, Shane instructed Beleth to be blindfolded and taken to the sub-basement jail. Beleth was both put in a cell and chained to the walls. Beleth in one cell and Sai in the other. However, Shane also ordered two guards to be placed outside the cells at all times. Shane had no idea of Beleth's powers, and he was taking no chances.

Alice was anxious to interrogate Beleth and asked to be part of the interrogation.

Shane replied, "Of course you can, but I want him to remain chained and blindfolded for a few days to let imprisonment and isolation take effect."

Just as they all recovered from the battle, Shane got an alarming message from Dalton. Dalton told Shane Sarah was missing. Back on Earth, Dalton had one thing going for him. His captors did not know he could communicate perfectly without devices. Grace and Shane McNaughton, Mufaro, Nancy Stoltz (the Masada Judge), and Noni all met in the Cuyahoga subbasement control room. Noni had his entire team working the scrying mirrors and trying to locate Sarah. They continued to build a list of places she might be.

They also researched Nancy Tolton and Bob Jones. It took them less than thirty minutes to figure out these were fake identities. Nonetheless, they used the fake identities to discover their homes, their financial statements, and some of their more public actions. With the locations of their homes, Mufaro and Nancy created portals to investigate. Luckily, within a few minutes, Nancy Stoltz had found Sarah at Nancy Tolton's townhouse. She was being interrogated by four people, and she was in tears as they pressed her. Mufaro also scouted Dalton's townhome and found there were ten armed men inside. Two armed men were outside in a parked car.

While the hour passed quickly on Masada, and within this universe, it was only a few minutes on Earth. The beauty of the multi-verse and the characteristic of time is it moved quite differently in each domain. This could be used to the advantage of rescuing those on Earth.

Shane told his team, "We have been nice to these people so far. This is a time we want to use lethal force. Attack with maximum effect."

Shane and Grace would take a team to rescue Sarah. Nancy Stoltz and Mufaro would take a team to save Dalton. They wanted to synchronize the actions, so there was no time to warn one location from the other location. At Sarah's location, Shane's team included Grace, Jack Dorsey, and Thomas Black. Shane felt it would be best to allow Sarah to see familiar faces.

A portal was opened into one of the townhome bedrooms. Within seconds Shane, Thomas, and others had neutralized the four men. Two of those men were killed. Grace immediately protected Sarah and released her from the chair she was tied to. Grace hugged Sarah to keep her shielded and protected. Jack attacked and captured Nancy Tolton. Grace, Sarah, and Jack moved back through a portal to Cuyahoga. Sarah was now safe within Shane and Grace's seventh-floor apartment. It would take Sarah a moment to realize she was not at the Lakewood Center.

Mufaro's team emerged from the portal he created at Dalton's home. They were all dropped in the middle of the living room. Dalton and Bob Jones were simply sitting on the couch. The ten men, plus the two outside, were all armed. Nancy immediately attacked Bob Jones with such force the blow fractured his skull. He was dead. Of the nine additional men, the Masadians killed seven of them and left two unconscious. The two in the car parked outside were captured without incident.

Mufaro took Dalton to Cuyahoga to join Sarah. He returned as the remaining followers cleaned up Dalton's apartment. The dead would be transported to Masada and buried where they would not be found. The injured would be healed and taken to the Cuyahoga jail. The jail was going to start getting crowded.

As Dalton was reunited with Sarah, he gave her a bear hug and told her how sorry he was. Sarah was crying and asking why this happened. Shane and Grace gave them some space to get through the initial emotions. Regardless, by now, Danny had heard about this attack. Noni had asked Danny to take a portal and come home. Noni was worried about a second attack on Danny.

While Shane and Grace were on the balcony allowing Dalton to calm Sarah, Danny entered. He had no sensitivity to the situation.

He caught Sarah's eye and said, "Man up, buttercup. Welcome to the family business."

Dalton looked at Danny with a "shut the Hell up" look. Danny continued, "Sarah, I guess now is as good a time as any to realize you are not in the world you thought you lived in. This is not Earth, this is not Washington DC, this is not Lakewood. You are now on Masada. Our home away from home.

Sarah looked at Dalton and asked, "What is he talking about?"

Danny continued, "You are safe here. Dalton, go show her around. She will get it. She is a smart girl."

Dalton did not listen to his brother often, but Danny made a lot of sense for once. They could sit there crying and soothing, or they could actually go see the wonders of Masada. Dalton told Sarah to come with him in as trusting a tone as he could muster.

Sarah and Dalton got two horses from the stable and took off to get a tour of Masada.

Grace laughed at Danny and said, "Thanks, I think you helped your brother out."

Later that night, Grace arranged a dinner in the great hall of Cuyahoga. Sarah would get exposed to the many Masadians who would attend, and she would get to know the Judges. Grace also made sure Sarah had a place to stay. She would stay with Alice and Nancy. She was given a wardrobe full of clothes to wear and her own bedroom. In her bedroom was a scrying mirror allowing her to keep in touch with her parents and others.

When Sarah came to dinner, she was refreshed and composed. She was wearing a cobalt blue dress with a white belt. She looked beautiful. There was no indication she was recently captured and interrogated. As they all sat down for dinner, no one really wanted to talk before discovering Sarah's thoughts. There was an awkward silence in the room.

Sarah finally broke the ice, "This is so cool! I cannot believe I am in a different universe. I knew something was strange, but this is incredible!"

Everyone laughed. With that, the dinner proceeded. Masadians and the Judges fawned over Sarah. She was to be loved and cared for. After all, this was the future daughter in law of Shane McNaughton, the Master Judge of the Order of Masada.

Grace finally said, "Sarah, as Dalton probably told you almost everything, we can't let you go back to Earth just yet. First, we need to make sure no other threatening people have gotten close to you two. Second, we never intended to be at odds with the United States. Initially, the Lakewood Center was opened so we could provide our services within the Ohio area. President Sands is an evil and possessed human intent on doing us harm. Unfortunately, if you are going back to Earth, then you will need training. You will need to understand the secrecy in which we operate."

Sarah replied without hesitation, "I am in. I am only upset Dalton did not tell me about this earlier." Sarah would be granted follower powers and would be trained. She was able to see her own Cherubs for the first time. Sarah remained in Masada for a month, which equated to roughly three days on Earth. Dalton and Sarah would not be missed, and the followers had cleaned up Dalton's apartment.

In Washington DC, Mick Gallow was meeting with the security firm he had hired to surveil, and infiltrate Dalton's lives. They had no explanation. The last communication they had from the team was about Sarah and Dalton's capture without incident. They were going to start the interrogation of Sarah.

Mick Gallow was waiting. He could tell things did not go as planned based on the security firm owner's body language. The man continued. "We did not hear anything more from the team. It went totally silent. After two attempts to contact them, we went on site. Our teams are gone. We have lost seventeen of our best security assets. No clue as to where they are. Both locations have been wiped clean. It is as if my entire team did not exist. These people have families. I have to explain why their father, husband, son, or daughter will not come home. Yet, there are no bodies either. No signs of violence. What did you get us into? This was not a simple intelligence-gathering mission."

Mick Gallow did not know what to say. He got out his checkbook and wrote a check for double the amount of the contract. Mick thanked the security firm owner for the update and reminded him everything was confidential per the non-disclosure agreement he had signed. The man was excused.

Mick Gallow did not relish going back to Scott Stanfield or President Sands with the news of failure. He did not want to tell President Sands the cost of the operation. He was worried about the failure, not so concerned about the money. After all, it was not his money.

After a few days of isolation, Beleth was led up to the Cuyahoga library. It was the first time many had gotten a look at him. He was roughly nine feet tall. He had a muscular physical appearance. His arms were as large as a grown man's thigh. He had no shirt on, and his armor had been imbedded or pierced into his skin. It was a layer of small square tiles that overlaid each other like roof shingles. On top of this was a leather harness with two sheaths for fighting knives. He wore creepy leather pants, looking like they were made from human skin. He had large biker boots on his feet. His face was European, and at one time, he may have been handsome. But like his great angel wings, his face looked worn, tired, and diseased.

He was escorted to and sat in the largest chair they had. Like Camuel, Beleth's wings simply disappeared as he sat down. All of the Judges were present. Angles Michael, Solomon, and Thomas were also present. These three angels were once Beleth's dear brothers. When God exiled Satan and imprisoned him in Hell, Beleth left with Satan. Michael, Solomon, and Thomas remained behind and continued to serve God.

Shane asked Beleth if he was comfortable or needed anything.

Beleth hissed, "I need nothing from you, human. I will soon be out of these chains, and then the tables will be turned."

Alice already had a spear by her side and was within striking distance of Beleth. She simply reached down and drove the spear into his leg. He screamed.

Alice calmly said, "I can do this all day. I look forward to your next dumb comment."

Beleth calmed down. Shane repeated his question. Beleth asked for a glass of water. When he was given the water, it was the first time he had drank a pure glass of water in thousands of years. Hell's water was polluted and acidic. Beleth drank the water as if it was the last act before he was to die. Shane left him have his moment.

Shane asked Beleth, "Why have you attacked us here in Masada? Why have you continued to send evil beings to Earth after we stopped the flow of them?"

Beleth explained what Michael and the other angels already knew. Beleth was banned from Heaven. There was no such ban on Masada. Beleth explained Masada is a paradise, like Heaven, and he desires to capture it for himself and his armies.

Shane thought this was a fair and honest answer.

Beleth continued, "I have been sending evil beings to Earth to corrupt humans for thousands of years. Remember, the original dispute between God and Satan was borne out of jealousy. God loved humans more than his loyal and faithful followers. Satan and my Hell-bound brothers all resented this. We all believed humans did not deserve a Heavenly domain for themselves. Over time, humans have proven us right. I send evil beings to corrupt them, and often, humans are already inherently more corrupt than the beings we send."

Beleth turned his attention to the angels in the room, "Thomas, Michael, Camuel. You all know we are right. History has been on our side, not God's. Humans have almost destroyed Earth. Yet, God continues to look the other way. Why give them more time? Does God think someday they will wake up and return his love? You know this is all false. Look at human entertainment. They occupy themselves with fantasies about evil. The evil they have no understanding of. Look at the false teachings in the Churches, which are rapidly decaying. Look at the whole population which has given up on worship? I am more right about this than you care to acknowledge."

Mufaro interrupted, "Yet we are now killing any evil being we detect crossing from Hell to Earth. Why would you keep sending them?"

Beleth replied, "They are simply pawns. They are human life forces, or as you call them evil beings, sent to Hell after their death. There are so many, it is of no consequence to me to repurpose them to corrupt the Earth. If they die again, they end up right back in Hell. You have only been stopping them for a few years. I have been sending them for thousands of years."

Shane appreciated this warm-up conversation. It allowed him to observe Beleth. On cue, it was Alice's turn.

Alice got up with her spear and walked very close to Beleth. She said, "I see you sitting here, and all I want to do is kill you right now. I want to run this spear through you and end your pitiful existence. You killed my husband, the man I loved. I have taken an oath to kill you in return."

With that, Alice extended her spear towards Beleth's unprotected underarms. She pierced his skin and dragged the sharp and blessed point down his side. If she had pressed further, she would risk disemboweling him. He screamed with pain. Alice withdrew the spear and stormed out. Shane kept his cool, but Alice had dramatically made her point. A point based on her honest desires, but a claim she would never act on without Shane's permission.

Shane said to Beleth, "We are at a standstill. I can imprison you or I can simply kill you. You could escape and go back to Hell. But since the portals are all locked and guarded, this would be highly improbable. Even if you do make it back to Hell, you are most likely now being blamed for your defeats at the hands of Masada. We have controlled the dark expanse between domains and stopped evil flowing to Earth. We beat you soundly when you attacked us here. Next to you in jail is your spy. We now have come into Hell and kidnapped you from your own fortress. I would suspect those in power are not going to easily welcome you back or return you to the command of Hell's army."

Beleth recovered enough to hiss, "You humans think you are entitled to all of God's riches and glory. You are not. You are like cockroaches. You have taken Earth, a replica of Heaven, and destroyed it. You are so easily corrupted with greed and power and trinkets. God may have created you in his image, but I see nothing resembling God. Even your worship of God is easy to corrupt."

Shane countered, "What you say seems twisted but does not discount your evil influence overall. You need to decide before Alice returns. At some point, she will torture and kill you. It is her right, as you killed her husband."

With that, Shane signaled Noni to have guards take Beleth back down to the jail. Once in chains, Noni would heal his wounds. When he was gone, Alice returned. Alice asked if she did good?

Mufaro laughed, "Remind me never to piss you off. You were very, very scary to me!"

120

Alice returned to her apartment as she tried to always be there in the evening for Joseph Junior. Most of the time, she would check and discover he was not there. She would climb a flight of stairs to Shane and Grace's apartment and find Joseph Jr. and little Christine playing together. They were always together.

This typically led to Grace asking if Alice and Joseph could stay for dinner. After this, if Nancy came to the apartment and found it empty, Nancy would be on her way up. Nancy would also stay for dinner. Shane, Grace, Alice, Nancy, and the children became an extended family in Cuyahoga. It was always easy to forget when Alice and Nancy became Judges; they were simply girls. Nancy was only a few years older than Danny.

Speaking of Danny, he had been forgotten at Ohio University. He was in his senior year. As December 2004 arrived, Danny moved home to Lakewood, Ohio. He became the sole occupant of their old house. As was customary each December, the entire extended family would travel back to Lakewood, Ohio, to have an old fashion Christmas. The holiday was approaching, and actually, there was a great deal to celebrate. Three battles with Hell's worst fallen angel and a 3 – 0 record. Successful defense against the US government and their constant attacks. The saving of three of the world's most persecuted populations. Continued harmony with the Catholic Church. The addition of Catholic missions in the Native American reservations. Everything was good.

As the Lakewood house came alive, Masada followers had carefully and quietly placed security guards around the McNaughton extended family. If someone went Christmas shopping, there were four followers discretely following at a distance. No one was going to ruin this Christmas.

Lisa and Lewis Boyle would also be arriving the week of Christmas. Lisa McNaughton Boyle was Shane's sister. It was always good to see them, and Shane had made sure one or two times a year they would get together.

Grace loved being home. On Masada, most of the meals and food preparation were done by the loving staff. Here in Lakewood, Ohio, Grace loved the idea of going grocery shopping and actually cooking. She would get in full homemaker mode of baking cookies, preparing a Christmas feast, and ensuring all in the house were fed. Nancy and Alice were always there to help. The three were like sisters. Since Nancy was Jewish, she had never really grown up with Christmas in the home. This was a great joy for her.

A few days before Christmas, Grace and Shane were enjoying a quiet moment in the family room. They were doing something else, not often part of the Masada life. They were watching television. It seemed strange to watch the sitcoms. They had on "Desperate Housewives," which Grace loved. It was in its first season, so Grace enjoyed the idea of being in at the beginning of the show.

Regardless, Danny and Nancy came in to sit down and watch as well. After a few moments, and waiting for a commercial break, Danny cleared his throat, "I have something to tell you. While you guys have been busy, I have actually been busy myself. I am not going back to school for the next semester."

Grace was puzzled, "Danny, why would you drop out one semester before graduation?"

Danny laughed, "Mom, I took extra courses and stayed at school for a few summers. You guys were not around, so I just stayed in Athens. The truth is, I got my degree long ago, and am now in a master's program here at home. I have moved home to Lakewood. I am not going back because I am done."

Grace and Shane were embarrassed they had not noticed but were happy. Danny accomplished his goal as a college graduate. And then some.

Danny had them on the run, so it was time to go for the kill, "I have given this a lot of thought. I want to be part of Masada. I have seen enough to know there is nothing on Earth with the same level of importance. I would rather be there, and if possible, be a Judge. I already have the same supernatural abilities as a Judge. Every time I have been up to Masada, I have trained with Michael or Zuriel. My energy casting is quite good."

Shane understood the risks and dangers, but he was not going to stand in Danny's way, "Son, if that is what you want to do, then go for it. I think we can consider you for a Judge."

Danny smiled and was happy, but there was more, "I also wanted to tell you something much more personal. Nancy and I have been seeing each other. She has been coming to Athens to visit regularly for the last year, and we are in a serious relationship."

Nancy was a fierce judge, but at this very moment, she was feeling awkward about her boyfriend's parents. Strange. A warrior who could mow down hundreds of evil beings, yet be extremely nervous about dating the boss' son.

Grace put Nancy at ease with a smile

There was a well-timed knock on the door, and in came Dalton and Sarah. They had just arrived from Washington, DC. All was well. Danny got off the hook pretty easy.

Christmas and New Year's were terrific for the McNaughton family. What they did not know was the security teams had been busy in and around Lakewood, Ohio. They had captured and detained at least twelve agents of different government agencies. Gently exposing and scaring them away.

After Christmas, Alice and Shane took a walk down by the lake. Shane started, "I think about him all the time. In fact, this house is where he transformed from a homeless man to a Masadian Judge. Joseph was the most valuable of all of us."

Alice did not tear up, as her year had been one of proving her own inner strength. Both as a warrior and as a mother. Alice asked, "What are we going to do with Beleth?"

Shane explained, "When we get back, I want something from him. I want to know about the demon possessing President Sands. The one who kicked our asses. We are facing some sort of higher-level beast. It looked like a dragon. When we get back to Masada, you, Noni, and I will get a lot of information from Beleth. I suspect that Beleth is going to choose to remain in Masada. Are you OK with this?"

Alice bravely responded as she had a tear ran down her cheek, "No, I want to kill him, and that will never change. However, I see the greater good if we can use him in some way."

After the Holidays, they all returned to Masada. Except for Danny and Nancy. Nancy had planned a trip to Buffalo, NY, to see her parents and family. She wanted to bring home her boyfriend.

On Masada, Noni had been making sure Beleth was comfortable and well-fed in his cage. The strategy was to keep him imprisoned but also to feed him. To provide basic comforts. To allow him to soak in the Renovare Pools. To remind him what it was like to not live in Hell. In January 2005, Shane met Beleth in the Library for a second meeting.

Shane was observing him on the walk. He was now magnificent in his appearance. His wings were snow white with Jet black markings at the wrists and tips. He had removed the embedded armor, and his skin had healed. He now appeared to be almost a twin of Michael the archangel. He had been given new clothing. His hair had been so dirty that Shane had thought it to be black. Instead, it was now almost a chestnut color. His muscle and skeletal tone and posture had improved. Beleth was a wondrous and mighty looking angel.

As they sat, Shane began, "I trust while we have been gone, you have been treated well?"

Beleth said, "Yes, I have been fine."

Shane replied, "I will not dance around, but instead speak to you plainly. God asked us to rescue his people. As I see it, we could extend this to include you. We have three choices. One, we can release you, and you can go back to Hell. Two, we can allow your freedom to live in peace here in Masada. Three, I can fulfill my promise to Alice and let her kill you."

Beleth thought, "I would like to stay in Masada. I now have a taste of what I have lost when cast out of Heaven. I would like to stay here and live quietly. My time as either God's or Satan's general is over.

Beleth turned to Alice, "What happened to your husband is unfortunate, but it was in the course of a battle. If I had not killed him, he would have killed me. I am sorry for your loss."

As they had agreed, Alice became angered by Beleth's answer and stormed out of the library. Shane wanted Beleth to always be wary of Alice.

Shane then asked Beleth, "As a sign of good faith, I want to ask you a question. We have been persecuted for some time by Jarrod Sands, the United States leader. He is an unusually angry, petty, and ugly man. I am not necessarily limiting this to his physical appearance but his behaviors, demeanor, and expressions. We attacked him, and sure enough, an evil being emerged from President Sands' body. However, it was a powerful creature that looked like a dragon. It was more powerful than you or Michael. Once exorcised, it did not fade to a ghost-like being on Earth. What can you tell us about this?

Beleth explained, "When Satan and God battled, Satan had created twelve dragons. These dragons were mighty. God's Seraphim was the only thing more powerful than the dragons. Prime angels like myself or Michael could not defeat a dragon. When God finally cast Satan to Hell and imprisoned him in the center of the planet, he also imprisoned the dragons."

"Over time, six of the dragons escaped to Earth. For thousands of years, they have disguised themselves and continued to commit great acts of evil. The humans they possess are not simply influenced to do evil. The humans they possess are eaten from the inside out. The dragon, if it chooses to, stays within the human. Of course, it will eventually consume and kill the human. If you want to look through Earth's history, the evilest events most likely involved one of these six creatures. You can't kill the dragons. Your weapons will not hurt them."

Shane asked, "Beleth, we think these dragons own four of the Earth's most powerful leaders. We need to defeat them."

Beleth smiled, "The dragons all have strengths. I cannot remember exactly, but the strengths are interesting. One dragon has the strength to parch the Earth, render it barren, and prevent humans from growing any food. One dragon has the strength to release diseases and sickness to entire populations of humans or other beings. One dragon has the strength to speak and put all under its obedient commands. One dragon is simply the strongest being in existence. I cannot remember what the other two can do."

Shane was frustrated, "Beleth, that is all good and well. However, since I have been doing this, I have discovered that no one is more powerful than God. I can go to Heaven if you cannot help me."

Beleth was surprised, "Shane, you have traveled to Heaven. Have you been in the presence of God?"

Shane answered, "I have."

To Beleth, this was amazing and profound. Beleth now had incredible respect for Shane, as he had never been in God's presence.

126

Beleth released the nugget of information Shane needed, "I don't see how this can help you. However, deep in Hell, there is a room. In this room, you may find God's weapons in the great battle against Satan and his dragons. There is also a book possessing the dragons' secrets, the fallen angels, and Hell itself. If man's scriptures tell God's story of creating the world, this book has the equivalent story of God creating Hell. I could lead you there to find it."

Shane was excited by this information, but now he would sentence Beleth. "No, Beleth. Your life will be lived here on Masada. Noni will be able to track you, and you will live with us. Your vow will be to never engage in battle against us and to never escape this domain. For this, we agree to allow you to roam free. We will ask nothing from you in our battle against evil. Is this agreeable?"

Beleth agreed. Shane asked his chains to be removed. Shane walked him out to the fortress. A large draft horse was provided with another packhorse filled with things Beleth might need. He was told to leave and avoid the villages. Beleth mounted his horse and disappeared. Noni was watching him from the Scrying tubes in the Cuyahoga control room.

A few hours later, Shane entered the control room and looked at Noni, "Well?"

Noni said, "He has just been wandering around. I think he is taking his time, no hurry. Interesting, but Michael is following him at a distance. We will keep watching."

Shane walked back out and said on his way out, "If he does anything suspicious, let me know. We will have to respond to his actions very quickly."

Chapter 8 – Masada expands and in comes evil

1 Timothy 6: 3 – 12 (New Testament)

"These are the things you are to teach and insist on. 3 If anyone teaches otherwise and does not agree to the sound instruction of our Lord Jesus Christ and to godly teaching, 4 they are conceited and understand nothing. They have an unhealthy interest in controversies and quarrels about words that result in envy, strife, malicious talk, evil suspicions 5 and constant friction between people of corrupt mind, who have been robbed of the truth and who think that godliness is a means to financial gain.

6 But godliness with contentment is great gain. 7 For we brought nothing into the world, and we can take nothing out of it. 8 But if we have food and clothing, we will be content with that. 9 Those who want to get rich fall into temptation and a trap and into many foolish and harmful desires that plunge people into ruin and destruction. 10 For the love of money is a root of all kinds of evil. Some people, eager for money, have wandered from the faith and pierced themselves with many griefs.

11 But you, man of God, flee from all this, and pursue righteousness, godliness, faith, love, endurance and gentleness. 12 Fight the good fight of the faith. Take hold of the eternal life to which you were called when you made your good confession in the presence of many witnesses."

Sri Ma and Nancy had been the Masada representatives most often visiting Creole and Baoule's outer settlements. A third settlement was created called the Dakotas.

Sri Ma was visiting Creole and was puzzled. Something was different, and she did not know what it was. At least right away. She sensed trouble, but nothing seemed out of place.

As she entered the city, there were many children there to greet her. Her destination, like always, was a church built in the middle of the town. The children walked with her. As they were walking, out of the corner of her eye, she glanced down an alleyway. In that alley, it seemed two men were beating on a third man. This was the first time she had ever witnessed this type of behavior. She was not sure she had really seen it. It surprised her enough to telepathically summoned Nancy. By the time she made it to the church, Nancy had used portals to arrive.

As they went to the church, a Creole man was teaching a group of people. He was using the Bible. A woman was also in the courtyard. She was leading a group of children to harvest and store food. There was also a man with a stand of handmade clothing offering them for sale. Sri Ma saw this and again had to look more carefully. This time, Nancy also saw it. They walked up to the man. He saw them coming and closed down his handmade cart and hurried off. Something was not right.

They followed the man until they had come to the town center. In the town center, there were several additional carts and stands. These people were definitely selling their goods for money. As Sri Ma and Nancy saw this, they were alarmed.

Across the market, Jonas was watching from a perch high up on a wall overlooking the courtyard. With him were roughly twenty young men. Sri Ma recognized Jonas and walked over to talk to him. She still had high hopes for him. As she came close, one of the young men stepped in front of her.

The man said, "What do you want, lady? Who did you come to see?"

Sri Ma carefully remained calm and said, "I came to talk to Jonas." As she replied, the man had now grabbed her arm to hold her in place.

Nancy was watching with some surprise. In a few seconds, she would intervene, but she was also curious about what would happen.

Jonas yelled at the man to let Sri Ma through.

Sri Ma walked the rest of the way to Jonas, "Jonas, how are you today? What is going on in the city square?"

Jonas replied, "It is just people selling their goods, and it allows others to get the things they need in life."

Sri Ma asked Jonas, "Do you think money and possessions serve any good purpose on Masada?"

Jonas said, "Certainly, how else would you make something for yourself?"

Sri Ma replied, "To make something for yourself, by taking advantage of the needs of others, is the basis of corruption and pursuit of wealth, is it not?"

Jonas thought for a moment and said, "What is wrong with wanting more. Is it not why you brought us here out of slavery? Is it not why you rescued us?"

A crowd was now gathering.

Sri Ma gently said, "The answer to your questions is no. If you see a man in need and help him, you give to him freely. If you have a talent, perhaps as a builder, then the talent is owned by all your neighbors."

Nancy noticed, just for a brief moment, that Jonas aura turned red. It was as if his evil flickered on and off. This disturbed her.

Jonas continued, "Those of you that live in Cuyahoga are given the best of everything. You live in a palace, and you expect us to live in these huts. You have servants and powers, yet we have none of those things. Why is that?"

The crowd was growing and was getting agitated.

Jonas saw the crowd grow to the size he desired. It was time. "I Jonas will now be the leader of Creole. I will decide what our destiny is and how we can enjoy our lives. There is no need for the Masadians to continue to be like our Gods. We do not need them."

Sri Ma shouted, "Enough. Your life and time on Masada are temporary. We relocated you to this place to protect you from the enslavement and torture on Earth. Do you not remember that? Do you not remember the time when you were sick and suffering? Do you not remember the false Gods which forced you into the sugar cane fields? If you live in Masada, you are only asked to obey God's plan for your lives."

Nancy added, "If you chose to exploit your neighbor for your own gain. If you chose to organize gangs of enforcers. If you chose to introduce money into your world … when all is provided for you. If you chose these things, then we can take you back to Earth. We can put you in places where you can accomplish this. Jonas, would you like us to do this for you and those following you? We will carefully place you back into Earth's society, free from your previous life."

Jonas was caught off guard, "I do not have a desire to return to Earth. I just want to make my life better here on Masada. Why can't I do that?"

Nancy replied, "You can. You just cannot do so with the concept of money or with the exploitation of your neighbor. It is simply not part of a heavenly way of life. If you stay here, we ask you to obey God when he said, "pursue righteousness, godliness, faith, love, endurance, and gentleness. Yet, you are always free to go. We do not hold you prisoner, and anyone choosing to depart simply needs to ask. We will take you anywhere you chose to live your life."

Sri Ma asked the crowd, "Is there someone who thinks they are better than the other? Is there someone who built a larger home? Is there someone who has more wealth? If one man or woman makes a larger house, what should you do? You have two choices. You can tear your house down until it is the same as your neighbors. This is an honorable thing to do, and it tells your neighbor you are no better than he or she. Or you can go to your neighbor and help them build their house as big as your own, should they desire. Those are your choices while here on Masada.

Jonas had not anticipated this line of conversation. He knew he was trapped. He could not continue the conversation and win the argument. Neither Sri Ma nor Nancy's logic would be impeached here today. He would have to take a different approach.

Nancy then told the crowd, "I have now talked about money. It will not be part of our Masadian way. There is a reason you are prevented from building wealth. First, it is because there is an abundance of everything you need here. Enjoy it freely. Second, it is because money is the root of all evil."

The crowd listened and seemed to be soothed by the conversation with Sri Ma and Nancy. Nancy carefully watched Jonas and those men seemingly drawn to him. As the crowd died down, Nancy walked to the group.

Nancy declared, "You men seem to be set apart from the others. Why is that?"

Jonas stepped forward, "We mean no harm. We are just friends."

Nancy pressed, "I will be watching. It is terrific you are a group of friends enjoying each other. However, the moment you prey on others, I will deal with you harshly. As a group, if you do positive things for your community, then I have no problem with you. Is this understood?"

Jonas said, "Yes, it is. We want different things than the others here. What should we do?"

132

Nancy replied, "This is a big world. Go out and start a new community with those all wanting the same things. I will not stop you. But be warned, do not take from others, or do not make war with other communities."

Jonas saw this as a secondary victory. He could now go out on his own, away from Creole, and build a community. His own army.

On Earth, President Sands was finishing his eighth year as President. No President had been as corrupt and as evil-minded. He was a master magician and hypnotist. With the left hand, Sands stripped taxes and regulations away from his wealthy friends. He fabricated many crises to divert billions of tax dollars to benefit his wealthy friends and corporations. President Sands artfully disguised promotions of his health care policies while enriching large drug and medical companies.

With the right hand, Sands underhandedly increased the taxes of the ordinary American. He lied about new economic policies to help the poor, which ultimately never materialized. There had never been such hunger and chronic unemployment.

He told farmers of his plans for billions of dollars of aid but only helped large corporate farms. Thousands of small farmers were devastated.

He set policies to reduce drug costs and free medical insurance to reach customers. A new deal. Yet, with unemployment, it only served to strip health care insurance from millions of people.

As obvious as all these tricks and deceptions were, President Sands' rhetoric was mesmerizing. His followers believed it. Even as they literally were driven from their jobs, their homes, and their farms. They still remained loyal to President Sands.

This loyalty terrified all in the government of the United States. Go against President Sands, and his loyalists would soon be at your doorstep to destroy your career. Suggest he was lying, and his henchmen would cut you off at the knees. Speak out against him, and he would make sure you never were heard from again. President Sands had destroyed the democratic heritage of the United States. He had tossed aside government ethics, the rule of law, and the legacy of public service.

Shane and Alice were in Ireland. They had worked in the St Audoen's Church located south of the River Liffey at Cornmarket in Dublin. This was the Catholic Church that Alice used as a base in Ireland. It was rich with a heritage as the oldest parish church in Dublin. Alice worked in the private areas of the church immediately adjacent to the Chapel of Saint Edmund. It was a sanctuary for her, and she felt peace at the church. It was a place she felt comfortable bringing Joseph Junior.

Shane and Alice were walking in the courtyard. Tourists busily looked at the distinct architecture and the great tower as they proceeded through their paid tours.

Shane asked Alice, "If President Sands is possessed by one of the dragons, which one do you think it is?"

Alice replied, "I think it is the dragon with the silver tongue. It seems no matter how incompetent, evil or deceitful President Sands is, his followers continue to be loyal. Look at the five televangelists appointed as his spiritual advisors. They are under his spell. They have completely ignored all of his sins and indiscretions. They even explain them away. I caught one of them on the news saying President Sands was a prophet of God. President Sands definitely is the dragon capable of hypnotic suggestion.

Shane said, "So do you want to finish your campaign in Hell? There is at least one more mission to be accomplished. We have to break into Satan's jail. We have to steal the weapons and the book telling us how to kill these dragons.

Alice smiled, "Of course, I thought you would never ask."

Shane replied, "Alice, you now have Joseph Junior to worry about. I will be happy to let you sit this one out. It is up to you.

Alice said, "Not a chance. I have reconciled my role as a Judge and a mother. If something were to ever happen to me, I know you would raise Joseph as your own. Little Christine and Joseph are like sister and brother, anyhow. Since my Joseph died, I have a mission to finish. I want to accomplish one complete victory against Hell. I want this to tell my Joseph I finished something we started together."

Shane added, "Then it is settled. I believe we should have Terry, Maggie, and you go. This might be the most dangerous mission we have ever attempted. Let's make sure we have three experienced judges and their followers on this mission."

Alice said, "Agreed."

Alice was thinking, as she walked, she was simply a young woman from Limerick, Ireland. She had many minimum wage jobs, mostly part-time. Her family and friends were close-knit from the neighborhood she grew up in. To be specific, Alice was raised in Southhill. This was an impoverished and crime-ridden area of the town. Her father was out of work often. Yet, her mother made sure she got an education. She attended an all-girls school, the Laurel Hill Convent. She was pretty typical. Alice was a well-behaved lass throughout her school years. Shortly after, her family moved in with her uncle and cousins to Dublin. It was exciting and a time to explore herself as she matured. Alice's good looks came late, and it brought with it a fantasy of being an actress.

Alice loved Constance Smith because they were from similar backgrounds and places. Her love really was cemented as she identified with the story in "Impulse" about a bad woman that ultimately finds redemption through unrequited love, for better or worse. Whether working as a waitress or a clerk or an administrator, Alice's mind drifted to fantasies about her own journey.

Then one day, a man named Shane McNaughton showed up at her door. He asked her to take a journey with him. While not a practicing Catholic, Alice had faith in God. When they portal-ed to Masada, and she met Camuel, she was hooked. Many months later, Alice became close to Joseph Magnum. Never comfortable with the warrior aspects of her role, she always felt safe fighting alongside him. He would protect her. It was not until she was faced with battle alone and successfully defended herself that she gave in to her love for Joseph. Joseph was no longer her protector. He was her partner. That changed everything.

To see him die was the hardest thing she had ever experienced. He died to save her in a terrible battle with Beleth. They had always discussed the natural end of being a Judge to sacrifice oneself for God. So, it had been something they tried to prepare for.

Now Alice was leading her own great mission. One of the most dangerous Masada had ever faced. Alice was going to fight for both her and her family. If she died, it was as if she could still hear Joseph say, "As a Judge, we are called to serve God first. Even if this costs us our lives." She could not love him so much and not respect his belief.

Chapter 9 – Alice breaks Hell

March 2005 Alice returned to Cuyahoga to prepare for the most dangerous and vital mission the Order of Masada had considered. She had gone home to Ireland. She had seen her family and had attended Mass at St. Augustine's Roman Catholic Church. She went to confession. It was part of her process to say goodbye to Earth if the mission was not successful.

She was going to break into Satan's prison. While this was a mission she was proud to lead, she was insanely troubled over what she had to do first. She had to seek out her sworn enemy Beleth for additional intelligence on how to break into the prison. Alice had asked Noni where Beleth was, as they tracked him at all times. Beleth was roughly 400 miles away in the middle of nowhere. Alice would travel there with Maggie and Terry. She wanted the additional support to keep her from killing him.

They created portals to get close to where Beleth was. It was a warmer climate with a desert landscape. They found Beleth on a plateau about halfway up a foothill to a mountain range. On the plateau, Beleth had built a cabin. He had surprisingly been joined by three wives. The four of them lived in the cabin, and their existence seemed to be relatively normal. There was a manmade pool of water, a garden, and a fire pit area with seating.

At least two of the women were pregnant. This was a shocker. Alice did recall one of the prequalifications of a Judge was to have been born of two parents with Nephilim blood in their veins. The Bible had talked about these beings; born from a human mother and an angel father, roaming the Earth. It seemed Beleth was creating a new group of them.

Beleth cautiously greeted the visitors. He did not speak but waved at them and nodded as they came closer. He motioned for them to sit near the fire pit.

Terry was the first to speak, "It seems you have settled into your new life."

Beleth said that he had, "Yes, I roamed Masada for a bit, met my wives along the way, and settled here." Beleth pointed to his wives and said, "Groupies is what I think you call them. Perhaps because of my time in Hell, this area felt comfortable."

As he talked, his wives worked as a team to start the fire, provide refreshments, and ensure all were comfortable.

Alice tried to be civil, "Well, it looks like you have settled in, given the opportunity to live out your life here in peace."

Beleth cautiously replied, "Alice, unfortunately, I cannot bring your husband back to you. Yet, I am sure you did not come here for your revenge. What is it I can do for you?"

Alice said, "We need you to tell us how to get into the lower dungeons of Hell, and eventually into Satan's prison, so we may retrieve what we need to kill the dragons."

Beleth said, "I will tell you what I know, but I have never been near there. Like you talk to your angels, I talked to Satan telepathically. I never was there. What I do know is if you go to the lake of fire, you will find an island in the middle."

Beleth drew a map in the dirt as he continued to explain, "You will go to the right once you reach the center of the lake of fire. You will find an island. In the middle of the island is a cave system. There will be no evil beings guarding the tunnels, but there will be terrible traps and dangers along the way. I will warn you these traps are so dangerous you will be fortunate to survive this journey."

Within a week, Alice, Maggie, and Terry had assembled a team of one hundred volunteer followers to go to Hell. The team was built based upon the individual ability to cast energy. Alice believed the nature of their mission would require them to use energy casting as a primary means of protection and security.

It was February 2005 when Alice was ready. The Judges had eaten dinner together the night before the mission. The dangers of tomorrow were real. Alice excused herself early to spend time with Joseph Junior. The mother in her was tormented. Why did she take on this mission and risk herself? Should she not be raising Joseph and being cautious? As she said this, she also remembered her husband, Joseph. They had agreed early on being a Judge would require the supreme sacrifice of their lives at some time. They had come to grips with this. She felt the guilt of wanting to fulfill her duty as a Judge more so than her duty as a mother to little Joseph.

Joseph and Alice played on the floor. Alice loved this moment with him as if it was the last. Joseph was crawling towards her with a toy in one hand. He had a smile on his face. For a split second, Alice saw her husband staring back at her. Somehow, this would work out.

Alice heard a knock at the door. It was Grace and Christine. Grace asked, "May we come in?"

Alice nodded. Joseph and Christine played on the floor. Grace and Alice sat on the floor, watching.

Grace slid over and hugged Alice. She said, "Alice, I know you are struggling with this mission. I wanted you to know regardless of where your journey leads, I will always consider Joseph as my son. He will always be part of our family, just as you are."

Alice and Grace enjoyed the rest of the night with the kids.

The next day, one hundred and three Masadians left for Hell. All the Judges were there to greet them, as well as many from the villages. Family and friends. On a hillside, overlooking the right wall of the Cuyahoga fortress, was a lone figure. Watching. It was Beleth. Alice recognized him as they were getting ready to leave. As she gazed at him, Beleth put a fist to his heart as a sign of best wishes.

In Hell, the trip proved uneventful. They had come through one of the fixed portals in Hell. They saw a few evil beings as they emerged. These scurried away upon sight. They made their way to the lake. At the lake, they discovered an oversight. There were not enough boats to take them all to the island. This slowed them down as they had to go in groups. Even using the Judge's portals, it took most of the first day.

Once on the island, Alice's advance team scouted and found the underground entry point. When the last boatload was on the island, they descended into the most infamous pit in Hell.

On Earth, Dalton and Sarah were nearing their wedding day. No one had bothered them since Sarah's kidnapping. Sarah no longer probed Dalton about what his parents and family did. She now bothered him on when they could go back to Masada. Nonetheless, they were settling into life in Washington, DC. Dalton's nonprofit had hired a new boss to replace Bob Jones, who had mysteriously disappeared. Things definitely settled down.

Scott Stanfield had quietly solicited Jarrod Sands' political appointee in the Department of Energy to keep an eye on Dalton's nonprofit. He asked that Dalton McNaughton be put on the radar and treated like a VIP whenever the opportunities arose.

Meanwhile, across town in Daniel O'Connell's Irish Restaurant & Bar, Frank Kotter and Rick Jones sat in a second-floor booth. The owners had allowed them to sit there based on Rick Jones' relationship with the owner. It was quiet, and they could talk. Frank Kotter was the Commissioner of the Food and Drug Administration. Rick Jones was a Director of the US Marshal service. They were soon joined by Tim Durante. Tim was a Special Agent in the Secret Service detail for President Sands. These three men were all true patriots experiencing almost eight years of President Jarrod Sands. They also had spent nearly an equal amount of time pursuing Shane McNaughton, on President Sands' behalf.

140

As Tim Durante was arriving, Frank Kotter was finishing a thought. "You have to be very careful around anyone in the White House and in conservative political parties. Washington public conservatives, with long-standing impeccable reputations, are now almost unrecognizable. Even their passions and personal goals have been supplanted with protecting and defending President Sands in many cases. He is a village idiot. He is someone who ten years ago would have been run out of the federal government. Now he controls it. He controls it. Hmmm. Now he corrupts it."

"Agencies like mine are no longer functioning on public policy. We are all simply actors in his reality television show. Truth is he gutted our agency and put in so many of his political appointees we are only doing about twenty percent of what we used to do."

Frank Kotter paused and acknowledge Tim's arrival, "Hey Tim, sorry I was venting, nice to see you."

Tim sat down and said, "All I can tell you is there is something very wrong with the man. It is what we are here to talk about?"

Rick Jones asked Tim, "Did you bring the audio recordings."

Tim shook his head, yes. He then unpacked his laptop, and he gave each of the men a wired earpiece allowing them all to hear the same thing. He wanted this secure, and he did not want it to be heard in public or transmitted over wireless technology. No risks.

Tim whispered, "What you are hearing is the audio files from months ago. While we don't intrude into Sands' private residence, there are listening devices all over the White House. In the past, the US Secret Service has caught many husband-wife arguments on tape. Actually, we have audios of things a lot more entertaining than the occasional argument. For the most part, if something is captured by the listening devices coming from the private residence, we destroy it."

"I have been part of a quiet group in the Secret Service, which started to listen. We did this because the President spends so much time in the residence. What is he doing? We have been asked and never answered. What you are about to hear is some very strange chatter. The first is a compilation of what he is doing by himself in the morning. When you hear this, I want you to know he is watching television for the most part. We have edited this out of the audios. Listen to this."

Tim played his computer audio player. There were some rustling noises initially, then you can hear President Sands voice, "Mirror mirror on the wall, who is the fairest of them all. Jarred Sands! Jarred Sands! Jarred! Jarred. Jar …"

Tim stopped the audio. Each instance, we pick up this weird chant President Sands repeats. It is obviously from Snow White. We think it is a chant pumping him up for the day. It is strange. We have a psychologist we trust who has listened to this. She does not think it is solely to pump him up. By listening to his emotion and speech pattern, she would guess he is meditating while looking at himself in a mirror.

Tim played his computer audio again, "You need to kill Shane McNaughton before it is too late. If you do not kill him, then he will kill you. This is your time. You only have a few months left to launch our plan. Shane McNaughton stands in the way."

Frank asked, "What the Hell was that? Who is talking?"

Tim said only Jarrod Sands was in the room. They could only conclude he was talking to himself.

Rick Jones said, "This confirms what we always believed. There is some unnatural obsession President Sands has with Shane McNaughton. Since he came into office, he has constantly attempted to destroy McNaughton."

Tim smiled and said there is more. "This next audio is from one single night. What you will hear are two voices and what appears to be multiple people fighting in the room. What is puzzling to the US Secret Service is that there was no detection of a breach or intruders. No one has any idea who was in President Sands' residency. It was the original reason we went back through these audios. We were trying to understand how anyone got into the White House undetected. Listen."

President Sands shouted, "What the Hell are you doing in my bedroom? Get out before I call my agents."

There was a skirmish. They heard what sounded like an attack, and someone was wounded. Perhaps someone had been shot or attacked with a knife. Then silence.

A minute later, they hear, "I am Typhon, and why have you come. You surely will die here and now."

After this, the noise of fighting escalates for over a minute. Then it quiets down.

The same voice as before says, "Human, do not attack me again. I am not like the other evil beings you so easily discarded of. I am Typhon and have survived for thousands of years. This man's skin is mine. I will do with him as I chose. Do not return. In time, I will come to you, and it will be your end."

Then there is silence.

Tim knew he had just blown the minds of his audience. Everyone sat quietly for a minute. Frank Kotter was shaking his head in astonishment.

Rick Jones was the first to speak, "You mean this recording came from President Sands private residence? It seems President Sands knew this Typhon character. He viewed him as a threat, and he was about to call his agents. That is the last we hear from President Sands."

"What troubles me is Sands goes quiet after this. If Jarrod Sands was truly threatened, I would expect him to be chatting up a storm. Curses. Threats. Begging. Crying. You name it. He is not someone who would suddenly go silent."

Tim was going to provide them two additional nuggets of information, "We analyzed this. We think that President Sands was incapacitated immediately after his comment. This Typhon person was actually fighting with others. We picked the sound up off two listening devices and did some crude analysis. The sounds were originating all over the room. We think there were at least four different people there. As we can hear, it appears this Typhon guy actually defeated the others."

Frank Kotter said, "If all this happened, then what about President Sands. Did he show up the next day injured?"

Tim said they checked video tapes of him exiting his room the next day. He seemed perfectly fine and normal. Also, they said the cleaning staff entered Jarrod Sands' bedroom to find damages to all the furniture. They had to replace it all.

Tim smiled as he knew he had reeled them in. "I saved the best piece of information for last. We analyzed the Typhon character's voice. Guess what? With roughly eighty-five percent accuracy, we believe President Sands and Typhon are the same person. Their voices matched."

Rick Jones was shaking his head. Frank Kotter was thinking. Could all the heaven and hell stuff Shane McNaughton had talked about all these years be real? Could President Sands be a possessed human?

Rick Jones looked at Frank and said, "I think we need to talk to your friend. Can you still get ahold of him?"

Frank said, "Yes. I have not talked to him in almost a year, but I will reach out."

Tim warned, "I brought this to you guys. We have several individuals in the Secret Service who are worried about President Sands' mental fitness. What is going on in the private residence? We can't find a good way to take this through formal channels. I am hopeful you two might be able to help." With that, Tim Durante got up to leave without another word. He left a memory stick for their use.

Back in Hell, at the entrance of Satan's jail, Alice had entered into the cavern. In the back was a nondescript tunnel. They walked around the entire cavern to look for other openings, trap doors, or hidden openings. Nothing. Just this simple tunnel. Alice was suspicious and said she would take thirty and move forward. Each group would wait fifteen minutes before entry.

Alice seemed to be in the tunnel system for hours as they traveled down. Although direction was useless, it did seem they were traveling in a tunnel which continuously turned. It was like traveling in a constant downward spiral.

Finally, they came out to a broad valley. It was a lot like the valley they discovered searching for Beleth. The valley floor was barren. Across the valley, and roughly a mile away, was another tunnel opening. This one was different. It was not simple. It had a set of columns and ornate carvings in the stone surrounding it. The large doors were bright and reflected light. Alice guessed this was the entrance to the real Hell. There were roughly ten guards. All appeared to be men. There were several buildings in front of the entrance. It was like a small town. On the road to the doors, there were probably another twenty evil beings wandering around.

Alice, Maggie, and Terry divided up the followers into three teams. Maggie would go first and scout out the area. If she found traps or threats, she would report back and continue. Maggie was off. She did not head directly for the doors but instead took a route giving her whatever high ground she could find. Maggie had almost made it to the village and reported nothing unusual. The other two teams were all in different locations to surround the town.

They huddled on a hillside outside the village. Alice would take a team to capture the doors from the guards. Maggie would take a team-up on the left side of the village. Terry would take the right side of the village. They would clear the buildings and detain all of the evil beings they encountered. They had no interest in a fight unless presented with one.

Within an hour, all human spirits and other evil beings were rounded up and placed in the largest building. Their arms and legs were bound. They were then also tied to walls or pillars in the building. In capturing and peacefully imprisoning these individuals, Alice did find one who appeared to be the informal leader of this community.

Alice asked him, "Are you the leader of this village and the doors into Hell?"

The man spoke in Tamil, "Āmām nāṉ irukkirēṉ, nīṅkaḷ ēṉ iṅkē irukkirīrkaḷ? Nīṅkaḷ niccayamāka antak katavukaḷait tirakka virumpavillai. Nīṅkaḷ oru tavaru ceytuḷḷīrkaḷ. Uṅkaḷai veḷiyē vaikka nāṅkaḷ iṅku varavillai. Katavukaḷai mūṭi vaikka nāṅkaḷ iṅkē irukkirōm. Eṉṉaveṉru yārum virumpavillai tappikka katavukaḷukku piṉṉāl." (Yes I am, and why are you here? You certainly do not want to open those doors. You have made a mistake. We are not here to keep you out. We are here to keep the doors closed. No one wants what is behind the doors to escape.)

Alice pondered this. Good answer. "What lies beyond the doors?"

The man replied, "Beyond those doors are tunnels leading down to Hell's prison. The dangers within are unknown. In thousands of years, I know of no one who has returned. You will die in there."

Alice asked, "If we go, and you escape your bindings, what would you do?"

The man answered, "I would send a guard to Beleth or one of the other fallen angels to tell them you are here. I will not do this if you return within a few hours."

Alice decided to leave a group of ten guards to watch the villagers so they could not escape. The remaining Masadians opened the door to Hell and began another descent down a tunnel system. The further down the tunnel they got, the more frequently they ran into snakes. Angry snakes. It slowed them down.

Eventually, they came out to a large room with a tiled floor. Across the room was a massive wall with one large set of double doors. The door was locked with a rather large, complicated mechanical lock. Alice and Terry were suspicious. This seemed too easy. Cross this open room and open that door.

The teams fanned out and carefully crossed. They watched the walls. They looked for pressure plates on the floors. Nothing. As they approached the doors, they saw an inscription. It said:

I love you, Lord, my strength. The Lord is my rock, my fortress, and my deliverer; my God is my rock, in whom I take refuge, my shield, and the horn of my salvation, my stronghold.

Alice telepathically read it to Noni. Noni replied in about thirty seconds, "The text is part of the Hebrew Bible and the Old Testament. It is one of the references describing Masada. Could God have intended us to be here at this moment? What else do you see?"

Alice replied, there are symbols on the wall in a circle, and there is a dial in the middle. I presume this is some sort of combination lock. I will describe the symbols as best I can. At the top is a symbol of a deer with horns, then a face with tears, a tree, mountains, a foot, a campfire with smoke, an ear, a rock, an eyeball, clouds in front of the sun, a nose, and a bird flying. After Alice described this, she turned the dial. When she did this, they all heard many mechanical sounds. As they looked, they saw small doors opening on the cavern wall opposite the locked door.

Hundreds of snakes were pouring out of these openings and down the wall. In a few moments, they would be surrounded. The snakes were headed straight for them. The Masadians presumed they were all hungry.

Maggie shouted for the group to form a semi-circle in front of the door. She commanded everyone to use their shield and their fire castings to keep the snakes back. Those with more potent energy casting abilities should be out front. Those not as strong should be behind and prepared to kill any snakes getting through.

Alice shouted to Noni to hurry up.

Noni had been right about the scripture. As he decoded it, he saw a pattern.

Noni explained to Alice, "This is a combination lock operating on symbols, not numbers. The pattern is tears, ear, mountain, nostrils, smoke, fire, campfire, clouds, feet. It is from Psalm 18, describing God's return to save us. Try that. If it doesn't work, then reverse the first turn and go the opposite way."

At this point, the snakes all continued to converge on the group. Shield and fire casting were keeping them at bay. They were killing the snakes. The problem was the pile of snakes growing in front of them made it hard to distinguish live from dead snakes. This created opportunities for live snakes to find their way through.

Ten followers had been bitten. Terry was healing them as Maggie commanded the defense. Ten more followers were down. At this rate, they would be overtaken in a few minutes.

Alice started the combination with a clockwise motion. Nothing. She reversed the combination. Nothing.

Alice screamed at Noni, "We don't have much time left. The combination you gave me is not working!"

148

Noni was silent for a minute. Then Alice heard, "Oh Shit." Noni continued, "I made a mistake. Try this. Tears, ear, mountain, smoke, nostrils, fire, campfire, clouds, feet."

Alice tried again, and she heard the lock open. She pushed the door open. Terry and a few of the followers moved the injured through the doors. Maggie signaled the retreat. Everyone made it through. Alice and Terry closed the doors behind them. The doors locked.

They were now in a quiet room. It was a pristine room with a rich arrangement of sculptures and paintings. It was a wonderfully designed greeting area. To Hell? This was strange but a welcome retreat. It was quiet, dark, and cool. A few of the followers used their energy casting to light lanterns on the walls. It was time for a rest.

Everyone was quiet and licking their wounds. Peggy pulled off her backpack and asked slyly, "Cookies anyone?" As she had stashed four packages of contraband, Oreo Cookies from Earth. It brought a smile or giggle to many of the follower's faces. A moment of indulgent humor in the face of death. You had to be a Masadian to get it.

On the other side of the room were two doors. These doors must lead to the next part of their journey. They were ready, and the snake-bitten followers were healed up. All were good to go. They split into two groups, and each took a door. Each door opened into a tunnel. These tunnels were not as long as before. They also did not notice any more extreme descent in the tunnel.

Alice led the left team, and they managed to avoid three traps. There was a hidden pit, there was a hole in a wall leading to a snake pit, and there was a booby trap with a swinging arm. They ultimately came out to a ledge area.

Terry led the right team. They came to a dead-end wall. As they were about to turn around, someone must have set off a trap. The entire tunnel caved in. It trapped them in a very small space. No one was hurt. Eight of the team needed to be dug out from under rocks.

Terry told Alice they were trapped, and he would set up portals to return to the lobby area. It would take them some time to catch up with her. Alice again decided to wait, as she expected more dangers. Alice went to the ledge and looked down. Roughly five hundred feet below was a molten river. She looked hard to see there were lizards of some sort swimming in the lava. They shot flames out of their mouths. There were three rope bridges to the other side of the cave. A ledge was there as well. Beyond the ledge were three open tunnels.

Alice suggested they take a rest break and wait for Terry. She was trying to keep everyone calm as the heat in this cave was very uncomfortable. Terry did catch up. When he locked eyes with Alice, he just shook his head. They would have to be more careful. It is going to get harder the closer they got. Maggie, Terry, and Alice were again divided into three teams.

Alice was about to head over one of the three rope bridges to the middle tunnel. Maggie shouted, "Stop!"

Maggie suggested they might use portals across rather than risk walking on rickety rope bridges. Perhaps purposefully built to fail. Maggie set a portal to the left tunnel. Terry set a portal to the right.

Maggie headed down the left tunnel with caution. There were a few traps along the way, but she discovered them first. One was a pit, and one was another snake hole. Maggie got to the end of the tunnel, and there was a simple wooden door. She opened it and saw some shelves. There were hand tools from long ago and a few ladders. She had struck out. A custodian's closet.

Terry headed down the right tunnel and found similar traps. Yet, when he got to the end, he found a set of locked double doors. It was not a massive or complicated lock. No traps and the doors opened quickly.

Alice went down the middle tunnel. She had no traps. However, when she got to the end, she arrived at a cavern. In the cavern was a lake of molten lava. There was an island in the middle. In the middle of this was a huge block building made of stone. The block building had barred windows. Alice wanted a better look, so she moved closer to the ledge. She saw there was another block building inside the other one. It, too, had barred windows. There was light inside the inner structure. The windows suggested multiple floors, perhaps a three-story building.

Six chained dragons were sitting or flying. The chains tethered these creatures equal distance from each other around the top edge of the large outer building. Every once in a while, a dragon would dip into the lake to eat lizards they saw swimming in the lava. Alice was amazed as these dragons looked very much like the dragon they faced when they attacked President Sands in the White House.

As she was looking, her head did a weird thing. She had the initial feeling of exhilaration. The type you get as you go down the largest hill of a roller coaster. She heard a loud voice, "Alice, it is nice you have visited me. I see your pain. Perhaps I can help you. Maybe we can find Joseph in the afterlife together. Why are you fighting a hopeless war for a God who does not care for you? Have you ever met him?

The voice continued, "Come with me. Joseph is here. Would you like to see him again? Would you like to tell him about his son?"

Satan now had placed a vision of her and Joseph meeting again. They were now greeting each other, both verbally and physically, with hugs and kisses. Alice completely gave in to this vision. Suddenly, Alice was up and walking towards the edge of the ledge. Two more steps and she would fall into the lava lake. Two of her followers saw this and tackled her.

Alice guessed this was Satan inside her mind. He was not shy, as he took over completely. She fell to the ground. Her followers picked her up as this vision continued in her head. They decided it was better to retreat. There was nothing here suggesting a library or storage room.

About halfway up the tunnel, Alice regained her focus. With it, she had a brief glance of Satan unleashing the fire breathing lizards to hunt down the group. She shouted at her team, "We only have a few minutes until all hell breaks loose. We must go.

Meantime, Terry had gone into a dark, large room. There were a couple of torches he lit. He saw a trough of oil and lit it. As the flame continued, it lit three more narrow troughs illuminating a room for about five hundred yards. The group was speechless. There were gold, jewelry, silver, and riches beyond anything they had ever seen. Weapons plated in gold—swords with ornamental jewels in the hilt. Fine furniture and paintings were stacked on the shelves. Even the shelves seemed priceless. Terry told Alice what they had found. It would take them some time to investigate.

Something was not right. Alice knew from Satan's invasion into her mind; there were only a few minutes to search for what they needed. Something was troubling her, but she could not see it.

Then in a flash of clarity, Alice knew what she had to do. Alice set a portal back up the tunnel. She moved everyone quickly. Maggie and her group were next to arrive at the ledge. Terry was last, as his team was resistant to tear away from the riches they had found. Alice directed Terry to get back to the lobby room with as many of the group as he could move.

Alice said to Maggie, "Come with me." Alice flew down the left tunnel at blazing speed. She busted into the small room. Maggie and a few other followers were with her, but they were puzzled by Alice's actions. "We looked in here; there was nothing."

Alice saw what she was looking for. On the bottom shelf, furthest away from the door, was a small dusty book. She grabbed it and tossed it to Maggie. Maggie began looking through it. Alice continued to look around the room. She was about to give up. Alice looked above Maggie and saw what looked like an air vent. It was high up, but Alice could stand on one of the shelves and reach it. When she did, she discovered several large bags containing tarnished weapons.

They had found what they were looking for. Alice told Maggie to retreat. They raced back up the tunnel to the ledge. All of them were carrying heavy bags of weapons, chains, or scrap metal. Alice said, "We need to get out of here now. Let's portal to the other side of this cavern and get to the entry room. From there, we can portal to the village outside where the rest of our team is on guard."

Just then, there was a screech. Two or three of the followers on the far edge of the group were enveloped in flames. They ran off the edge of the cliff and were killed. The lizards down in the molten river were crawling up the sides of the cliffs. Rapidly. Alice looked down and saw hundreds of these lizards crawling up the walls. They had about thirty seconds to get to the outer room and escape.

Alice and Maggie created portals to the other side of the cavern. The team got through very quickly, but precious seconds had passed. Alice and Maggie realized they would have to turn and fight. They had to slow the lizards down to get everyone safely away.

Alice shouted to Terry to keep his portal open and wait for their arrival. Many of the followers were exiting through the portal now, two or three at a time. Terry remained and could now see the light from the lizards' flames. Light danced off the tunnel entrance walls. Followers started to come out of the tunnel carrying bags of weapons. They needed no coaxing to jump into the portal and go.

Alice and Maggie were behind everyone else and using energy casting to hold the lizards back. They used energy and water bursts to hold the lizards back. Water was effective against fire lizards. It worked. When they were hit with water, they stopped advancing. As Alice and Maggie walked backward up the tunnel system, the lizards were still coming. There were too many of them. If they stopped two lizards, five would take their place.

Once in the room, there were still about twenty followers jumping into Terry's portal.

Alice shouted at Maggie, "Create a second portal, or we die. Get everyone out. I will hold these dragons back." Alice did not enter the room but remained in the tunnel opening, determined to not let even one lizard get by her. Alice focused her energy casting down the tunnels leading to Satan's jail. She was using every last bit of her energy.

Everyone was now through to portals except for Maggie, Terry, and Alice. Terry shouted at Alice, "Alice, retreat, and we can get out of here.

Alice shouted, "I will be right behind you. Go!"

Alice turned to dash for the portals just as two large lizards were about to pounce on her. She gathered all the energy she had and created a shield. The dragons shot fire from their mouths, which enveloped Alice and her shield energy. It prevented Alice from moving towards the portal. If she did, she would be exposed and burned alive.

She attacked the two dragons with her sword and killed both of them. Again, she turned to head for the portal. Alice did not have enough of a gap between herself and tens of lizards now pouring into the room. All intent on her destruction.

Alice turned to fight and to send a telepathic message to all, "Tell my son how much I love him and tell Shane how much Masada has meant to me."

Maggie and Terry's portals to the village remained open for only a few seconds more. Terry and Maggie waited on the other side as the portal energy faded. No Alice. Terry wanted to go back, but as he moved towards the portal he created, a dragon came through. Maggie's portal also was filling with dragons. They had to shut them down. Alice saved them all but could not get out herself. As they were waiting for Alice, they got her last telepathic message, as all the Judges did.

The Masadians collected themselves, released the villagers, and left. After they were far enough away from the village, they created portals to Masada.

Terry and Maggie were met by Shane. They had accomplished their mission but had lost another Judge. Alice was killed. Shane was distraught and broken. The other Judges, no matter where they were, converged to Cuyahoga to comfort each other. In the Cuyahoga main room; Grace, Danny, Terry, Maggie, Noni, Arunta, Nancy, and Mufaro gathered. Their pain and grief were raw and profound. It was unbearable to have lost Alice.

As they sat at a table in the great hall, others slowly gathered. Grace and Nancy held tight to little Joseph Junior, who was still too young to comprehend what had happened. Sri Ma, Camuel, and Michael all came in to quietly share the grief. Guard Angles floated above and around the group. They provided protection and comfort as Masada was heartbroken.

Alice was loved by all. When she joined the Order, she was simply a young and reckless Irish girl. When she died, she had turned into a fierce warrior and a compassionate healer. She had saved thousands in the name of God.

At some point, Shane whispered something to Grace and left. Shane had gotten on a horse and left Cuyahoga. No one heard from him. Shane rode up to the mountains where the portal to Heaven was located. This is also near the mountains where the waterfall hid the cave containing the jewels and rare stones, generating most of Masada's earthly wealth. Shane contemplated a trip into Heaven. He got off his horse and released it. It would find its way back. He took his backpack and gathered some food. Fruits, berries, and convenient foodstuffs found on the trail. He filled a canteen with water from the fresh mountain streams. He headed for the fixed portal to Heaven.

Approaching the portal, Shane saw the Guard Angel Thomas. He said, "Hello my old friend. I hope you are well. I need to pass."

Thomas replied, "I know you are troubled. Do you want to talk? I think it is perhaps the wrong time to approach Heaven. Your grief and your sorrow should not be carried into Heaven. It would be unwise. If unburdened while there, you do not honor Alice. You forget her sacrifice. Are you sure you want to enter?"

Shane said that he did.

Thomas asked again, "What if you do not return to Masada? Are you prepared for this?"

Shane had never thought of this. Yet, as he did, he understood God could simply reward him with eternal life. God could take away his pain by forcing him to forget Masada, his family, judges, and experience. At that moment, Shane had genuine fear. He was not ready for this.

Shane was frustrated in his grief. Like most people, grief is complicated. Yes, there is sadness, but there is also the frustration that many don't talk about. The disappointment of the illogic. Why this person? Why not me? What did we do to deserve this? What do I regret? Unfortunately, when losing a loved one, the answers to these questions do not come easily.

He finally faced Thomas again and said, "Thank you, my old friend, I will not be going to Heaven today."

Shane walked away into the forest. He found a clearing with a rock in the sunlight. He decided this was an excellent place to think. It was an excellent place to pray.

"God, why have you abandoned me? Have I not brought all I have on this journey? Have I not healed and rescued thousands, as you asked of me? Have I not fought every battle you put in front of me? Why have I lost both Joseph and Alice? Why will Joseph Junior grow up without knowing his parents?"

Shane heard a sound and looked up from his prayer. Once again, it was Jesus standing in front of him. Jesus was crying as Shane was praying. Jesus said, "I feel your pain, my brother. I know this is not easy for you. You have been challenged by more than even I expected. You have done well."

Shane replied, "I don't know how much more I can take. Dragons, corrupting Earth. Evil beings are creeping into every crack of darkness. How do we go on? It has now been over ten earth years. Grace and I cannot even go to our family home in Lakewood without President Sands sending his goons to attack us. My children are being attacked."

Jesus said, "To those who can do, much is given. I told you when this began, it would be difficult. The dragons are going to be a tremendous challenge. I wish I could tell you there will not be more suffering or death, but there will be. You just have to know you are making a difference. You have rescued thousands upon thousands. Remember, God would have asked and been pleased if you had simply saved one. You have done so much more. For this, I am very pleased."

Shane asked, "So what would you have me do? Do I keep fighting demons and politicians? Do I keep running from corrupt corporations and governments? What am I to do?"

Jesus replied, "Humanity will always be corrupt. It is what makes them worth saving. You need to push forward, as you have not even grown to full strength yet. Honor Joseph and Alice's sacrifice by getting these dragons back into hell. Rid the world of the most powerful source of corruption to ever exist. You can do this, brother."

Shane got up as if the pep talk was over. Jesus had one last thing to say, "The key to your future is Christine, Joseph Junior, and others born to Masada. They will not be on Earth. They will be masters of the multiverse. Their strength and abilities will save generations from inevitable destruction. You are the beginning of it all. Press on."

Jesus continued, "Shortly, you will soon discover ways to use the power bestowed to you and the Judges in even greater ways. You will find a need to rescue those on Earth with the talents and knowledge to further Masada's power and technologies. Another era of your journey will soon be upon you."

Shane closed his eyes for just a second as if to gather the strength he needed to move. When he opened his eyes, Jesus was gone. Shane opened a portal back to Cuyahoga.

Once again, Masada had a memorial service for their Judge. Alice and Joseph were both gone. Shane had disappeared the night of Alice's death, and he only reappeared before her memorial service. He now had a beard and looked much older than his usual youthful and effervescent self. Grace put her arm around him as if to hold him up.

Shane spoke, "I can still remember a time when I was a sporting goods store manager. Grace and I were raising two young boys. We had a normal life. Alice was a young teenage girl from Limerick, Ireland. She was carefree and had her life ahead of her. I think she wanted to be an actress. Yet, here we all are. Once again, we have been reminded of the serious and grave nature of our mission. None of us sought this great burden out. Yet all of us answered the call. God, please help us in our moment of sorrow. Please heal our broken hearts."

With that said, Shane ended the service by walking up to the burial pedestal. They did not have Alice's body but instead had placed flowers, memories, and a few pictures on the pedestal. Others followed. In the end, they laid a torch on the wooden pedestal. Miraculously, a vision of her sleeping body appeared on the pedestal. Just for a minute. And then her life force simply raised up and took flight. The appearance of her faded. Hopefully, she would join Joseph in Heaven.

Shane was mourning, but he also knew he had to get new Judges. After talking to Sri Ma about what happened with the Creole community, Shane believed he needed additional Judges to work exclusively on managing Masada societies. Judges ensuring heavenly societies without strife or corruption. Judges presiding over these communities as they self-govern. Understanding how to build them, so they were always in harmony with the land and goodness.

Shane had an even bigger idea. Maggie actually had provided it. She had rescued and restored the Native Americans living in perhaps the worst situation in the Western World. She had then gone beyond this mission to heal their land. Finally, she enabled them to stand up and expand their footprint to further success. She took weakness and made it strength. She took poverty and made it wealth. She took prejudice and made it superiority. By empowering these people, they could move bodily into the world.

Shane believed this model could be used anywhere on Earth. More importantly, Shane thought that even Masada could use it to reemerge in Lakewood, Ohio. It was not their mission to bring everyone to Masada to start over. It was their mission to take back the Earth. Masada was their temporary home. Speaking of that, Shane also wanted to seek out those in Masada that were best suited to return to Earth. To lead a re-emergence that would be capable of restoring God's presence to Earth.

Shane asked Sri Ma to find four to ten people from each community who were natural leaders showing a strong commitment to Masada and what it stands for. Sri Ma agreed to do so. She was troubled because there was one man who stood out to her. Jonas of the Creoles. Yet, for all of his potential, his behavior showed a thirst for power and riches. Could he be one of those recommended?

After Alice's death, it seemed Shane's life did not hit pause. He was consumed with activity. In March 2005, Jack Dorsey told Shane, "The Catholic Church phone in Rome rang. A man named Frank Kotter is trying to get ahold of you. Thomas and I can travel back to the United States with you."

Shane telepathically contacted Dalton, "I have a business in Washington, DC. Is it possible for you to put up a group of six people at your place in the next week?"

Dalton answered, "Yes, come in on Monday, and you can stay as long as you like. Some of those people will have to sleep on the couch."

Shane asked Jack Dorsey to arrange a meeting with Frank Kotter. Either has the meeting at a church or arrange an out of the way location. Shane wanted Jack to travel back to Washington, DC, to arrange the details.

It was late Spring 2005. The Washington cherry trees were in full bloom, offering a panacea of color. A few more weeks, and it would be exploding into a beautiful summer season. Shane loved this time of year. Masada had seasons like Earth, but they were on different cycles.

Shane and his team traveled Monday night. He told Dalton of his vision for Masadian societies on Earth. He asked Dalton if he and Sarah would want to lead the Lakewood Ohio initiative. Go public, go strong and populate with the overwhelming goodness of Masada. Dalton said he would think about it.

Regardless, Frank Kotter had agreed to meet at St. Joseph's Roman Catholic Church, which was in the south on 2nd St NE. On Tuesday at 10:00 AM, Shane arrived at the church and was escorted by Thomas Black to a room on the second floor in the back offices. Jack Dorsey was outside of the church, waiting for Frank Kotter. Frank arrived about fifteen minutes later for their 10:30 AM appointment. He was with three other people. Jack watched them enter and remained on watch for any people following them. Nothing happened.

A follower named Sam Sarpinski worked in the church. Sam approached Frank and asked who the others were. Frank told him these men were Rick Jones, Tim Durante, and Arlen Wright. Shane telepathically told Sam he knew all of them except for Tim Durante. Regardless, Sam was to escort them back to the office to meet with Shane.

As they entered the office, Shane greeted Arlen Wright. Arlen was the only one of them who had always treated Shane with respect. He welcomed the others, and Tim Durante was introduced. Thomas Black and Jack Ramsey entered late and were also introduced as Shane's associates.

As they settled in chairs, Shane asked Frank, "What can I do for you?"

Frank was uncomfortable with blurting out the sensitive information he was about to uncover, so he stalled, "Are we sure this location is safe and confidential? What I have to discuss is something of the greatest importance. Hearing it or speaking it could get someone killed."

Jack Dorsey replied, "We have been in control of this church and this room for three days. Nothing has penetrated the security. The Catholic Church in Rome has secured the perimeter. My team has secured the meeting room and all of the adjacent areas. The church staff was asked to vacate the property for the duration of this meeting. We have done our best to provide a discrete and secure location."

Frank was impressed. He had come to know Shane as always thorough and careful. This was no exception. Frank continued, "Since the last time we talked, we have noticed a dramatic change in behavior of President Sands. Inadvertently, we picked up some troublesome recordings from the White House private residence. I wanted to know if you are somehow involved in all of this.

Shane guessed at the evidence but asked anyway, "What are you all concerned with, and perhaps I can enlighten you."

161

Tim Durante went through the materials he had briefed the others on a few weeks back. After playing the audios and talking for about thirty minutes, Tim finally finished. He looked at Shane as if the answers were forthcoming.

Shane thought about the answer. Would the truth hurt or help? Finally, Shane spoke, "In this world, have you ever wondered how a single person in a single moment can change everything. In history, you can view it with all the hindsight you want. Yet, the emotion of the day is gone. None of us know what Margaret Thatcher, Nelson Mandela, Adolph Hitler, Mother Teresa, or Osama Bin Laden thought when they woke up each morning. Yet, we all see the results of their good or bad, without the context of the why or how. We can only guess. None of us know what the silent voice inside said to the person in the mirror. You simply have gotten a peek into President Sands' emotional makeup or character."

"Tim, let's take this a bit further. What if angels and demons were invisibly interacting with all of us. In most, there is a subtle influence we might call a good mood or a bad mood. If you believe this, then is it also possible that an unfortunate person is possessed by a mighty evil being? If you can follow me for just a moment longer, what if President Sands is possessed by evil? Think about what you have observed. Angry, vindictive, narcissistic, indulgent, self-aggradations ..." Shane paused for effect.

"What if President Sands spends so much time in his room because he is planning the next evil act? Objectively, he has stripped wealth, jobs, health care, senior benefits, and much more from the American people. He has also lied at every turn about doing it. He has often singled out some defenseless victim to take the blame for him. He has victimized people, families, political parties, countries, unions, and so much with his divisiveness. Do you think one man, however smart, could be this consistently evil without some higher power help?"

"More importantly, look at the people surrounding and protecting him. Most of these people were not bad or evil people before they got involved with Jarrod Sands. Most of them were pretty levelheaded. Most of them would never have been in the same room with President Sands, let alone clinging to him. How does this happen, unless it is supernatural? How does a Christian leader with a long history of righteousness and integrity suddenly change their stripes? They go as far as calling this man Godly. The old Christian in them would never even shake his hand."

This happens because, whether we like it or not, evil does influence the world."

"Now, to your question. What you caught in your audio was President Sands interacting with the demon possessing him. The demon would love to see President Sands imprison or ruin as many people as he can. The demon would love to see President Sands somehow start a massive war. The demon would love to see President Sands tarnish goodness in the world. This is what the audio is catching."

"When President Sands spends all his time in his private residence, he is simply scanning the world for the next thing he can destroy. I take that back. The demon within is scanning the world. The demon indiscriminately seeks the next evil act he can engineer, through President Sands."

"What do you think is happening when the majority of the population sees a President Sands' rally always promoting right-wing, older, whiter people screaming at the top of their lungs? Screaming they are protecting their God-given rights as Christians to carry their automatic weapons and injure those not like them. All presume God has somehow sanctioning hateful and bigoted behaviors through these so-called Christians. The opposite is true. These Christians are condemning themselves by knowingly following evil. President Sands rallies cost God thousands upon thousands of good Christians, Jews, Muslims, and others."

Rick Jones spoke up first, "A very compelling story, but it does not provide hard evidence to work with."

For the first time, Thomas Black spoke, "I represent the Catholic Church, and I have a law enforcement background. I can tell you Shane McNaughton is giving you a better explanation than anything you have at this moment. You do not live in the world you think you live in. There is good and evil all around you. Furthermore, this idea of Heaven and Hell as some abstract future reality is crap. They are both real places, existing right outside of your human ability to see them."

Arlen objected, "This might explain President Sands, but it does not explain you. We have been watching your band of merry men and women for years now. We have arrested you. We have kidnapped you. So, are you all angels? Are you possessed as well?"

Shane shook his head no. Shane added, "We are simple people like you. If President Sands has been influenced one way, let's just say we have been influenced the other way."

Rick Jones spoke, "I have never said it, but I am sorry we went after your sons and family. It was uncalled for."

Shane had a clock in his head. It was time for this to wrap up before someone noticed, "All I can tell you is your concerns are very real. The danger is genuine. I imagine you all could get into deep trouble if you had these audio files. Destroy them. Jarrod Sands will be out of the office in a few months. We need to go."

Shane got up as a sign that this meeting was over. Shane did not tell them he was already planning to deal with President Sands. The Order of Masada was trying to understand the dragons and track them down, like President Sands' dragon, Typhon.

In early July 2005, Sarah and Dalton got married. They had returned to The Homestead for their wedding. It was a good time. Several from Masada attended. A wide range of people from their lives in Washington DC attended. Sarah's family attended. They had the wedding at the Hot Springs Presbyterian Church and the reception in the Homestead Crystal Room. As Shane sat in the Crystal Room looking out over the friends and family gathered, it made him homesick for Cuyahoga and his own great hall. Despite the expense and the effort put in, this was a hollow representation of what Masada offered.

Shane also wondered how many people at this wedding were here under false pretenses. People who had weaved their way into Sarah and Dalton's lives to get close to Shane and the Order. Jack Dempsey and Thomas Black were again in charge of security for the event. There were followers whose sole purpose was to look for any threats. This was the first time both little Christine and Joseph Junior were on Earth. They had both grown but were still toddlers. Always together.

Sarah's parents were charming people. Grace and Sarah's mother had worked at the wedding. At first, Sarah's parents were nervous about the expense of a destination wedding. Grace told them Shane, and she was going to pay for the wedding. They should just enjoy it. At first, Sarah's parents objected. Sarah talked to them and explained it was fine. They ultimately agreed, and Sarah's mom actually was the one who planned most of everything. She did this at Grace's insistence. Grace explained to Shane and she was always traveling.

Nancy and Shane had found a moment alone at the wedding. This was coincidental, but the first since the announcement of her relationship with Danny. Nancy nervously started, "Yes, I remember us meeting for the first time in a crowded shopping area at Christmas in Ohio. One person out of a crowd. I was no older than these recruits we are training. Just a few years older than Danny and younger than Dalton."

"Shane, I have two things to talk to you about. First, with Alice departed, I think we need to recruit more women Judges. Maggie and I are both feeling a bit lonely."

Shane said, "Sure, yet I am not the one selecting Judges. This has been done by God, pointing us to those who are his choice. They all have Nephilim blood, and the crystal tells me where to go. What is the second thing?"

Nancy casually replied, "I feel a bit awkward because of my relationship with Danny. It was not something that happened suddenly or as a plan. It just sort of evolved."

Shane tuned out everything else and turned to Nancy, looking squarely into her eyes, "Nancy, you are already my family. I love you and trust you unconditionally. I have watched you grow up to some extent. Your relationship with Danny is great. With it or not, you would always be part of our lives. No worries."

Nancy smiled and gave Shane a large bear hug. "Do I have to start calling you, dad?"

Shane laughed and shrugged.

Later, Shane watched as Danny and Nancy danced the night away. It was one of those moments too far and too few for the Order of Masada. Shane thought this has to change. After all, it is still a life to live. Joy and happiness need to be sprinkled in. He knew exactly what he wanted to do. He telepathically reached out to Sri Ma, Barachiel, and Zuriel to help him. The Order of Masada was going to have an annual festival at Cuyahoga.

Back on Masada, Sri Ma had brought new followers from the settlements. Ten from the Creole settlement and ten from the Baoule' settlement. Jonas was one of the trainees from the Creole settlement. Maggie added ten from the Dakotas. Mufaro brought some of his closest earthly followers from Africa. The plan was to introduce these people to Cuyahoga, train fifty potential followers, and hope one Judge might emerge. This was designed to connect Creole, Baoule', Dakotas, Africa, and Cuyahoga into a more unified multiverse community. Shane believed this could be a supplemental process in their ongoing recruitment.

Michael and the other angels did the training. Jonas stood out in every way. He was the best warrior. He was the most engaging leader. Sri Ma was so proud of her personal sponsorship of such a wonderful young man. In the next few weeks, if no issues arose, the forty men and women would join various Judges' groups to become full-fledged Masada followers.

Sri Ma asked Camuel and Michael how the recruits were doing? Both gave them high marks and complimented her for selecting them. Sri Ma and Nancy made sure to provide news back to the settlements for maximum effect. The settlements were cheering on their chosen followers from afar.

In August 2005, President Jarrod Sands sat in front of his mirror in the White House Private Residence. It was a Tuesday at 1:00 PM. He was carrying on "a conversation" with his mirror, which had now lasted three hours.

Jarrod Sands said, "Why must I deal with this? I am going to be gone in a few months. Why me?"

Jarrod Sands' inner voice, "You fool, if you don't take action, Masada will hunt you down like a cornered animal. Once you have left office, you will not have the protection of the United States government. Your skin will be ripped from your body one strip at a time. Your fingernails and toenails will be burned from your appendages. After this torture, your fingers and toes will be cut off one at a time. Your eyelids will be cut from your eyes. You will have your bones broken, one at a time. You will be forced to see things you can never unsee. At least until Masada finally grants you the mercy of your death."

Even a courageous man could not have listened to this description of his fate without flinching. Jarrod Sands cried out, "I have tried. We have done everything we can legally do. We have threatened, imprisoned, tortured, and chased Masada and Shane McNaughton for years. Nothing has changed."

Jarrod Sands' inner voice, "Do what I tell you. Give Masada no place to go. Track them down and kill them. Find them all. Spare no expense."

Chapter 10 – Saving of the Presidency

Jude 1, 4 ~ 21 (New Testament)

4 For certain individuals whose condemnation was written about long ago have secretly slipped in among you. They are ungodly people, who pervert the grace of our God into a license for immorality and deny Jesus Christ our only Sovereign and Lord.

8 In the very same way, on the strength of their dreams these ungodly people pollute their own bodies, reject authority and heap abuse on celestial beings.

10 Yet these people slander whatever they do not understand, and the very things they do understand by instinct—as irrational animals do—will destroy them.

12 These people are blemishes at your love feasts, eating with you without the slightest qualm—shepherds who feed only themselves. They are clouds without rain, blown along by the wind; autumn trees, without fruit and uprooted—twice dead. 13 They are wild waves of the sea, foaming up their shame; wandering stars, for whom blackest darkness has been reserved forever.

16 These people are grumblers and faultfinders; they follow their own evil desires; they boast about themselves and flatter others for their own advantage. 17 But, dear friends, remember what the apostles of our Lord Jesus Christ foretold. 18 They said to you, "In the last times there will be scoffers who will follow their own ungodly desires." 19 These are the people who divide you, who follow mere natural instincts and do not have the Spirit. 20 But you, dear friends, by building yourselves up in your most holy faith and praying in the Holy Spirit, 21 keep yourselves in God's love as you wait for the mercy of our Lord Jesus Christ to bring you to eternal life.

With Alice gone, Maggie had picked up the slack. She took extra patrols in the dark expanse. She recruited more followers. Most importantly, she perfected energy casting with Zuriel. Maggie saw Shane in front of the Cuyahoga entrance. She asked him to take a ride with her. They got two horses and headed out. Maggie took them to climb a large hill, and they stopped at a point where many of Maggie's followers were gathered.

Maggie said, "We have come up with a new way to use energy casting. Take a look at what we have been training to do." Maggie handed Shane binoculars. She pointed down to the valley below. She continued, "This is roughly 3,500 meters or 4,000 yards to the targets below." Watch what we have been able to master.

Maggie signaled followers to begin. They had a weapon Shane had never seen before. It looked like a long rifle. It had a rifle stock, a handgrip, a rifle scope, and a very long barrel. It did not have a trigger. Instead, the user put their entire hand into a harness of some sort. Shane also noticed something else about the barrel. It started with a cylinder about the size of a tennis ball can. This then tapered to a barrel more like a rifle barrel.

The follower Shane was watching was humming and then said a casting word for fire, "Gorag." As he did this, a very brief flicker came out of the rifle. Within a fraction of a second, the target in the field below exploded. Another follower repeated this but used the casting word for water, "Buwa." The same thing happened below. Another follower demonstrated pure energy using the word "Centine."

Maggie explained they had now perfected a way to use energy casting for long-range attacks like a military sniper. Maggie pointed to the followers shooting and described the distant targets were all further than the range of a gas-powered, centerfire snipper rifle.

Shane was really impressed, "Maggie, this is amazing. We now create long-range weapons allowing us to extend our attack. Will this work in the dark expanse and on Earth?

Maggie confirmed it would. She had already traveled to different domains and tested it. She was selecting and training followers to be part of special sniper teams she would lead.

She then smiled and said, "There is more!"

Maggie took Shane to another group looking like they were practicing martial arts or dancing or both. As they neared, Shane heard them chanting. They were coordinating the chanting with hand signals used in energy casting. "Gorag, Centine, Gorag, Yosa, Gorag, Centine, Gorag, Yosa." The chant and physical movements were matched with four blasts of fire. As the fireball traveled through the air, it seemed the wind chant exploded the fire like a napalm blast. The last chant was "Yosa" or shield. It protected the follower from being caught in the fire explosion.

Maggie told Shane, "I am borrowing from my Native Sioux culture and our war dances. By incorporating rapid energy casting, the blend can provide almost a machine gun effect. Rather than simply one fireball, we repeat the energy casting and combine it with other casts, each amplifying the effect. What you are seeing is the repetitive use of fire, wind, and shield. This can be taught to all followers."

Shane was again amazed, "Work with Sri Ma and Zuriel to incorporate this into training. This demonstration should be part of the festival Sri Ma is organizing. Speaking of the festival, isn't it coming up soon? Your followers could do some fascinating demonstrations."

Sri Ma had organized a festival at Cuyahoga. The Cuyahoga sporting fields and first floor rooms were vividly decorated with colorful streamers, flowers, and decorations. Beyond this, it provided anyone who traveled to the event a grand celebration of Masada and its culture. The villages around Cuyahoga were welcoming to all. These villages hosted thousands of travelers, providing places to eat, sleep, and forge new friendships. Throughout the festival, people who attended could find all sorts of opportunities. Villagers provided lessons on gardening, hunting, cooking, sewing, crafts, and much more. Less obvious, the Judges watched the socialization and the behaviors of people. People were bonding with each other regardless of their background.

Sri Ma invited all of the settlements, followers, and their families to attend. It gave villagers who had never seen Cuyahoga a chance to travel here. The Baoule', Creole, Mufaro's African villages, and the Dakotas Native Americans were all invited to attend. Maggie had ensured representatives from Mufaro's African towns and the Dakota's on Earth were able to portal to the event. For some, it would be the first time they had a real sense of togetherness. It was an opportunity to demonstrate God's meaning of his chosen followers to them all. Even though many remained in their own groups, they also saw Masada had no distinction by color, race, orientation, tribe, or sex.

Shane opened the week with a speech of sorts, "Many of us are here today after being selected and saved by our heavenly father. We are here in the sanctuary. It is a place we can see all is possible with God. If nothing else, Masada promises life, healing, love, and goodness in our lives. It is a place of remembrance. Remembering Earth was once a place such as this, full of abundance and promise. We are here to celebrate with each other and to forge new relationships. These relationships are not based on skin color, sexual orientation, ethnicity, or beliefs. They are based upon a shared love for one another. Enjoy yourselves but remember the potential of your visit to Cuyahoga."

"This reminds me of a story I heard. It was a story of an Israeli Jewish man. He said that his ideal neighborhood would be to live beside a Christian family and a Black Muslim family. To live across from an Indian Hindu Family and a Hispanic Catholic family. Down the street, have a neighbor that is gay, an atheist family, and any other diversity that could provide cultural diversity. He said this neighborhood would make him a better Israeli Jewish father, husband, leader, and man. Without diversity, how can you enrich your own beliefs and character?"

In the last week of the festival, the main attraction was a team competition emphasizing Masadian followers' skills. Sri Ma had created eleven teams of twelve competitors each, selected by each Judge or each village. The competition included one hundred and thirty-two people trained, competing, and working as teams. The real purpose was for Judges to observe and find a large new group of followers. Shane wanted to see if this festival benefited the sense of belonging and promotion of Masada's purpose.

Those selected to be competitors in the games were given additional training. Archangel Michael was an intense drillmaster in combat training. Zuriel was an equally fierce instructor in energy casting. Beyond this, there were general skills taught by Noni, Mufaro, Nancy, and Sri Ma. Camuel, Jeremiel, and Barachiel provided the competitors instruction of the multiverse; including Heaven, Hell, Masada, and Earth's domains.

As the competition began, the first level of events were oriented towards physical speed, strength, and coordination. Teams Terry (Gault) and Mufaro were by far the strongest competitors. Jonas, from the Creole team, was individually near the top. Maggie's team included Sioux reservation participants such as Jason, Hansko, and Mato. They were all very fast, although not as strong as some of the others.

One of the competitions was an obstacle race. Two tracks around the facility had obstacles requiring jumping over hurdles, climbing up walls, hanging & crossing rope bridges, crawling, and running. Jonas and Hansko were leading the race. As they came to a hurdle, Jonas elbowed Hansko just enough to throw off his balance near the end of the race. Hansko fell and had to quickly get up again. Jonas won the race. When Jonas elbowed Hansko, just for a few seconds, a red aura appeared. It disappeared as quickly. Yet, Sri Ma had noticed it. She momentarily worried about her "favorite son" from Creole. Did he have the character to be a follower? Did he belong in Masada?

The second day was about energy casting. Maggie was excited because this was not a fair competition. She had drilled her team in energy casting, and she had also perfected the new skills. She was excited to introduce them at the festival. Maggie was the most refined energy caster.

Nancy was also skilled at energy casting. It could be said Nancy was the most powerful energy caster, as were her followers. It would be interesting if their training benefited their teams. Every other team was way behind Maggie and Nancy's groups.

One of the last challenges was to blast a hole into a wooden wall. On the wall was a large circle. The goal was to target this circle, with little damage outside of it. This was difficult because it required the energy cast powerful enough to cut through the wood but not wide enough to extend beyond the circle. Emmitt was Nancy's follower, and Mato was Maggie's follower. They were all tied as they came to this last challenge. Emmitt was first up, and he used a Gorag fire cast. He had shaped the energy casting to be a long burst of fire, but not quite as powerful. In the end, Emmitt had burned too small of a hole through the wall. Yet, he had not gone outside the target area. Mato's turn was next. If he won, he would take this competition. He danced and chanted, "Gorag, Gorag, Gorag, Gorag." Instead of a stream of energy, Mato had cast four pulses of energy. When they hit the wooden wall, each pulse was slightly more powerful. The fire spread out over the wood wall until the hole had completely burnt everything inside the circle. Mato and Maggie's team won the day.

After this, Maggie had her team give a demonstration of their new long-range weapons. Everyone wanted trained and wanted a gun. Jonas was particularly interested in this technique. He often hunted in the forest areas near Creole and thought targeted energy casting could be used in his hunts.

The third day was about team activities. These included a traditional tug of war, Masada style. The Masada twist required teams to pull a rope while balancing on a single elevated beam, fifty feet in the air. If a teammate fell from the shaft, they were eliminated. What made this interesting is teammates could telepathically communicate. They could coordinate swinging the rope left or right. Pulling hard or allowing slack. By this communication, they were pulling the other team in unpredicted directions. In the end, Mufaro's African villages team won the event, beating Terry Gault's team.

The final event of the festival was a paintball war between teams, Masada style. A battlefield had been constructed with obstacles, uneven terrain, and two forts at opposing ends. The participants had been given weapons Maggie had created. Each gun could shoot small, focused energy bursts coupled with colored powders. If a ball of energy hit the other team, it would leave a small circular colored mark. Maggie had made two types of weapons. The first was a short pistol for close-range firing. The second weapon looked like a rifle. The rifles were for long-range and accurate shooting. It was exciting to watch this last event as the teams were gradually eliminated.

The last two teams were Maggie's team versus Shane's team. Shane's team was a mix of competitors from Lakewood, Ohio, from the Catholic Church and Masada villages. In the end, Shane's team won the final paintball competition. Overall, Mufaro's followers won the competition. Jonas was named the most valuable follower. Mato was named the most valuable energy caster. Mufaro's African team was named the most valuable remote team.

The final day concluded with a banquet in the Cuyahoga great hall. It was fun for everyone who traveled and participated in the three-day events. Beleth and his wives were invited. While it was common to see angels in Masada, Beleth was still a hated adversary by many. Being at the banquet was a surprise, but Shane had invited him.

Shane greeted him, "Beleth, nice of you to join us. Did you bring your new family?"

Beleth replied, "Yes, I did not want to leave anyone behind. I enjoyed watching the events today. It seems Masada is growing and growing. You should be proud."

Shane said, "I am, and it is always good to use our skills without being in real combat."

Beleth was scanning the crowd, "Do you think it is OK that I am here. I was hoping to spend some time with Solomon and Thomas, my old angel friends. It has been …"

Beleth paused. It was as if he saw someone important. He continued, "Excuse me, I see someone I want to say hello to."

Beleth left and slowly made his way through the crowd. He got something to eat along the way. It seemed he was not in a hurry to find whoever he had seen. Beleth moved to the side of the great hall, standing and watching. Eventually, he saw who he was looking for. As the crowd moved and exposed the person, Beleth was shocked to see their eyes connect instantly. They had both been searching.

Beleth motioned to move outside, and he walked out towards the Renovare Pool. Most everyone was inside except for guards along the Cuyahoga fortress walls. They were looking outward, not inward. As Beleth approached the Renovare pool, he moved to his left, towards the mansion's side where the farm buildings were. He found a nice quiet place to stand against a farm building wall. He was out of the guards' sight, and at this point, no one could see him. If they did, he was merely a large angel eating outdoors.

Beleth waited only a minute or so. The person he was looking for had also exited the front door. It was Jonas. Jonas scanned the courtyard until he saw Beleth standing in the dark. He moved towards Beleth, slowly.

Jonas said, "Hello, my old friend. I thought you were dead. How is it I find you here among the humans."

Beleth replied, "They attacked me in Hell and kidnapped me. My choices were death or peace. I chose peace. I live quietly on a settlement far from this place. I only came back at the invitation from Shane. My days as a commander in Hell are over."

Jonas said, "I have also been here for a long time. I have taken this human form until I can find a way to serve our master. I am slowly getting closer to a trusted position with them. Although I grow tired of being trapped as a mere human."

Beleth cautioned, "I would not take the humans as weak or as ignorant. They will discover you at some point. I am surprised you have not already been found by the archangels or guard angels. I saw you immediately for who you are."

Jonas boasted, "I am not you. I can conceal my true nature from all. I am like a fox, walking among them, and gaining their trust. I will find a way to attack them. Will you help me?"

Beleth forcefully replied, "No, I will not help you. I have found a place I enjoy and am at peace. However, I will watch with amusement as you try to spin your treacherous trap. Beelzebub, you were always a dangerous and cold-blooded monster, even by Hell's standards."

Jonas laughed, "I will do the bidding of Satan, but I will also come for you. You have betrayed our father. I will not let you merely live here in luxury."

Beleth laughed and shook his head as he walked off.

With that, they parted ways. Nancy and Danny were out for a walk. They had stopped at the edge of a garden and in a romantic embrace. Danny was observant of their surroundings as he did not want to be noticed by others. He looked over into the dark by the farm building and saw Beleth and Jonas talking. While not alarming, it was an unusual sight to see two beings, with no apparent relationship, speaking in the dark. Yet, something else stood out. The glow surrounding both of them was red. It was strange because everyone in Masada typically had a green or blue glow around them. It was one of the things the Judges and followers always looked for before allowing anyone to enter Masada. Beleth was the exception. Jonas was not.

Danny asked Nancy, "Are you seeing this?"

Nancy replied, "What are you talking about?"

Danny whispered and turned Nancy slowly, "Look over my left shoulder into the darkness by the farm building."

Nancy did and remained quiet, but she gently nudged Danny back into the bushes they happened to be standing in front of.

Nancy watched the same thing Danny had. Both Nancy and Danny observed the red glow as the two of them departed. Beleth's own aura dimmed to a dull yellow, which was normal for the new and improved Beleth. What disturbed them was Jonas walked away with a red glow. For just a moment. Then it completely turned to green. No one could do that. One's aura did not change like that. Not like Jonas did.

Nancy was the first to speak, "I understand Beleth, but not Jonas. My eyes saw Jonas with an evil aura distinguishable from Beleth. Although it disappeared within a few seconds. I have known Jonas for a long time and have no explanation as to why he would be talking to Beleth."

Danny replied, "Well, it is over now. And I have you in the bushes. Let's take advantage of this."

Nancy laughed and pulled Danny to her.

After the festival, Shane prepared for a trip. He would be away for some time, at least Earth time. Barachiel had long ago given Shane a crystal directing him to find worthy people. It was time for him to travel to Earth to search once again. He worked with Noni to locate potential Judges on the scrying mirrors in the control room. Three locations lit up. The first was in Boston, the second was in Saudi Arabia, and the third was in Germany.

Shane went to a portal and floated in the dark expanse towards Earth. He used the locating crystal to direct him where to go. When he passed through a portal, Shane found himself in Boston, Massachusetts. It was always difficult to exit a portal in a populated area. Shane would stop short of the doorway, and he would peer through it. He would wait until a moment when it was safe to slip through. Even times when his appearance or disappearance was witnessed by someone, it was typically this momentary event. They did not trust their eyes.

He looked at the Crystal. It was pushing him out to the northwest of Boston. Shane hailed a cab and asked the driver to drive towards Cambridge. Eventually, the crystal changed direction, and as it did, Shane asked the taxi to stop. Shane's crystal took him to the Harvard Center for the Study of World Religions (CSWR) building at 42 Francis Avenue. How interesting he would begin his hunt for a Judge here.

Shane entered the building and picked up a brochure. Since the late 1950s, the Center was at the forefront of promoting understanding the world's religions. It was integrated with the study of religion at Harvard. As Shane often found, God put him in one of the most appropriate places.

As Shane stood in the lobby reading the brochure, a young man walked by him. The crystal followed the man. Shane caught up with him on the sidewalk and asked, "Excuse me, I have traveled a long distance and was wondering if you could give me a moment of your time."

The young man was friendly. He agreed he would help. Shane noticed a bright blue glow about the man.

Shane introduced himself, "I am Shane McNaughton, and I am here to find someone."

The man introduced himself, "I am Terry Guererro, and I am a grad student here at Harvard."

Shane asked what he was studying. Terry replied, "I am finishing up a Master of Theology and doing some work with the Center for the Study of World Religions. How can I help you?"

Shane took a deep breath and said, "I have been sent to find you."

Terry laughed nervously but did not pull back. Shane continued, "What if I could translate your studies into an opportunity of many lifetimes? Would you be willing to give me half a day to show you?"

Terry said, "Why me? Is this some type of con job, or do you want money?"

Shane said, "No, I want nothing from you. In fact, if you take a walk with me, I can show you everything."

Terry declined, "I don't know you and am uncomfortable going somewhere with a stranger. Sorry, good day."

Shane was disappointed, but he was not giving up. He had another idea and hailed a taxi. He asked to be taken to Saint Anthony Parish, 43 Holton St, Allston, MA.

Saint Anthony Parish was a beautiful church with a cobblestone front and three beautiful arches. The sanctuary included a rounded pulpit area with six beautiful stained-glass windows. Overhead was a balcony with the pipe organ. Shane saw an attendant and asked to see a priest. He was greeted in a few minutes by Pastor Reese Jones. Shane asked the Pastor to call Father Bennie on a private number he had been given. He explained once the Pastor had called, all would be revealed.

Pastor Jones invited him along a corridor back to some offices. He made the call, and his facial expression changed dramatically. Finally, he said a rapid succession of yes's. He hung up the phone, looked at Shane, and asked how he might be of service. Shane explained he needed to influence a graduate student at Harvard Divinity. This student was someone vital to Shane. Shane needed Pastor Jones to reach out and see if a local hand could guide this person to Shane and his cause.

Pastor Jones said he knew some influential professors at Harvard, and he would see what he could do. In the meantime, he offered food, room, and anything Shane needed to feel comfortable. Until Pastor Reese Jones delivered Terry Guererro on a silver platter, Shane was his most valued guest. He didn't say it, but it is what he meant.

Shane decided to wait a day and see if Pastor Jones could work his magic. Until then, Shane asked Pastor Jones if he were active with a hospital or other place with individuals needing help. Shane explained he wanted to do some good while he waited.

Pastor Jones thought for a moment and then said, "I know just the place. Are you ready? I will get my car."

Pastor Jones drove Shane to a homeless shelter at 112 Southampton Street in Boston. It was a large brick building capable of holding hundreds of people. They walked into the large hall where meals were served. Pastor Jones and Shane got coffee and sat off to the side of the flow of traffic.

Pastor Jones asked, "If it is all right, may I bring people to you needing help?"

Shane agreed.

For the next three hours, Pastor Jones worked out in the crowds. Every few minutes, a new person or people would visit with Shane. In each case, he would heal them generally. Sometimes there was something specific. For instance, many of them had either addictions and/or mental health problems. In these cases, Shane would lay his hands on their heads and heal them specifically. In other cases, a family would have a sick child. Often the child's sickness had driven them into homelessness, to begin with, as they could not afford to pay the bills. Shane would heal the child and create healing in the parents, worn down by the circumstances. Finally, there were old-timers. These were men and women who were on the streets and were elderly now. Broken and merely surviving. Shane would make a concerted effort to repair their bodies and reverse the aging process to give them more time. Pastor Jones worked tirelessly finding and escorting people to Shane.

After three hours, they had seen many people. Shane knew he had healed many, but unfortunately, their circumstances did not magically change. He wanted to do more. He had kept notes of particular cases where the people also exhibited goodness. They had a green or blue aura, which Shane had seen. He explained to Pastor Jones that Masada may return for these people. The Order of Masada would make their lives better. Shane's intent was to offer some of these people financial support or even passage to Masada.

The afternoon of the next day, Pastor Jones called Shane into his office, and Terry was sitting there. Terry's body language was a bit more relaxed than the last time they met. Shane suspected meeting some guy on the street had unnerved Terry. He could not blame him and told him as much. Shane asked Pastor Jones if he and Terry could meet privately. Pastor Jones excused himself.

Shane started, "Terry, I know you are focused on your religious studies. As an academic, what if I could provide you an opportunity of a lifetime? An opportunity to study the nature of God and Heaven?"

Terry did not understand.

Shane said, "I was not just running into you on the street, as you might have thought. You were somehow chosen by God."

Shane took out the crystal and showed it to Terry. Shane commented, "This is the crystal I use to find people God has chosen." Shane moved the crystal around to demonstrate it was always pointing to Terry.

Terry continued to object and moved back.

Shane understood Terry was cautious, and it would take a lot to convince him of his destiny. Shane created a portal both Terry, and he could pass through. Shane was wondering if he would have to force Terry through. Terry got up and slowly approached the portal. Shane gave him the time Terry needed to take that first step.

Terry would be the most educated Judge Shane had recruited. Shane and Terry were in Masada. As an intellect, Terry was amazed and willing to explore. As a Judge, he was less inclined to agree. Camuel would have to do the convincing. Shane said goodbye to Terry and promised he would be taken care of while in Masada.

Shane headed to Berlin, Germany. Berlin was always a favorite city. It was one of the most interesting places on Earth. It was a reminder of the devastation of World War II. It was also incredibly representative of different historical points of view. Germany always gets lost as a cultural hub of Europe. Roman empire. Greek mythology. British Golden monarchy. Spanish explorers. Danish Vikings. Berlin was a tale of two cities, separated by the Wall and a communist government. It was a modern city with hope for a great future.

Shane created a portal to the Ludwigskirche Catholic Church. As sometimes happens, Shane lost track of Earth time while on Masada. It was 9:00 PM in Germany. Shane asked Thomas Black to arrange for a room with the church Pastors. When he got to the church, they instead had reserved a hotel room at the Hotel Seifert. It was a clean, no-frills hotel. Shane was hungry, so he walked to Weyers Restaurant. It was too cold for their outdoor seating, so he sat by the bar and ordered Wiener Schnitzel and a beer. He enjoyed German food and remembered his mother cooking some of the dishes on the menu.

This brought back his childhood in Galion, Ohio. Shane McNaughton was one of three children born to Judy and John McNaughton in 1954. He had an older brother Sammy and a younger sister Lisa. Judy and John divorced in 1959, and John disappeared from their lives. Teddy and Christine Bridgewater were Judy's parents and the children's grandparents. They had a German heritage even though they were part Irish. As with most families, the adopted culture stems from the family cook's heritage. Christine Bridgewater was mostly German.

Teddy was a lay preacher at a local church. It was a Christian fundamentalist church believing in a rigorous discipline of literally following God's Word. Beyond that, Teddy worked in the local General Motors factory and provided for his extended family. He adored the three grandchildren and always spent time with them. This was particularly important after Judy's divorce.

The food had brought back this memory. As he thought about it, he was fortunate to have reconnected with Teddy and Christine on Masada. They had somehow found their way from Heaven to Masada, as they worked at Cuyahoga. While not instantly, but over time, they realized who each other were.

Regardless, as Shane finished his late dinner, the crystal began to vibrate and glow. He looked at the time, and it was 10:30 PM. The person he was looking for must have been near. He glanced around the restaurant, but there were no clues. He paid and decided to walk back to his hotel.

He glanced at the crystal, and it was pointed in the general direction of his hotel. He would follow and see where it led. He turned up Uhlandstraße, towards his hotel, and the crystal was still pointing the way. He reached his hotel at the corner of Lietzenburger Street. The Crystal shifted slightly to the right but continued to point forward. He decided to follow it. At the very least, he would walk off his dinner. He was now headed to the right on Kurfürstendamm. He followed this for several blocks until he came upon the Kaiser Wilhelm Memorial Church. This was a church that had been bombed in World War II. It was now preserved as a war-ravaged skeleton of the great church which had existed. Large holes riddled the walls and structure. Scars from the war. On this chilly night, Shane almost forgot his mission as he gazed upon the structure. A memorial to war and horrors of it.

Regardless his crystal shifted, and it tracked to a Polizei. Shane was not thrilled to approach a policewoman, at night, in Berlin. Regardless, he had learned to follow when called upon. Shane approached the woman. Shane greeted her, "Guten Abend, darf ich für einen Moment mit Ihnen sprechen." (Good evening, may I talk to you for a moment) As with most languages, Shane had the gift of tongues and could speak and understand German.

The police woman replied, "Womit kann ich Ihnen behilflich sein?" (How can I help you?)

Shane introduced himself and explained he had been specifically looking for her. He wondered if she would have a moment to talk to him. She was hesitant but agreed. Her name was Jody Troutman. Shane was impressed by her physical build. She was around six feet tall. As a policewoman, Shane assumed she was in good shape.

Shane tried to explain the opportunity to join Masada. After Boston, he was a bit rattled. Terry had almost turned him down, which shook his confidence. He decided to technically explain the crystal. He took out the crystal and explained this was a holy relic. It was used by his Order of Masada to find particular people. People predestined for great things on behalf of God.

Jody interrupted, "Is this some sort of trickery. Is there a hidden camera somewhere? If there is, I will not treat you gently. Besides, I am both gay and an atheist."

Shane laughed and replied, "No, I am serious. I would like to take you somewhere if you are willing to give me five minutes of your time." He regretted it as soon as he said it.

Jody refused as she was on duty. However, she agreed to meet him the next morning at his hotel at 7:30 AM.

Shane got a good night's sleep and was downstairs at 6:45 AM. Thomas had gone the extra mile by having the pastors arrange for a change of clothing in his room, as well as all the essentials he would require. There was a buffet breakfast, but he planned on waiting for Jody to arrive. By 9:00 AM, she had not shown up. Shane concluded he was stood up but not defeated.

Shane got a taxi and used the crystal to direct him. It took him to the corner of Fraunhoferstraße and Kohlrauschstraße. This was a neighborhood street with apartments. He got out and paid for the taxi. Using the crystal, he proceeded down Kohlrauschstraße to apartment building number seven. This was a five-story, concrete building. At the door, he found a door entry system and saw Troutman listed. He was about to buzz the door and then smiled. Instead, he simply used a portal to get through the security door.

He walked up to the fourth floor and Jody's apartment on the left. He knocked on the door, and she answered. She was shocked to see him there, but also on guard. From the noise, Shane could deduce that others lived in the apartment. Her family, or her girlfriend, or roommates … he did not know.

Shane said, "I am sorry to disturb you, but we had an appointment. This is of the utmost importance. May I ask you to meet me at Café Südwind, down the street? This will only take a few minutes.

Jody seemed upset and embarrassed by Shane's intrusion. After all, she said she would meet this man. She agreed to meet him this time. When she agreed, Shane apologized for the interruption and left.

He got a table in the Café and waited. Fifteen minutes later, she arrived.

Shane apologized, "I realize how strange this is, and for my persistence. I have been directed to recruit you for something important. Can I get your trust for just five minutes?"

Jody agreed. Shane asked her to follow him. Next to the Café was a small green space. It was at the rear of an apartment complex on the next street and served as the residents' parking lots. Shane asked Jody to follow him to the most discrete location in this lot. He looked around, and there was nobody to disturb them. He created a portal, reached out for Jody's hand, and they headed to Masada. Two down, one to go.

Shane was about to make his last and, by far, most dangerous trip. He was directed to travel to Saudi Arabia tomorrow. There was Masada business to attend to.

In the morning, Shane found a safe place to create a portal, Yamamah Park, in Riyadh's diplomatic region. Shane thought he would walk. He was wrong, and the heat was oppressive. He found a taxi and directed it to the location of The Ritz-Carlton, Riyadh. As he exited the taxi he was impressed with the Ritz. A large three-sided building around a massive fountain in front. Inside, it was luxurious and impressive. Of course, like most of Saudi Arabia, tobacco smoke permeated the hotel. In his room, he found fresh clothing and toiletries. He had a terrace and a hot tub on the balcony. He could live like this. It was nice.

Yet, he got a shock. As he walked out on the terrace, he experienced a surprising vision or trance. It was as if the landscape had changed from buildings, sand, and desolation to a lush tropical landscape. Trees, vegetation along the grounds, water flowing in rivers and pools. It was as if God was showing what was or what could be. He did not know.

After being refreshed, and after his vision, Shane looked at his crystal. It directed him to the east. He took a taxi to the city. He again exited to walk the last leg of his journey. The crystal reoriented. Shane continued until he was in the Al Bawardi Gardens. This allowed him to then walk to the front of the Al Bawardi Mosque. Here he looked for any sign of a person he was supposed to meet. Instead, it just pointed inside the Mosque. Shane did not know what to do.

Shane was relieved that his American clothing was not terribly out of place. Businessmen who had come to pray had on similar attire. He took off his shoes and proceeded slowly and with purpose through the first entry to a lobby. He then entered a large prayer room. Men were seated in groups, but it was spread out. There was not a large crowd. Prayers appeared to be over. He took out the crystal and surprisingly located a young man. He estimated the man was about thirty years old. He was wearing a white thobe and a traditional keffiyeh. He looked about six feet, five inches tall, and had a neatly trimmed beard.

Shane thought, here goes nothing, "Medhrtan, hal yumkinuni alhusul ealaa lahzat min waqtk?" (Excuse me, could I have a moment of your time?)

The man's name was Raji. He was a school teacher. Raji's posture left Shane with an impression of natural curiosity. Shane tried to appeal to this curiosity. With this, Shane was able to convince Raji to take a trip with him. Raji and Shane walked to the Garden, and Shane pretty much drug Raji through the portal. Camuel was there to greet the third of the Judges.

While in Cuyahoga, Shane took a swim in the river behind Cuyahoga and refreshed himself. He spent time with Grace, Christine, and Joseph Jr. He talked to Noni about any issues needing his attention. Danny had wanted to speak to him, but he was in a hurry.

It was now September 2005, and time was running out. The Judges had examined the book they recovered from Satan's jail and the weapon cache they had brought back. The book told a story of the six dragons having escaped to Earth. They wandered the Earth, taking possession of humans over time. When a human was possessed, there was a distinct brand. It was a pentagram within a circle.

When they did not have a human, they often hid in Earth's deep belly and slept. Yet there was always at least one of them wandering the Earth. Their mission was to corrupt the Earth. While the Bible Book of Revelations described God's view of the end of time, the dragons had a completely different version. In their version, they possess powerful people in the world while at the same time accumulating wealth and power. The goal is to stay hidden to prepare for the days of the Anti-Christ.

Each dragon had special powers.

- Erebus - Ability to hypnotically control humans.
- Typhus - Brute force and strength in war
- Aerico - Ability to release sickness and disease
- Ayax - Ability to burn the Earth, leaving a barren wasteland.
- Boreas - Ability to freeze the Earth, leaving an ice age.
- Thanatus - Force a lasting nighttime and release lower demons over the Earth

They could all be exorcised and defeated with the blessed weapons. The weapons were made of the same metals used in the chains securing the six dragons to Satan's jail. The metal is in the bars and walls containing Satan, himself. This is what is so special about these weapons.

There was some horrible news, as well. The book said the twelve dragons in Hell and Earth were all telepathically wired to hear each other's thoughts. This means if Masada were to kill the dragon within President Sands, the others would know. This might trigger them to create destruction and more evil.

Nothing was mentioned, but Shane wondered if bringing President Sands to Masada and then dealing with the dragon might throw this communication off. Even for a moment. After all, Masada was not even created when the dragons roamed the universes. Maybe, just maybe, Masada might hold an answer.

In the long run, the decision was made to kidnap President Sands and bring him to Masada. If the Serpent tried to extricate himself, kill the demon with the blessed weapons. Otherwise, exorcise the demon on Masada and return the President to Earth before it was noticed. That is presuming they did not kill the President first.

The Judges all agreed it was worth the risk. It was decided to repeat their plan from the last time they attacked President Sands in the White House private residence. After all, he seemed to be hiding in his private residence most of the time. As they talked, Shane directed each of the Judges to their portal and attack responsibilities.

Shane was discussing the attack plan for the private residence entrance into the bathroom and dressing areas. "Alice, you had the experience. Maybe you could …" Shane stopped as he realized Alice was no longer among the living. A moment of silence ensued. He started again and gave Alice's role to Jody.

They would again attempt to get into his bedroom in the dead of night and whisk him away to Masada. This time, they would leave Nancy and Terry behind in the private residence. Once they had President Sands in Masada, Nancy and Terry would guard Jarrod Sands' private residence. If anyone entered, they would attempt to neutralize them until President Sands returned.

Danny interrupted and spoke up. He was a Judge in training but participated in most of their planning. "I think the first plan was flawed as the dragon had time to exit Jarrod Sands. Would it not be better to tranquilize Sands? Put Jarrod Sands to sleep with the idea the dragon is then somehow trapped.

Wait until he finally does go to bed and goes to sleep. Sneak in very quiet with only a few people. Tranquilize him. Put him asleep. Have the teams waiting if something goes wrong, but otherwise, hope you get him to Masada without stirring his inner dragon."

The room was silent for a moment, and then Shane replied, "Danny, I think your idea is a winner. We can just check on him periodically until he is in bed. No guarantee he would be deep asleep. Noni is there anything we can do to detect this?

Noni replied, "No, the White House would notice any sensory or wireless devices placed in the room. We would just draw more attention than it is worth."

Shane looked at everyone, "If there is no objection, then we will go with Danny's plan."

On November 15, 2005, it was a slow news day. Presidential debates were scheduled for the next election cycle. The Dow Jones Index fell 733 points. A few days earlier, suicide bombers attacked three hotels in Amman, Jordan, killing at least 60 people. President Sands had spoken today about building up the military and blamed this on Islamic extremists. All in all, it was a quiet day for President Sands, as his second term was wrapping up. In fact, he decided to head to his residence early to watch the Presidential debates.

Around midnight, Jody Troutman stood outside the White House behaving like a typical tourist. She was with six followers and was the relief should things go astray. Shane and Nancy would portal into the bedroom. Each carried a syringe filled with a tranquilizer. Noni and Nancy had prepared a dosage of midazolam, based upon a rough calculation of President Sands' age, weight, and health. Then they added a bit more.

Shane opened a portal into the room to peak at Jarrod Sands. He had just gotten into bed. Shane started a timer believing they would have to wait at least thirty minutes for him to fall asleep. Thirty minutes later, they checked again. Still awake. Thirty minutes later, and he was sleeping. It was go time.

Nancy entered first. President Sands was on his left side facing the bathroom. Nancy circled around the bed to the other side. She leaned in to reach his buttocks, which was partially exposed. Slowly and gently, she administered the shot. He stirred and reached around to swat or rub the area where he got the shot. By then, Nancy had withdrawn back into the portal. It was as if the Judges were not there. They waited roughly another twenty minutes for the drug to take full effect.

Everyone was telepathically told it was time. Mufaro, Shane, Razi, and Terry Guererro all entered through a portal into the bedroom to secure and transport President Sands. So far, so good. No sign of the dragon. Shane had prepared him by binding his legs and arms, covering his mouth, and placing a hood over his head. They quickly carried Jarrod Sands to Masada's basement jail cells. The entire abduction was over in less than five minutes.

President Sands was securely tied to a chair in the middle of the cell. The judges were quietly gathered outside the cell. Fifty followers were on guard throughout Cuyahoga. Shane thought this was overkill, but he did not want to take any chances. As the drugs worked, Shane believed he would be asleep for a good hour or two. He left the hood on President Sands' head.

It took a bit under three hours for President Sands to awake. Shane pulled the hood from President Sands' head. President Sands was fearful. He scanned the jail cell and the Judges surrounding him. He was screaming like a drunken sailor one minute and crying like a baby another. A far cry from the tough-guy bravado he projected on television. Profane threats and spittle were coming from his mouth. President Sands was a hot mess.

Shane had instructed all to stare at him but not speak. It was a form of intimidation, not for President Sands, but for the dragon inside. The Judges did not say a thing. They positioned themselves against every wall in preparation for something they had never seen. Each was armed with weapons for the dragon. Shane and Mufaro had two large daggers from Satan's prison. First, they sliced his clothes off, and President Sands was sitting in the chair naked. They inspected him to ascertain if they could find a birthmark. Sure enough, Mufaro found it on his left butt cheek.

Upon this confirmation, Shane nodded to Noni. Noni sent a telepathic alarm bell to all Masadians. It was the signal to all that the dragon was about to be released. Followers were on guard. Families locked themselves in their houses. Shane and Mufaro approached President Sands and sliced two deep cuts into President Sands' forearms. He howled.

A massive serpent-like, evil being pulled itself out of the back of President Sands. President Sands had either died or passed out in the chair. The being was enormous, and all were amazed. It had emerged from the relatively small President Sands. It raised itself up to the ceiling.

Hissing at them, it said, "Why have you disturbed me? Do you know who I am? I am Nasham's son and one of the most powerful demons. I am Typhon. If you let me go now, I will not kill you all. Surely you do not want to die here today. Let me pass, and I will travel on."

Shane was the first to attack, and he was able to severe the lower left arm. The demon used the adjacent arm to throw Shane easily against the wall. Mufaro had a spear and drove it into the abdomen of the serpent. As the serpent lowered itself instinctively, Terry Gault jumped on its back and drove a sword into its shoulder. The serpent raised its head and smashed Terry into the ceiling. Any of these three attacks would have mortally wounded a lesser demon.

At this point, the demon did not want to fight but to flee. The serpent bent the jail cell bars out and smashed them to the floor. It passed through the crowd and up the stairs. It mowed over any followers standing in its way. Followers outside engaged it, but even when wounded, it was able to swat its attackers away. However, Typhon left a blood trail to follow. The Judges and their followers immediately gave chase. It headed through the villages and towards the mountains. It was very confused as this was not Earth. As it got to the river, it was again surrounded by the Masada warriors. Energy casting held it in place.

The followers and the Judges took turns attacking it with the weapons from Satan's Chamber. The serpent was mighty. Any attacker seemed to only get one lunge in before the serpent would send the attacker through the air. Each landed blow did weaken it. It was starting to slow down. The judges realized this was like chopping down a tree.

Shane grabbed a spear, circled the demon, and wanted to strike low. He took a running start, launched himself at Typhon's lower abdomen, and fully extended to drive a spear into the serpent. As he did this, the serpent did not throw him but took two hands and drove Shane into the ground.

Typhon stood over him and shouted to the Masada warriors, "Halt, or I will tear this human from limb to limb."

It was the first pause in the fighting since it began.

The serpent asked no one in particular, "Where am I, this is not familiar to me? Where am I?

Maggie spoke first, "You are not on Earth. You are in a domain called Masada."

The serpent was still confused, "Masada, where is that?"

195

The demon held Shane in a crushing grip, like a rag doll. He used Shane as a shield as he limped away from the fight. The Judges and followers were cautious. They followed the demon allowing him to put distance between them. Typhon headed out of the forest and towards the barren terrain. This was the area of Beleth's plateau home.

Beleth has just emerged from his cottage for another day in Masada. Quiet and peacefully spent by himself and his wives. Beleth was alarmed as this large dragon was coming right at him. He had a dagger with him and his sheathed sword. He was debating whether to leave the ugly monster pass. Just turn around and go back to his cottage.

As he was thinking, he saw Shane in the grips of the dragon. Beleth stepped into Typhon's path. The dragon did not see him, as his eyes were fixed on those pursuing him from Masada. Shane and Beleth's eyes did meet. Beleth threw his dagger into the dirt along the path the serpent was taking, handle sticking straight up. Beleth let the demon come to him. The demon had still not seen Beleth blocking his way when Beleth swung his sword with all his strength and struck a fierce blow across the back of the serpent. The serpent dropped Shane to turn and face this new threat. Beleth retreated out of the serpent's reach. Shane allowed gravity to drop him to the ground, where he reached the dagger. Shane returned to face the serpent one last time. He gutted the demon completely open. From there, Typhon was not dead but was incapacitated. As this was not a special weapon, Typhon would heal himself.

Shane immediately instructed others to bring up the shackles and chains found in Satan's jail. They bound the dragon and drug it off to Cuyahoga. It was not dead, but it was seriously wounded and in pain. The shackles rendered any healing properties or magic useless. Once in Masada, Shane instructed those with medical training to stitch up the wounds. They would have to heal Typhon the old fashion way.

The Judges and followers cheered their victory, as Shane thought to himself, five more dragons to go. No way!

Regardless, Shane realized they were on the clock. He shouted to the Judges, "Judges, we need to get back to the fortress. We have little time left. They all raced back, quickly cleaned themselves up from the battle, and headed out to the Renovare Pool. Debbie and several others had been using wet towels with the water from the Renovare Pool to revive President Sands. When Typhon was defeated, it suddenly brought President Sands back to life, barely. He was awake but not talking.

Shane returned and pulled a chair up to face the President. Shane started, "How are you feeling?" The President nodded. He was OK.

Shane continued, "Do you know who I am?"

The President said, "You are Shane McNaughton. I presume these are the other people who we have been hunting. Have you abducted me? Are we in Lakewood, Ohio?" Some of the Judges smiled.

Shane continued, "President Sands, you have been an evil and corrupt leader in the World. We are the Order of Masada, selected by God to fight evil on Earth. This has always made you and I adversaries." Shane paused to let it sink in.

President Sands asked, "So are you going to kill me?"

Shane said, "No, President Sands. We brought you here to extract a mighty demon which possessed you. We have now accomplished this. You have spent a life of greed, lust, and persecution of those less fortunate than you. This demon filled you with hate. I am curious, how do you feel at this moment?"

President Sands was quiet and then said, "I feel strange and different, but have no anger or hate in me. I should be furious for what you have done, but strangely am not."

Shane continued, "Your time as President is wrapping up in the next few months. Our simple goal was to exorcise this demon. It will not make you a good person. It will only free you to choose. That is all God wants from any of us. After you have been restored in a few minutes, we will send you back to Earth as if this never happened. But the demon within you is gone. Your time is short. I must warn you to leave us alone. We are not your enemy."

Shane expected President Sands to protest, scoff or reject his explanation. Surprisingly, Jarod Sands seemed to accept this explanation and remained very quiet. Shane told Mufaro to let him soak in the Renovare Pool for a while and then get him a clothing change. Keep guards on him. Shane had an ulterior motive.

Shane went outside to the farm area where they were keeping Typhon. He grabbed the chain leash and pulled the dragon to the Renovare Pool. President Sands was sitting in it and became very frightened of the dragon. He was more than afraid. He was terrified as if seeing the worst thing in the world. He jumped up and got out of the pool. Using the pool to separate himself from the dragon.

Shane said, "You may never believe this, but this dragon had possessed you. We captured it. It will never do this to any other human." The only reaction that Shane got from President Sands was fear and a continual whimper.

Shane was about to continue but was interrupted.

Typhon hissed at President Sands, "Hello, my puny and pitiful puppet. Call you forces and defeat these people. Kill them all. You were not worthy of my attention. I have put up with your cowardly and ignorant ways for tens of years. Without me, you would have ended up a desk clerk in one of your ugly and dirty slums. Get your people to free us. Now!"

Shane and others were laughing. President Sands was not. He was weeping and had urinated down his leg.

When this was done, Shane returned President Sands to his bedroom in the White House. Only a few minutes ticked off the clock on Earth. Things went according to plan. No one had noticed. No one had entered the rooms. Jarrod Sands went over and sat on a couch. He was completely exhausted.

As Shane got ready to exit through a portal, President Sands asked, "What do I do now?"

Shane turned and said, "God has given you a chance to live the rest of your life. Chose to be righteous, faithful, and loving. Chose to fight for those who cannot fight for themselves. I charge you with this mission. You still have time. By the way, I would fire all those so-called religious leaders you have trotted out into the public. They are frauds."

With this, Shane disappeared. He now had a pet dragon to deal with. Shane also sent messages to Frank Kotter, Rick Jones, and Tim Durante. The message simply said, "Please monitor the situation, and inform me of any changes you observe. Things should get better."

As for President Sands, he indeed became a changed person. He was only in office for a few more months, but he laid the groundwork to have a fulfilling life after office. Many had thought he would sabotage his successor, but he did not. Many thought he would vilify the liberals as he left office. He did not. One could only hope he indeed achieved change.

Chapter 11 – Pieces of the Puzzle

Philippians 2: 2 – 11 (New Testament)

"2 then make my joy complete by being like-minded, having the same love, being one in spirit and of one mind. 3 Do nothing out of selfish ambition or vain conceit. Rather, in humility value others above yourselves, 4 not looking to your own interests but each of you to the interests of the others. 5 In your relationships with one another, have the same mindset as Christ Jesus:

6 Who, being in very nature God, did not consider equality with God something to be used to his own advantage; 7 rather, he made himself nothing by taking the very nature[b] of a servant, being made in human likeness. 8 And being found in appearance as a man, he humbled himself by becoming obedient to death, even death on a cross!

9 Therefore God exalted him to the highest place and gave him the name that is above every name, 10 that at the name of Jesus every knee should bow, in Heaven and on Earth and under the Earth, 11 and every tongue acknowledge that Jesus Christ is Lord, to the glory of God the Father."

1 Samuel 16: 6 – (Old Testament, Hebrew Nevi'im)

"6 When they came, he looked on Eliab and thought, "Surely the Lord's anointed is before him." 7 But the Lord said to Samuel, "Do not look on his appearance or on the height of his stature, because I have rejected him. For the Lord sees not as man sees: man looks on the outward appearance, but the Lord looks on the heart." 8 Then Jesse called Abinadab and made him pass before Samuel. And he said, "Neither has the Lord chosen this one." 9 Then Jesse made Shammah pass by. And he said, "Neither has the Lord chosen this one." 10 And Jesse made seven of his sons pass before Samuel. And Samuel said to Jesse, "The Lord has not chosen these." 11 Then Samuel said to Jesse, "Are all your sons here?" And he said, "There remains yet the youngest, but behold, he is keeping the sheep." And Samuel said to Jesse, "Send and get him, for we will not sit down till he comes here." 12 And he sent and brought him in. Now he was ruddy and had beautiful eyes and was handsome. And the Lord said, "Arise, anoint him, for this is he." 13 Then Samuel took the horn of oil and anointed him in the midst of his brothers. And the Spirit of the Lord rushed upon David from that day forward. And Samuel rose up and went to Ramah."

(The last Sermon of Prophet Muhammad)

"All mankind is from Adam and Eve, an Arab has no superiority over a non-Arab, nor a non-Arab has any superiority over an Arab; also a white has no superiority over black, nor a black has any superiority over white except by piety and good action."

With the threat in the United States disappearing, Shane and his team could return to the Earth. The Lakewood Center was opened again. Shane, Grace, Noni, Danny, Terry Gault, Terry Guererro, and Nancy worked from this facility. Arunta also became the Lakewood Center Manager, and Noni's family re-established themselves in Lakewood. This group alternated in having two Judges always in Lakewood and two always in Masada. Their followers would do the same.

President Sands had now passed the torch. He was out of office, and no longer a problem for the Order of Masada. His replacement was a liberal President and a good man. All who knew of him conveyed his goodness and his respect for the Rule of Law. As a liberal, he would have the oft-repeated historical responsibility of rebuilding everything President Sands had so cavalierly torn down.

President Sands had returned to private life. From afar, Shane could not determine any changes. President Sands seemed to continue his life in New York but did not seek attention. He had toned down the rhetoric and did fade from the public eye. The jury was still out. Shane did not care, so long as the dragon was gone.

In the meantime, Geneva, Switzerland, was the location of a very secret meeting. It was to occur at the Hotel Metropole Geneva, located on the left bank facing Lake Geneva. It is ideally situated in the heart of the financial and shopping districts. A week before the meeting, the Saleve and Jura rooms and the adjacent rooftop terrace had been booked for three weeks. A security and administrative team had arrived. They had completely isolated these rooms from the hotel staff. They created a physical and electronic fortress around and within the rooms. The five luxury suites in the hotel had also been booked. They were also given the same electronic configurations. No one could enter these facilities without passing through a wall of security guards and the hidden surveillance electronics.

On March 19, 2006, at 11:00 PM, three black SUVs pulled up to the hotel's front entrance at Quai du Général-Guisan 34. A security team of five men and one woman surrounded an older couple, who slowly walked into the hotel. They were led through the lobby and up to the Calvin Suite. Before midnight, this arrival was repeated four other times, each with another group of important guests.

The next morning at 9:00 AM, the meeting room had been re-decorated to include five comfortable chairs with various furnishings around them. End tables, telephones, ottomans, coffee or tea service carts, and so on. The chairs had been arranged so that each could speak in a normal tone and easily hear the others.

The guests were revealed to include:

- Illyia Rankochev, Head of the KGB, Moscow, Russia possessed by Erebus
- Peter Sterling, CEO and Founding Family Member of the EuroCocoa Corporation, Brussels, Belgium possessed by Aerico
- Sunny Wang, CEO and President of China's Zang Electronics Corporation, Beijing, China possessed by Ayax
- Roman Santegio, Drug Lord, Columbia possessed by Thanatus
- Chester "Jess" Wagner, President of Alistar Defense, Washington DC, USA, possessed by Boreas

These were the most unlikely cast of five people to ever be in the same room together. If fact, if the secret of this meeting ever became public, the world would be scratching their heads. Two high ranking and influential members of the Defense Industry. A drug lord. It made no apparent sense these people were together. Sunny was the only woman among them.

Illyia was the first to speak, "Let us take a moment to remember our brothers and sisters imprisoned in Hell."

After the prayers, Roman was first to speak about their purpose, "We are the five remaining dragons of Satan freed to roam the Earth. Typhon has disappeared. I cannot find him, and I cannot sense his presence inside Jarrod Sands. Something or someone is hunting us."

Sunny replied, "It would not be the first time some human has stumbled upon our secret. It will soon be revealed to us. I have put a team of my best operatives on discovering what happened. And discover who caused this."

Peter spoke with anger in his voice, "I suspect it is the same people who made our Industry's labor disappear from the cocoa and the sugar cane fields. These are all large events otherwise impossible. This indicates a very powerful intervention. Our conversations with Typhon suggested someone, or something, called the Order of Masada."

Jess Wagner added, "That is correct. President Sands was hunting an organization called the Order of Masada. He was absolutely convinced this group and their leader would be a lethal threat to our reign on Earth. It was an organization run by a man named Shane McNaughton. In the last six years, President Sands tried to repeatedly attack them with no success. I have to believe the answer to these many questions is right in front of our noses."

Roman replied, "They are human. Simply kill them and ask questions later. Why is this so hard?"

Jess said, "They appear to be supernatural and appear to be empowered by God himself."

The room went quiet as they all considered this. Could their days of freely wandering this domain be coming to an end? They all knew the Word of God suggested they would be imprisoned again. They would once more be thrown into Satan's jail.

They spent the next hour going from person to person to explain their individual accomplishments seeding the world with chaos and evil corruption. What evil and what destruction had they caused? What society or people had rejected God based upon their efforts? These were artists who painted the canvas with broad and bright brushstrokes of evil.

Illyia had continued to promote corruption and unrest in neighboring countries to Russia. His most recent actions were an effort to escalate the Russian-Georgian aggression to full-scale war. Best of all, the United States was getting involved with the Georgia Government, and a well-placed event could cause war to break out.

Illyia promoted similar unrest in Ukraine, Azerbaijan, and Moldova. Whether they pulled away from mother Russia or moved closer, chaos was always introduced, which created more violence and exploitation. Illyia, from his position in the KGB, controlled the puppets without them knowing.

Illyia was also "encouraging" the corruption of Russia's new-found capitalism by support for billionaire businessmen. Men like Mikhail Khodorkovsky and Vladimir Potanin. The idea was to allow them to strip Russia of its wealth and further impoverish the general population. An impoverished population who rejected any form of Godly worship. Illyia was successful, either way.

Those around the room congratulated him on his work and the impact he was having. The dragons had patiently promoted themselves to high ranking officials in powerful governments like the United States, China, or Russia. This did not happen overnight. Years in advance, they would have to observe and possess someone ascending the government's power structure, a business, or the media. It was rare to have Illiya, or Erebus within, be this successful as Head of the KGB.

Peter had been busy trying to salvage his empire built over 1,000s of years on the backs of poor African or Central American workers. Whether cotton, sugar, tobacco, cocoa or any other crop needing harvesting, he and his associates had perfected the exploitation of slave labor. Even when slavery was outlawed, Peter had found a way. Over hundreds of years, he had continued to rebuild the slave labor pools from distressed countries like Haiti, Ghana, Togo, Nigeria, El Salvador, Nicaragua, and other impoverished locations.

Peter was directly or indirectly responsible for millions of enslaved people who lived in Hell on Earth, hidden from the world's view. Once every twenty years or so, someone would notice. Yet, Peter and those like him simply paid off the politician or non-profit organization to go away. The sheer number of desperately poor and starving people in the world easily supplied more labor for Peter's very public exploitation of entire populations. Peter was not as ambitious as the other dragons but was significantly more successful at spreading evil and corruption.

Sunny said China continued to resist freedom in religion and remained communist controlled. Sunny was well positioned within the communist structure, as she often corrupted the political officials with prostitutes, drugs, and illegal wealth. Sunny believed she would facilitate the destabilization of surrounding countries, and she was promoting China to spread its dominance. Sunny had no small part in China continuing to have the world's most significant irreligious population. The Chinese government and Communist Party continued to declare themselves as atheist.

Sunny also promoted intellectual property theft from the United States and Europe. She maintained control of a vast network of paid contractors, always given rewards for the intellectual property they stole. They had been able to seize control of entire billion-dollar industries. Telecommunications, information technology, energy, personal computing, automation, robotics, and many other industries were now dominated by China. Steal the intellectual property. Build vast manufacturing facilities. Offer the products at half the cost. Destroy competitors that could not keep up. This was the formula.

Sunny laughed about the fact governments and corporations were so helpless in their resistance. They did not ever see the grand plan. Massive job losses. The collapse of businesses in other countries. Sunny knew economic devastation was just as lethal as a bullet or a bomb.

As in other meetings, she simply reported the industries, the companies, and the statistics of loss accomplished by her underworld of spies and thieves.

Sunny also said that it was time for her to release another disease on mankind. China was a petri dish of human over-population. It was time to scare them once again. She took the hand of Aerico and asked for his help.

Roman laughed and said he continues to provide the world with drugs. While Roman was not a drug dealer himself, he was the master planner. He was creating darkness over the earth through illegal drugs. He did this by remaining in the background and controlling all of the kingpins and cartels. If a drug lord was not under the influence of Roman, he simply killed him. His name was never spoken, but the most powerful people understood their allegiance and subordinate responsibilities to Roman.

Chester commented the United States greed and self-centeredness always makes it easy to inject evil and corruption into their lives. Yet, Chester was patiently climbing the ladder of the US Defense Industry. The dragons often called this the cocoon stage. When they embed themselves, often for tens of years, until their real power can be used. While Chester had little to report, all of them had been in this cocoon many times over thousands of years.

As this wound down, Chester stood to address the group. It was an unnecessary gesture, but he wanted something. Chester asked if he could seek out this Order of Masada and take the lead on squashing this threat. He wanted to know if he could act on behalf of everyone and assume this leadership position. They all agreed. After all, he had his fingers in the world's largest military.

The group took a break and then reconvened to hear from their business advisors. How much wealth had they accumulated? How was it being used to provide influence and power? This presentation continued for about two hours. The entire meeting took about six hours. They adjourned to their suites for the day.

When they reconvened for dinner, the hotel room had been rebuilt. It included five comfortable couches. In front of each couch was a feast of food and drink. Servers and guests had been hired explicitly for this feast. They were hired for their physical beauty and for their skills. They were scantily dressed and were available to serve the five dragons. To sit and play with the five dragons. For three hours, the dragons dined and played with their human toys. It was a time for simple pleasures.

At 11:00 PM, a chime rang out. As it did, the servers and guests were ushered out of the room. At the front, a specifically designed marble pedestal had been placed. Two guards brought one of the guests, a young girl, back into the room. Upon the pedestal, they laid the naked, young woman. They secured her in place by binding her hands and feet to the table. Each of the five gathered around. At the head of the pedestal was a satanic priest. He was reading some type of scripture out loud. At an appropriate time, he stopped, nodded to the five, and bowed down in respect.

The five dragons all shed their human forms. It was obviously liberating, as they all let out sighs of sheer joy. The two guards gathered their human skins and gently laid them out of the way. The dragons then took ornamental daggers in their right hands and placed their left hands on the woman. Each left hand was placed strategically over a satanic symbol. Symbols were placed upon her stomach, heart, eyes, left arm, right arm, and left side of her torso. They each drove the dagger through their left hand from the back to the palm. The dagger then continued down into the woman at five of these six locations. Their blood was mixed in the wounds and poured to the table. The five wounds were lethal to the woman, and she was killed in this moment of terror.

The five dragons immersed themselves in the woman's death, in the blood, and in celebrating the ritual. The Priest who had continued to chant now was silent. The blood ran to a trough carved into the edge of the podium. From the trough, the blood was collected in a challis below. The Challis was passed to each one, who drank from it. The Challis was symbolic as it mixed each dragon's blood with the sacrificed women. This was their ritual to celebrate evil and their connection to one another.

As it was over, they spent the rest of the early morning continuing the feast and talking with one another. Not as humans, but as the dragons they were. Before the city awoke, they all returned to their human form.

Two days later, each of the five people had left Geneva, and there was no trace of them ever having been there. The most important outcome of this meeting was Jess Wagner being given the job to infiltrate Masada's Order. Unlike the missing Typhon, Jess would not fail.

Chester "Jess" Wagner was a powerful man in the Defense Industry. His former role as Director of the US Navy Intelligence Division connected him with everyone. Years of work as a US government director meant that he had been responsible for billions, if not trillions, of dollars of defense contracts during his career. He was endeared to the Defense Industry. Unlike his colleagues, he never had his hand out for anything. Not once. Through the years, this meant his political capital and Industry clout had piled high with favors owed.

Furthermore, Jess Wagner had been a close confidant to President Sands. He did not divulge, in Geneva, his knowledge of how worried President Sands was. He knew the fear Shane McNaughton had created. He also knew that Frank Kotter, Rick Jones, Scott Stanfield, and Mick Gallow were knee-deep in the persecution of the Order of Masada. He intended to quietly put each of these individuals under a microscope.

Jess Wagner also would not use the military for what he had in mind. He needed an assassin. A team of assassins. He wanted Claire Yang-DiAngelo to be this assassin. She was his former US Deputy Director of Intelligence – Asian Pacific Field Operations in the US Navy. She now was responsible for Alistar Central American Operations. She was of Chinese descent but had married a US Naval Officer. For most of their careers, they were ships passing in the night. Away from each other for long periods. They had decided early on children were not a good idea. Their careers were their children.

Claire was not afraid to go deep undercover as a field operative and not afraid to get her hands bloody when needed. While others were good at their jobs, she was lethal. No place was too light, too dark, too high, or too low for Claire. It made her perfect.

Claire was briefed on every activity associated with Shane McNaughton and the Order of Masada known by the US government. She had been made aware of their vast network, including the Catholic Church.

She asked, "What are my objectives?"

Jess said, "Surveillance and infiltration of the Order of Masada. Identify the key operatives. Once we know more, then execute kill orders to destroy this organization." Claire knew the team she picked would have to be lethal. She also knew that she was dealing with supernatural forces.

Jess Wagner grew dark, "This group of people are highly skilled and have been attacked by forces well beyond your understanding. In each and every case, Masada was victorious. Regardless of the force, not even a fingernail was harmed on any of them. Study the files, approach them cautiously, and remember your adversary is invincible."

Jess concluded the meeting by saying, "I wish you and the team happy hunting. I don't want to see you in this office after today. It will be announced you have taken a personal leave of absence."

Jess Wagner reported back to the dragons what he began. All were supportive and excited. If for no other reason than to find what had happened to their dear brother Typhon. All Jess Wagner could tell them is Typhon was no longer in possession of President Sands. He had disappeared.

Shane had his own plan. He intended to repopulate Earth with strength. He was convinced Maggie had discovered the key. By strengthening the Dakota Reservations, it enabled this group of people to take over the geographic footprint surrounding them.

210

With the Native Americans, Shane took people weakened to the point of near-death and restored them. He healed their lands. He provided them wealth. Finally, he re-educated them and restored their spirit.

Second, he wanted to extend this formula to Liberia, Togo, Guana, Haiti, Puerto Rico, and many other devastated populations. Repopulate these areas with strong, capable, and healed Masadians. Gain affordable access to equipment, fuel, food, and housing. Encourage and enable (through Masada's riches) the introduction of Christianity and Catholicism. Help these areas evolve from cursed to blessed.

Third, and perhaps most important, Shane wanted to return to Lakewood, Ohio. He wanted to create a United States center for healing. He wanted to invest in building his Ohio homeland into a paradise. He wanted his neighbors to be cared for and nurtured. He wanted to create a contagious and rapidly spreading case of good fortune from Lakewood, Ohio, to as far as he could imagine.

Shane hoped that he would be able to accomplish these things, and more, without threats from the government or others.

Shane and Terry Guerrero were visiting one of the remote cities. They were walking along a footpath between the city and a stream. Terry spoke, "As I have learned, I have to admit you understated the magnitude of this experience. Each day has brought a new and amazing discovery. I cannot thank you enough."

Shane replied, "You can thank God or Heaven or whatever pointed me to you as a Judge. I simply followed a crystal until it pointed to you as a candidate. I think that there has to be a very specific reason for you to be here."

Shane was looking out over the landscape as they walked. In the distance, he saw two men walking. He could vaguely make out Jonas as one of those men. Suddenly, and without explanation, the other man seemed to transform into a dog; no, it was too big. Perhaps a wolf. Shane thought his eyes were playing tricks on him.

211

As Shane was thinking, Terry spoke up, "That was strange. Did you see that? The man on the horizon seemed to disappear, and a dog took his place. My eyes must be tricking me.

Shane motioned them to step into the cover of vegetation off to the side of the path. Jonas was headed towards them down the footpath. The wolf-headed off to the right on the crest of the hill. They could track him. Shane nudged Terry, and they sped off in the forest to track the wolf.

They tracked the wolf about five miles. Shane and Terry were easily able to keep up with the wolf. They had climbed about 1,500 feet as the hill gradually moved up to the base of a mountain. At some point, the wolf disappeared.

Shane and Terry cautiously moved to the point where the wolf had disappeared. From here, they saw a box canyon. In the middle of the box canyon was a mountain stream and a small village. As the wolf approached the village, it transformed back into a large man. This was something new; werewolves on Masada.

Aamon had been careful in selecting both the village and the people he transformed into his followers. Much like the old stories of werewolves, Aamon could transform a human into one of his wolves. He did not have to bite him. He simply possessed him.

Aamon would capture the person. He would starve, torture, and weaken their spirit. At some point, they would ask Aamon to save them. Upon their request, Aamon would simply touch them, and a small part of his spirit would "infect" them. They would transform soon after.

Aamon had grown his community or wolf pack to include twenty-five men and sixteen women. The men and women were typically mated to each other for life. The single men were always on the prowl for unsuspecting females. They preyed mostly on the Creole villages.

Much like Beelzebub running into Beleth, a similar coincidence accidentally brought Aamon to find Beelzebub. Both disguised as men. Aamon and his people would sneak into villages at night to steal what they needed. One night, they were captured by Jonas' soldiers. Upon being marched to Jonas for their crimes, Aamon and Beelzebub recognized each other.

Beelzebub, for his part, now had a loyal soldier. Aamon would build an army for him. Beelzebub, disguised as Jonas, could now use Aamon without exposing himself. This was perfect.

Meanwhile, Shane and Terry spent about an hour observing the Aamon's village before carefully backtracking and heading for Cuyahoga. This was another unexpected development they would have to comprehend. Shane asked Nancy to get a message to Jonas to join them at Cuyahoga.

As they reached the Cuyahoga fortress, Noni had already raised a mild alarm. Shane could see guards on the walls and followers assembled within. All had weapons and armor. All the Judges had been told to return to Cuyahoga as soon as they could.

Nancy had created a portal and was bringing Jonas back to Cuyahoga directly.

The Judges assembled in the first-floor meeting hall. Shane and Terry explained what they saw. They left out the beginning where they say Jonas and the other man talking. After about ten minutes of discussion, Shane slipped in a test for Jonas.

Shane asked, "Jonas, you are in all of the Creole villages. Have you ever come across these people or these dogs or whatever they are.?"

Jonas passed the test, "Yes, I have. The leader is called Aamon, and he is part man and part wolf. We trade with him, and he leaves us alone. Once in a while, a man or woman comes up missing."

Nancy angrily asked, "If you have known this, why did you not tell us about this threat? We are here to protect you."

Jonas empathetically said, "You have enough on your plate. We were handling this. If it had gotten worse, you would have been the first to know."

Jonas passed Shane's test.

One of Noni's followers rushed into the room and whispered to Noni something. Noni immediately said, "I don't think we have to wait too long to face these wolves. We have picked up a message from Beleth that he is being attacked by them."

Shane directed a force of fifty, with Mufaro, Nancy, and Jody, to get ready for battle. They opened portals to Beleth's encampment. As they came through the portals, they saw these werewolves surrounding Beleth. Beleth was wielding a large, broad sword and dagger. Beleth was wounded, and at least two of his wives were motionless on the ground.

The Masadians raced to the battle and immediately turned the tide. These wolves were strong and quick but still no match for many of the Masadians. The Masadians split into three groups. Shane took group one and joined Beleth. Intermittently, the Masadians cast fire and fought directly in front of them. The second group attended to Beleth's family. Protecting and healing them. The third group set up a flanking skirmish line and began using their weapons to fire at the wolves retreating from the battle.

Shane deduced that their leader, Aamon, was the wolf they had tracked. He located Aamon midway through the battle. Aamon was now slowly moving to the rear while pushing his wolves into action. Shane anticipated that Aamon would try to escape. As the thought came, Aamon broke into a running retreat.

Shane took off, alone, after Aamon. It would take less than a few minutes to catch him. Aamon turned to fight. Shane did not slow down but directly charged into Aamon. Aamon tried to bite and claw at Shane, but it happened too fast. Aamon was mortally wounded. Shane's sword entered below his rib cage and exited his lower back.

Shane knelt down and healed Aamon's wound as he slowly pulled the blade out. Aamon shrieked in pain. Shane said, "I will now heal you, but you will explain yourself.

In the aftermath of the battle, Beleth was severely wounded. Two of his wives were dead. The third would recover. His children were hidden away. The Masadians secured Beleth's encampment. They got him to his Renovare Pool, along with his remaining wife. Everything else was put back in place.

Chapter 12 – Beelzebub Returns

Aamon was taken back to the jails. He was questioned night and day. The Masadians discovered that Aamon had come through a portal opened between Hell and Masada. He had kidnapped or recruited all that lived in his village. He explained how he turned them into werewolves. A process he alone could accomplish.

Shane heard Aamon's continued banter about serving Beleth and about the destruction of Masada. He heard about being cast out of Heaven. He heard all the things that others before Aamon had believed.

Shane had one question, "If you were so loyal to Satan and believed all you have said, then why were you here trying to kill one of Hell's greatest generals? Why were you trying to kill Beleth?

Aamon was trapped. He remained silent as he sensed this was a trick question. Aamon finally said, "Beleth was disloyal to Satan, and it was my responsibility to kill him.

Shane again spoke, "That makes no sense. You came to Masada through the very same portal that we brought Beleth through. You knew he was our prisoner. You had no indication he was disloyal, or he would not be your ally. Why would you kill him? Who told you to kill him?

Aamon said what Shane was fishing for, "I was told that Beleth had betrayed all of us. I was told that it was my duty to kill him and his family.

Shane jumped up and approached Aamon. He grabbed his shoulder and dug into it to almost collapse his collar bone. Aamon screamed.

Shane asked with anger, "Who told you to do this!!!!" I want a name.

Aamon was in extreme pain, and through clenched teeth, he said, "Beelzebub told me too!"

216

Shane asked, "Where is Beelzebub? How do we find him?"

Aamon had said too much and not enough. He realized now that he had one valuable piece of information. Enough to bargain with. "If you let me go, I will return through a portal to Hell. I will tell you then who Beelzebub is."

Outside, Jonas was doing everything he could to remain calm. Would Aamon give him up? How could he kill him to stop him from speaking?

It was nighttime now; the Judges and their advisors had closed themselves in the library to discuss what had transpired. Shane began, "Aamon has been directed by Beelzebub. We do not know who Beelzebub is disguised as. Aamon has said that he will reveal the name when he is delivered back to Hell. I find this a good deal, the elimination of two primary evil beings. What do you all think?"

Terry spoke on his point of view, "We don't need to know who Beelzebub is. It is only essential for us to decide on returning Aamon to Hell or not. If we do, we will eliminate a need to guess who Beelzebub is. It will be revealed to us. In the meantime, since we have no idea, everyone is to double up, and everyone should be guarding our most precious people and assets."

The room was silent for a minute. Terry did not speak often, but he had a way to cut through to the heart of the issue. Shane and the others agreed with him.

Shane agreed to send Aamon back to Hell. There were two conditions. The first was to identify Beelzebub. The second was to be a Masadian spy in Hell.

Aamon protested but eventually saw this as acceptable. After all, his once esteemed leader, Beleth, was sitting in the lap of luxury on Masada. He, himself, had enjoyed his time here. The universes were not as black and white as he once believed.

It was decided that Shane, Nancy, and Danny would return Aamon to Hell. Upon his return, we would divulge the identity of Beelzebub. Shane considered this might be futile, as Beelzebub could take on another identity between now and then.

They created a portal. Just before entering, Jonas approached and asked to join the group. Shane agreed. Upon entering Hell, there were no evil beings in sight. Aamon did howl upon his return. Shane suspected Aamon was calling his wolves to him. Time was limited.

Suddenly, Aamon broke free and took off at a dead sprint. He was attempting to escape before concluding his business with Shane. Shane, Nancy, Jonas, and Danny simply watched as he crossed the flatlands in front of them. Suddenly, Aamon was violently knocked to the ground. He tried to get up and was knocked down again. At this point, he remained still.

Within a few minutes, Mufaro, with a long rifle, trotted towards Aamon from his sniper position. They had anticipated Aamon's treachery. Mufaro picked him up and returned him to the group.

Shane saw that Mufaro had broken Aamon's leg. Shane healed him as he exclaimed, "Well, that was fun. Please don't try it again. You agreed to identify Beelzebub, and you agreed to be our spy here in Hell. Is this correct, or do you need another painful lesson?"

Jonas had slowly moved up to within reach of Aamon. He grabbed him and slapped him across the face. He angrily said, "You coward, you are lucky to be alive." Aamon had a desperate and frightened look on his face as if he was about to be executed.

Jonas moved back. As Aamon turned to Shane, Jonas slowly drew his blessed dagger. While the group of Masadians formed a semi-circle around Aamon, Jonas moved quickly to be immediately behind Shane. He raised the blade above his head and drove it downwards. Shane's back was exposed and vulnerable.

218

At this point, Jonas suddenly stopped in mid-air. He slumped as a distant "crack" was heard. An ice shard was protruding from his left chest. Beelzebub gradually revealed himself as Jonas was lying with a critical wound.

Beelzebub asked, "How?"

Nancy replied, "Your disguise as Jonas was not infallible. We had been suspicious. We also believed Beelzebub would not allow Aamon to reveal his identity.

Nancy yanked the ice shard from Beelzebub's chest. He screamed. Danny put blessed shackles on Beelzebub to transport him back to Masada. Like Mufaro before her, Maggie came trotting up to the group with her long rifle.

It was time to leave. Aamon was released. Aamon looked at Shane in as respectful a posture as he could muster, "I can see why God has entrusted you with his mission. I will be your ally here in Hell. Yet, my wolf brothers here are still a threat to you. If they knew our relationship, I would be torn from limb to limb.

Shane nodded acknowledgment. The Masadians returned home.

For a time, Peace fell over Masada. Beelzebub was in the sub-basement jail. Beleth was grieving but left to care for his family. On Earth, President Sands was gone from office. Typhon was in a special cage and shackled. His wounds were slowly healing.

One glorious Masada morning, as Shane was contemplating his day, Noni and Maggie entered the apartment. They both had big smiles on their face. Shane was relieved. No dragons to fight. Not attacks to defend. No patrols to rescue. Yet, Shane knew something was up because these two and their followers had been mysteriously busy and absent at the same time. He suspected they would show him another weapon they developed.

Maggie asked if they could have a minute. Noni created a portal to the Lakewood Center. Whatever they wanted to show him was covered with a large tarp. It was about the size of a semi-truck.

Maggie was first to speak, "Noni and I have been working with a team on our technology. If we could focus our power to create a sniper rifle, what other ways could we amplify the energy that we possess? I believe our invention represents a revolution for Masada. It will open up the domains to us in ways we never thought of."

As Maggie was talking, a vehicle of some sort was being wheeled out into the field. It reminded Shane of a cross between a Jet fuselage, a Volkswagen Bus, and an Airstream camping trailer. In fact, Shane could not make out which it might have come from. Regardless, it was shaped like a large tube (a Pringles can) with a tapered nose in front and a squared back.

Noni could not contain his excitement, "Please, let us get into the shuttle. It is quite special."

Shane laughed, "Shuttle, you mean you want me to take a drive in your gadget with you? Which one of you is driving. I have driven with Maggie before, and she is dangerous."

They laughed.

As they approached the Shuttle, the squared back opened up, and it became a ramp. Noni signaled followers to wheel supplies onboard. With a forklift, two crates were driven into this cargo hold.

Noni explained, "With the shuttle, we can now bring supplies and machinery from and two different domains."

Once through the cargo area, Maggie opened the door to the front of the shuttle. As they entered, there were three distinct areas. The first were lockers. In the lockers were weapons and gear. The second was an area with two couches along the sides. Above each couch was a large screen scrying mirror. In front of each couch was a narrow table.

220

Finally, the front included two rows of two captain's chairs arranged left and right. The front two captain's chairs seemed to be for the drivers or pilots. On the left was a wheel or yoke. In the middle was a console of some sort and on the left was a smaller scrying mirror.

Shane was amazed, "This is fantastic. Between all we have been doing, how did you find the time to develop this?"

Maggie replied, "It was really a simple extension of our work from building the sniper rifles to the concepts making this shuttle work." She gestured for Shane to sit in one of the captain's chairs.

Maggie took the left pilot's position. She swiveled the chair to talk to Shane and the others on board. "This is a prototype of what we believe we can do. First, each of the Judges can create portals and travel from domain to domain. Second, we know that we can amplify and direct this power, as we have with weapons development. Third, Noni and I have developed a way to focus a Judge's power times 1,000 percent. Not only that, but we found a stone on Masada which actually stores a Judge's energy casting. It allows the energy to build up. We learned to work with it. It was quite by accident."

"We can now travel within a vehicle, as we did when we floated between domains. Everyone strap in."

Maggie smiled as she turned around. She put her hands into two devices that were very much like winter mittens. On the dashboard, in front of her, they all watched as a translucent globe lit up. Noni had turned around as well and did the same. At some point, an audible alarm sounded. When it did, Noni removed his hands and turned around.

Noni explained, "One or both of us are required to charge the energy system running the shuttle. We just did that, and the craft is now functional."

Maggie added without turning around, "If there are two Judges, then it only takes a few seconds. A little bit longer if there is only one of us. Please look out the front windows."

Outside, some of the Lakewood Center staff had taken the tarp off the large device in the middle of the field. It included three large rings that lit up.

Noni explained that the three rings were the equivalent of an airplane's runway. At some point, a large light on top of the nearest ring turned green. As this happened, Maggie used her steering wheel to raise the craft and accelerate quickly through the rings. Before they were through the last ring, the shuttle was in the dark expanse.

Maggie explained that they had a set of rings like this constructed within the Cuyahoga compound on Masada. This is where they were traveling to. Noni had a display screen, and different points were glowing. Shane presumed that these were various portals.

Noni explained once in the dark expanse, they could use the magnetism of the various portals. They again found ways to magnify it and to use this for ship maneuverability. Maggie did a barrel roll and a few other types of maneuvers similar to a jet.

Shane was amazed.

Maggie explained they could now use a vehicle like this to patrol the dark expanse. Noni excused himself and exited out the rear. Soon he was floating in the dark expanse in front of the shuttle. He floated several beach balls and returned. Maggie retreated in a large circle and then flew towards the beach balls. She used a trigger on her steering yoke to cast energy pulses towards the balls. She hit all three of them, and they exploded.

With that, Maggie stopped the shuttle. Noni got up and walked to the back couches. He asked Shane to join him.

Noni asked the scrying mirrors to turn on. As they did, everything was lit up. Noni explained, "From the back of this shuttle, I can do almost everything I can do from the sub-basement control room in Cuyahoga. I can track the dark expanse. I can see evil beings, Masadians, or heavenly beings crossing from one domain to another. I can even watch television or access the Internet on Earth. Can you see how this is a game-changer?"

Shane was speechless.

Noni continued, "I think the future is for us to build a station in the dark expanse. A station where we can control everything occuring between and within the domains. Yesterday, we could magically float in the dark expanse, one of us at a time. It was like treading water in a large and unwieldy ocean. When we wanted to move towards or away from something, it was difficult; like swimming, not running. This shuttle is like comparing the tortoise and the hare."

Noni continued, "We can move things and people from one domain to another without effort. We can use vehicles like this to patrol the dark expanse. We can put an entire "squad" of Masadians into a shuttle and complete a mission in this way. The domains, as we know them, will become one space for us to master. This will change everything."

Shane listened but was nervous. Would God and Heaven approve of this evolution? Did it put too much power into the Order of Masada? What would be the downsides? Shane could not think of any right now.

Noni when back to the right captain's chair, and Maggie continued their short trip to Cuyahoga.

Noni and Maggie's arrival was noticed. The word spread like wildfire. There was now a shuttle service between Earth and Masada. Many asked if they could go visit relatives or could they get something from Earth that they missed.

Shane took his horse and headed to the heavenly portal connecting Masada to Heaven. He was troubled in that he could inadvertently introduce technology to Masada to begin its corruption. Would it merely follow Earth's path of technology, greed, and power?

He found a familiar "rock" he had sat on several times before. He had hoped that somehow Jesus would find his way to this place for another needed conversation. After about an hour, nobody showed up. His heart and mind were still unsettled.

He was just about to head back to Cuyahoga when several distant figures were seen walking up to his location. As they approached, he recognized his heavenly counselors; Camuel, Jeremiel, Sri Ma, Barachiel, and Zuriel. They all sat in a circle with him. Jeremiel quickly built a large fire.

Barachiel was the first to speak, "Shane, you have a new technology. We know you are troubled. It is simply like any tool, do not worry. Yet, believe us when we say the problem is the same. When fighting evil, corruption, and greed, remember the issues are as old as time. When fighting the five dragons you still have to face, your new technology will not reduce the risks, dangers, and challenges.

Camuel asked if he could show Shane something. Shane nodded. Camuel got up as all of them watched. He walked slowly to Shane and touched the middle of his forehead.

Camuel and Shane were transported to the dark expanse instantly. Except for this time, Camuel sped them to a domain. The domain was desolate. There were abandoned machines and crumbling cities as they looked on. Camuel said, "This is a domain other than Heaven, Hell, Masada, or Earth. It has been destroyed millions of earth years ago."

Camuel touched Shane's head again, and they sped to another domain. It was the same. In this case, vegetation had enveloped the decay of a civilization long gone. There were animals that Shane did not immediately recognize. Lizards and large flying animals. Camuel said, "This is another domain older than the other."

Camuel touched Shane's forehead once again, and they were back sitting at the campfire.

Jeremiel asked Shane, "If your technology advances your ability to move between domains, how is this a bad thing. Particularly since you have now witnessed the remnants of failure in other domains. In saving the Earth, you are going to have to come out of the shadows. Go boldly towards a future of saving humanity. It is time."

Shane thought of this on his trip back to Cuyahoga. As he viewed the mansion, he saw baby Christine looking at him from afar. He wondered how her life would be fifty years from now. He hoped, filled with love and people.

A thought flashed into his mind, and he thought about the domains he had witnessed. I can no longer just think about the worst situations on Earth; I have to save everyone. And I have to do it quickly; the devastation is coming.

At this moment, Shane heard a booming voice command, "Shane, Come Home!"

Epilogue

Shane was returning to Masada, when he heard the call to come home. He had listened to this before in his life and now understood it was always God calling him to return to Heaven. Shane was puzzled. He had sat outside the Heavenly portal for hours with no activity. Now he was almost to Cuyahoga, and he was told to turn around. It was not his to question, just his duty to obey.

Shane passed through the portal to Heaven. His Cherubs were always excited to return. Seth, Bartholomew, Rogan, and Ned were all running and flying around like crazy Cherubs.

Ned told Shane, "Come with me, I know the way!" And off he went.

After traveling for about an hour, the Cherubs stopped at a small cottage along the path. It was just outside a village. What Shane saw was amazing. In front of the cottage, a man was working to build something. As Shane comprehended what he saw, a woman emerged from the front door carrying a tray with drinks. She looked at Shane and motioned to him to come over.

Shane was looking at Alice and Joseph. His Cherubs were now by his side and smiling.

About the Author

Steve A. Day is a business owner and entrepreneur with a distinguished career in technology businesses. He has worked for a wide range of Fortune 100 companies to startups, including Sprint, Times Mirror, ADC Telecom, and Marconi PLC. Throughout Steve's career, he has traveled and gained a world view perspective. As a sales and marketing professional, Steve has always had a strong aptitude in communications, content creation, and creativity. He also has a master's degree in public policy and management from the University of Pittsburgh and a bachelor's degree in business economics from the College of Wooster.

He has spent the last few years focusing on writing books, short stories, and poetry. At the same time, Steve is a born-again Christian. He has a great deal of interest in Christian religious history and alternative beliefs, including Far East Asian religions, Islam, Judaism, and other spiritual beliefs. Heavens Portal is envisioned as a portal fantasy genre series of books. To date, this is the second book promising a thought-provoking and delightful journey.